THE LANZIS III

THE LANZIS III

Dreams and Disillusions

GIANCARLO GABBRIELLI

Copyright © 2021 Giancarlo Gabbrielli.

All rights reserved. No part of this book may be reproduced in any form or by any electronic or mechanical means, including information storage and retrieval systems, without permission in writing from the publisher, except by reviewers, who may quote brief passages in a review.

ISBN: 978-1-63795-418-8   (Paperback Edition)
ISBN: 978-1-63795-419-5   (Hardcover Edition)
ISBN: 978-1-63795-417-1   (E-book Edition)

Some characters and events in this book are fictitious. Any similarity to real persons, living or dead, is coincidental and not intended by the author.

Book Ordering Information

Phone Number: 315 288-7939 ext. 1000 or 347-901-4920
Email: info@globalsummithouse.com
Global Summit House
www.globalsummithouse.com

Printed in the United States of America

- I -

SOUTHBOUND

Roberto knew this time it would be much more difficult to leave, but he could never have imagined it so hard.

His previous journey south, with the certainty of a speedy return home from the tests at the Air Force Academy, had seemed almost painless. Now though, following the official acceptance letter from the Ministry of Defense, his departure felt more like a long-term sentence, an exile, albeit voluntarily taken.

How dear and necessary now seemed all the people he was leaving behind, how cherished his home near the gentle slopes of the Tuscan hills. But he had to leave, for only that way could he aim towards a better future. Yet, right now, instead of owning his future, it felt as though the future possessed him.

Even the weather, this time, seemed to have conspired against him, as rain poured from a laden sky making the night seem sinister, the moment gloomier.

On the train, Roberto placed his bag on the compartment rack, then moved to the corridor and stared at the drenched landscape through the sheets of water washing the surface of the glass window. Trees and houses appeared as smudges in the blurred field of vision. Despite the late hour, a few orange lights pierced the darkness, revealing the location of invisible farmhouses dotting the countryside, where people were still awake. Soon, even those people would go to bed, sleep, and in the morning attend to their usual chores, simply, content with their own existence, the sameness of their days, and their predictable future.

Why couldn't he?

Was it because he wanted more from life? Was it for the challenge that his yearning implied? Yes, he thought, but at that moment, he would have liked to be like those people: at home, serene and satisfied with their lot.

He knew it could not be the life for him. He had known it since his early youth, when his family found refuge and waited out the passage of the war in the countryside. He met Mario, a boy about his own age, who seemed so much in harmony with his environment, his fields, his life. Though strong and talented, Mario did not long for much, other than, perhaps some day bringing electricity to the house, or adding a small parcel of land to the farm. He seemed quite content with what nature and destiny had given him, while Roberto already yearned for more; travel, adventure, position.

It was that way then, and it was going to remain so forever.

Resigned, Roberto closed his eyes, and from the veiled mist of his memory, summoned up Silvia's image. How sweet and intense had been their last moments together, how hard and painful it was to go away from her with still the smell of her skin over his body. It would be months before he could see her again.

Months! He thought in dismay; he couldn't even conceive such a length of time, now that every minute felt like an eternity. His vision of the bright but far-off future he dreamt of seemed too far away to lessen the pain of his present.

He would gladly forego five years of his life, just to distance himself from this moment.

He remained at the window for a long time, unable to sort out the web of feelings inside his head. Nevertheless, the decision was made, and now he must continue on the path he had chosen.

The train continued its relentless run south… Ta-tam, ta-tam, ta-tam, pulled by a force as inevitable as gravity. Roberto vaguely registered the names of towns and stations they passed, as he mentally charted the slow descent towards the lower end of the peninsula. Ta-tam, Ta-tam, Ta-tam, moving closer to his destination and farther from his love. At every station, the familiar screech of metal against metal braking, the jerky stops and then, after a short pause, the run resumed.

Beginning in Rome, more and more young people got onto the train, most likely headed for the Air Force Academy as well.

Towards evening, he finally reached Caserta.

He left the station and stepped into the square, surrounded by a boisterous bunch of young men of about the same age. The Royal Palace, where the Academy was lodged, loomed before him.

Twelve hundred rooms, two dozens state apartments, a library and a theater modeled after the San Carlo of Naples, he thought scanning the formidable exterior.

He shouldered his gear with a sigh and followed the others to the gate.

- II -

DAY ONE

Salvatore Marciante, Toto to his friends, had arrived in the early afternoon and was sent to room number 289. Several people were already there and had by now selected their bunks. Some were reading local newspapers, car or sport magazines and some were playing a game of rummy. Salvatore threw his small bag over an empty cot and mumbled a quick hello to those who looked his way.

"Are we all in the same course?" he asked no one in particular, "Jet engine mechanics?"

"No. I'm in the navy" said one of the card players with a coarse Roman accent, "I'm here waiting for embarkation."

Several people laughed.

"Don't listen to him" said a tall guy with a northern accent, "we are all *Motoristi* in this room. Sixteen of us, all listed on the sheet posted at the door."

"Mind your business *polenton*" the roman shot back.

"Better be a polenta eater than an ass hole like you."

The size of the northerner discouraged a reply.

Toto walked to the door, read the list and recognized the name of one who had passed the exams with him, returned to his bunk, dug out a *New Wings* aviation magazine from his bag and immersed himself in reading.

At the gates, Roberto was checked against a long list with other recruits, as when he had come for the tests a few months earlier. Then, made to join a small group and escorted to pre-assigned dormitories on the top floor of the palace.

"Ehi, Roberto, do you recognize me?" said Toto upon seeing him.

"You're the fellow from Leverano if I remember correctly."

"You surely do."

Roberto shook hands with him and then moved to the last free bunk. He didn't feel like talking. Silvia's blue eyes and sweet smile kept on appearing in the screen of his mind. These were his toughest hours and needed all his strength and concentration to resist the temptation to grab his bag and run home.

* * * * *

A bell rang and a senior airman appeared out of nowhere.

"Everybody out" he yelled.

They recruits were gathered in the corridor and marched in platoons to the mess hall.

It was like walking into a beehive, as the buzz was loud and constant. Several warrant officers and staff corporals walked up and down the hall, directing the recruits to tables marked with the same number as their dormitory. Once everyone was in place, they were called to attention. The metallic voice of a loudspeaker recited the Aviator's prayer, then told them to be seated.

They were going to eat their first chow.

The tables were already set: dishes, cutlery, a glass a bun an apple and three water jugs. The first ones to get there had already started nabbing the largest bun and the best looking apple. One of the guys tried to grab Roberto's apple but he nailed his wrist to the table. "Leave it there!" he said decisively.

"Eh, you're breaking my wrist" said the guy. He too had a roman accent.

"I'm not touching your things, and you don't touch mine. Understood?"

"What a fucking guy" said the thief releasing the apple and massaging his wrist, "I was only joking."

"And so was I. Believe me, otherwise I would have broken your arm."

Some of the fellows looked at Roberto curiously and then laughed at the misfortune of the roman guy.

"You stupid" said the one who had told Toto he was in the navy, "next time take the apple from someone smaller than you."

The service airmen arrived with large aluminum mess tins and served a dish of overcooked pasta beside a dark stew with hard chunks of meat.

"*Aho, aint'you eatin'?*" said the guy who had tried to snatch the apple.

"No" said Roberto pushing the plate away, "the look alone makes me feel sick."

"Can I have it?"

"Go right ahead" said Roberto. He hoped this would balance his earlier aggressive gesture.

Toto was eating with gusto and seemed surprised that others didn't. He had kept quiet for a while, then, turning towards the tall northerner who had taken his defense in the dormitory asked, "What's your name?"

"Livio Piccinin. And yours?"

"Salvatore Marciano, but back home they call me Toto."

"How does one come up with Toto from Salvatore? I could understand Sal or Tore, but Toto…?"

"Dialects and small towns' habits" mused Toto. "My grandfather's name is the same as mine and they call him Tore. Children and youngsters in general they call Toto. For some of us it sticks for life."

Roberto made a mental note of several names and accents around his table. Franco, Giulio, and Michele, were definitely from Rome or thereabouts. Nicastro, definitely from Sicily, Alberto, the smart-ass *navy guy*, probably from one of the destitute areas of the capital. Livio and Carlo from the northernmost area, Patrizio, who sat several places away from Roberto, seemed to have the familiar vernacular accent of a Tuscan; from Pisa or Lucca. As did Renzo, who had the look and manners of a truck driver and sprinkled his phrases with as many colorful profanities as regular words. Roberto couldn't tell about the ones farther away from him; he would soon enough.

Back to the dormitory, they were given twenty minutes to wash and do personal grooming at the multiple showers down the corridor. Then the lights were switched off. It was time to sleep.

From the corner of the dormitory, one of the fellows whispered a few verses from a known Neapolitan song:

"*Santa Lucia, luntan da te, quanta malincunia…*"

Judging from the accent it must have been the short, curly fellow from Naples who sat near Patrizio. Despite the closeness to his city he was homesick as well.

"Fuck you and your *santalucia*" yelled Renzo, "go and whine somewhere else, we need to sleep."

The singing stopped and the noise of springs and metal rubbing together signaled everyone adjusting to the new accommodations.

Other than during wartime, Roberto had always slept in his own room, alone. Now he was with all these people from all different regions and walks of life, irreversibly embarked on his new venture.

He was restless. The thought of Silvia's distance, the time that separated them, and negative impressions of his new environment were grating inside his head. He was disheartened and begged for the obliviousness of sleep to come and relieve him of his thoughts.

- III -

DAY TWO

When reveille sounded Roberto had been awake for a while, staring at the pale light coming from the open window and thinking of home.

It was six o'clock and after a quick run to the lavatory and an even quicker breakfast, the recruits were escorted to the stores. The personnel who distributed the gear seemed to enjoy making fun of the new recruits and handed over outfits disproportionate for their size. Arguments were heard all over:

"Hey, what the fuck you want me to do with this tent?" yelled a little fellow holding a huge shirt, "I can fit four of me inside."

"Just tuck it in a bit, it will be just fine."

"You, smart ass" Livio boomed nearby, "The boots you gave me won't even fit my big toe."

"Here, give them to me" replied the smallest fellow of the group, "the ones they gave me look like boats."

Roberto was given a pair of trousers that barely reached his ankles. He threw them back without saying a word. The fellow behind the counter looked at his strong build and unsmiling face changed them for an appropriate size.

"Feel the fabric of this underwear" said a chubby fellow, "it must be concocted by the same chap who invented sand paper."

"Don't complain, Vito" someone answered, "at least you won't have to ever scratch your ass again."

Then there were the high uniform's caps, rigid black visor and a high peak, kept spread and tensed by an inner circular steel wire. Because of its size, it was nicknamed 'Saratoga', after the famous American airplane carrier.

"What's the circumference of your fat head?" the service airman asked.

"How the hell should I know? I never measured it, but certainly not as big as your mother's ass."

There were those whose hat barely balanced at the top of their skulls and those with the hat rim down to their eyes. Exchanging with comrades was the simplest solution.

Then came marching boots, with hard-leather soles, and an elegant pair with Vibram soles, to be worn with the high uniform, plus a pair of wooden clogs to be used at the showers.

Lastly, they were given two coveralls in grey fustian cloth. One of them had an internal flannel lining and the collar covered with synthetic fur. It had several pockets and on the upper left arm there were several small pocket-holes suitable to hold pencils or small utensils. These mini-pockets were lined with aluminum casings closed at the bottom and shaped like bullets.

"This is your flight suit" said the airman to Toto.

"Flight suit?" yelled Toto enthusiastically, "we fly, we fly."

Several people looked at him stupefied and someone said:

"Hold your horses, Von Richthofen, you *ain't* the 'Red Baron' yet.

The day after the outfitting, they were taken to a building near the southern wall of the park. It housed a dozen or more civilian tailors who worked for the school and who, at the recruits' request and at a modest cost, adapted the uniforms for a better fit. With as little as fifty lire, they could also alter the stiff look of the ceremonial hat. Roberto tried to explain how he wanted his, but couldn't make the tailor understand.

"If I bring you a picture" he finally asked, "would you be able to do it exactly the way I want?"

"*Si* – Yes. But if it's too different from the norm *we'gotta do it a umma, a umma.*"

"What on earth is he saying" Roberto asked Gennaro.

"It means on the sly" replied the curly Neapolitan. "You stick around me and I'll *learn* you my language."

The following day Roberto returned with a book that showed a picture of Rommel in Africa and explained to the tailor he wanted his visor as low and inclined as that, and the peak high. "Don't worry about the steel wire" he said, "I'll reshape it myself".

"I understand" said the tailor, "*you wanna look like uno tedeshco*"

"No! I don't want to look like a German, but not like a rubbish collector either."

He detested the way some of the older warrant officers wore their hats; flat like pancakes, almost undistinguishable from that of train conductors, bus drivers, mailmen or even garbage collectors. Well, since he had joined the military, he might as well look like a real soldier!

The tailor was surprised at the unusual request but, since he was being paid, he agreed to do it.

Next door to the unusual *atelier*, a horde of white-robed barbers had organized a veritable production line and were busy shearing locks, curls, manes and pride from the previously manicured heads of the new recruits. For some of the young men, it seemed a humiliating experience and they tried to sweet talk the barbers, or used monetary inducements, to try and minimize the damage.

For the few like Roberto, who already wore a very low cut, it didn't matter. In fact, he took pleasure in telling his barber, who clearly expected a bribe, to follow rules and cut even deeper at the sides; "*alla tedesca* – German style" he told him.

Next stop the showers.

The white tiled room was like a gigantic steam bath, where the naked bodies of the recruits twisted and turned under dozens of high power heads. Thoroughly washed and sanitized they walked back to the dormitory. Their wooden clogs resonating against the high vaulted ceiling like cavalry returning from a watering trough. Within minutes they were all spread out over their cots waiting for the 'silence' and for the lights to be turned off.

Suddenly, the door of the dormitory was thrown wide open and an airman first class entered and yelled:

"Everyone down. Dress up again and take all your civilian clothes down to the store."

"Why didn't they tell us before?" Toto asked.

"Shut up and move."

Perhaps still imbued with a 'civilian' spirit, Toto placed his right hand over his mouth to produce a loud fart. The airman noticed the jest and yelled:

"You, smart ass, give me your name. I'm *gonna* show you what happens to people like you in the military."

Toto obeyed, took his belongings and followed the others to the store.

- IV -

DAY THREE

Roberto's group was aligned outside the dormitory ready to go to breakfast. The senior airman in charge asked:
"Whose turn it was to serve at the table?"
No one replied.
He asked again and the cadets looked at each other. Their expression said: who on earth knows? Nobody told us.
After a few moments of embarrassing silence, Roberto called:
"It's okay senior airman, I'll go."
"What's your name?"
"*Allievo Motorista* Roberto Lanzi."
"Get moving, you're late."
Roberto was about to answer that it wasn't him that was supposed to go, but changed his mind. He rushed down the stairway, caught up with the others and was among the first ones to serve his table. All seemed resolved, but when they read the order of the day, he discovered that he had been punished with two days of confinement. The motivation said, "… for his delay in the execution of his duties."
Angered by what he perceived to be an injustice, he immediately requested to speak to the company commander. He was sure, once he heard his explanation, the punishment would be revoked.
"Lieutenant, sir" he said, "our group was not advised about who was supposed to serve at the table and I simply volunteered to avoid delay. Therefore, I have been unjustly punished."
"If you volunteered it means you knew you'd be the designated person. Don't tell me you volunteered solely for your good sense of duty."

"You can call it what you wish, sir, but it is the truth."

"Don't be impertinent, otherwise I'll add three more days of confinement for insubordination. You must learn that in military life discipline is not a topic of discussion."

"Not even when applied in error?"

"Airman Lanzi" the lieutenant yelled, "remove yourself immediately from my presence and tonight get your blanket and present yourself to the cell."

Roberto was indignant, but given the circumstances he thought better to abstain from further replies.

* * * * *

DAY FOUR

The company was taken to a large auditorium that seated about 500 people1. Several officers were on the elevated stage and one of them, after adjusting the microphone, introduced the next officer as the Commander of the *Gruppo Allievi* – Air Force Cadets. He was a pleasant looking man of about fifty, of average height and build. On his chest, below the colorful ribbons indicating his campaigns, he wore the cross-swords emblem symbol of a field promotion. He bent the microphone towards his mouth, smiled and said:

> "I'm major pilot Rovato and your commandant officer. This here morning, I am very content to welcome you at the school. Both me and the Generale Gatti I am very secure that if you will do what is expectant of you, you will receive a good career. You'll have a fine lively hood, and you will feel like you are at your home..."

"What on earth is that?" said Roberto to Toto. The fucking guy is either senile or illiterate. Maybe both!"

"Well... maybe he is a good pilot."

"He *was* you mean. All the same, he has no business talking." He was going to add more but a loud applause crashed upon his unspoken words. Obviously, he thought, at this latitude the Italian language does not account for much.

After major Rovato, a chubby officer, lieutenant stripes stitched to his clerical garb, came to the mike.

"I'm Padre Dante" he said in a *Bolognese* accent, "I'm the school's military chaplain and I'm supposed to take care of your damned souls. I perform holy mass on Sundays and I don't care if you attend it or not. BUT… if you know what's good for you, you'll be there!" He paused until the giggling faded away, then, in a telltale mellifluous tone, added: "From the windows of your dormitory, looking to the right, you can observe the magnificent park and the fountains of the Palace. Many tourists visit these grounds, especially on Sunday. If you happen to see a pregnant lady with a big belly, don't put your left hand over the right arm and yell out of the window, "You got it!"… "You got it!"

When the laughing subsided he concluded: "And I beseech you, be careful when masturbating, because if you damage your bed springs the quartermaster-sergeant will charge you."

There was a thunder of laughter.

As a well navigated priest in military waters, Don Dante, had managed to gain the sympathy of the audience.

Toto looked towards Roberto who raised eyebrows and shook his head, but made no comment.

That evening, and for the following three nights, Roberto was to collect his blanket and present himself for consignment to the cell. With anger for what he perceived as an unjust punishment and Silvia in his mind, the hardness of the plank was the least of his concerns.

* * * * *

DAY FIVE

As soon as reveille sounded Roberto returned to his room. Everyone jumped out of the bunks and began to make the bed to precise specifications: pillow flattened and smoothed, sheets and blanket perfectly parallel and tight enough to bounce a coin. Then, they dressed in the new uniforms and lined up in the corridor. Under the sameness of their outfits, they were almost unrecognizable from what they had been only days before.

At breakfast, the service airmen were already at the head of every table with the aluminum mess-tins ready to serve coffee. Eight minutes to drown a couple of dry buns in the dark watery solution someone had already renamed 'sludge' and then, at the order of the service warrant officer, down for the first lessons.

* * * * *

In the classroom a textbook titled "Military Culture" sat on each desk. It was going to be the first subject of the day. Minutes later, an officer entered the room.

"I'm captain Cricchi" he said in a soft voice, "during the next two hours I will explain the ranks of military hierarchy, the difference in names and equivalence between air force and navy ranks, the correct way to salute, and the concept of *esprit-de-corp*."

He paused, looked around the classroom as though to familiarize with the eager new faces staring at him, then continued: "Soon you will start your drills, which are the basis of all teamwork. Our ancient predecessors, the Romans, used cadence marching for their tactical formations. And although through the centuries technological innovations of armaments have changed, drills are still used to move troops in an efficient manner as well as for military displays and ceremonies."

He paused and calmly scanned the classroom again. Then continued, "Military formations in order of increasing size or numbers, are: platoon, company, battalion and division. The troops move, rest or execute commands given by an instructor or a company commander. These words are divided into two sections; cautionary and executive. The command 'attention' for instance, as all others, will be pronounced as 'Att- tention', the first part will alert the troop and the second will tell them to execute the movement."

He further explained that only officers should be addressed as 'Sir', while all others were to be spoken to by calling their rank; corporal, sergeant, sergeant major, etcetera.

"Until your oath of allegiance – two months from now –" he concluded, "the entire company will march, study, eat and sleep at the same command; you will become a single unit."

Captain Cricchi dismissed the class.

He seemed a good-natured type, rather quiet and solemn faced, his subject was basic and easy to digest. Roberto liked the mild mannered captain, his mentioning ancient Romans. In his early grades, it had been his favorite dream to imagine himself marching with Caesar legendary Tenth Legion at the conquest of Gallia.

Military Culture was going to be easy to apprehend and didn't even require taking many notes.

- V -

MARCHING

After the lesson, they were taken to the main square, to start learning the nuances of proper marching. The instructor was a warrant officer of about fifty. His name was Iovine, had a pronounced belly, a red nose and pants that hung well above his ankles. He told the squad to align themselves in rows of ten in order of height.

After a lengthy shuffling of feet, pushing and pulling, swearing, and vying for position, they were finally ready.

"Atten--tion!" Iovine commanded with a sharp voice. His pronunciation of *Ts* as *Ds* betrayed his southern origin.

Most sergeants and warrant officers at the school, were locals or from nearby towns. Due to advanced age and limited education, their primary aim was that of remaining stationed at the school until retirement. Close to home, the family and, for many of them, the only environment they had ever known. The best way to insure that, was by being good instructors. Which meant, being mean to the recruits, yell commands, invectives and abuses at the top of their voice, and march the men till they had covered every inch of the parade-ground and worn out the soles of their boots.

Generally speaking, the recruits disliked them, even this sentiment however, was considered good medicine, the catalyst which awakened in every man the type of comradeship soldiers called *esprit-de-corp*.

During the next two hours Iovine yelled and swore at the top of his voice: "I'm *gonna* make you the best bloody platoon of the course if it costs *you* the last drop of blood!" "Left-right, left-right, left-right. Squad-halt!"

Stamping of feet, pushes, screams of 'ouch' and other expressions of pain followed by profanities, came after the command. It was badly executed by the recruits and the back lines collided with the forward ones and forced everyone out of sync.

"You are worse than a bunch of sheep" Iovine bellowed, "realign again!"

Then he approached the first man of the first row and yelled. "Can you see the nose of the far man on your right?"

"No sir."

"You don't *calle* me sir. Only officers are called sir."

"Yes sir."

"You are an idiot! Run around the square five times, then rejoin the platoon. Maybe by then you'll smarten up some." He then moved in front of another airman.

"Son, do you see the nose of the last man on your left?"

"Yes, warrant officer."

"And how can you possibly see *dat* bloody nose if I stand in between? You think I'm *drasparent*? Go run five *dimes* around the square."

"Cadet!" he then yelled turning to Roberto.

"I get it" he replied, "I'll run five times around the square."

Amused, Iovine looked at him run away and after a moment he turned around to face the platoon and said: "At my command *Avand*-march, shoot your left foot forward half a pace, toe *poinding* ahead. *Den*, when you *sdrike* your heel down, swing *de* right arm straight onward and the left straight to the rear; and when I say the rear I don't mean your ass."

When the laughing subsided he added, "And do all of you monkeys know which one is *de* right arm, or should I *pud* a yellow ribbon around it?"

Finally he ordered 'Ad- liberdy'.

During the short break, the cadets devoured a bun and a piece of cheese delivered by service airmen. Afterwards, under the guidance of the class leader, they were taken to a second floor classroom.

No one knew when, how or why, Proietti, the *navy-guy* had been selected class leader. Several people voiced their concern.

"He is neither intelligent or likable" said one.

"Judging from his peculiar lingo" said another, "he must be from the sewers of Rome."

"Perhaps all the 'romans' voted for him."

"He is just a typical bully" added Livio.

"The only reason he is even considered fucking suitable for enrollment" suggested Renzo, "is because of the fucking five-pointed star stitched to the right arm of his shirt. His father must have died during the goddamned war."

At that remark, Roberto was glad he had kept his status undisclosed. He wanted to achieve whatever possible not because of his father's death, but on his own merit.

When they reached the classroom, a civilian instructor named Fucile entered the classroom and immediately began unloading onto the students notions of algebra, geometry, physics, and electronics.

True to his name, which in Italian means 'rifle', he shot with his shifty eyes any person who caused the minimal disturbance. He did not allow any questions and if one did not understand a concept, he had to wait for the break between lessons and hope in the goodwill of a friend. His rushed and unorthodox manners did not suit the subjects and Toto, who had never taken algebra, was soon in trouble. He was so desperate that he began to cry.

Fortunately Roberto had recently refreshed his memory by reading the old notes dictated by his beloved Federica and could solve those equations with his eyes closed.

Now, going over those yellowing pages, Roberto thought dreamily of the young and beautiful substitute teacher who had arrived at his Santa Chiara school. She was an excellent teacher, very beautiful, and he had immediately fallen in love with her. He brought her flowers, wrote her poems, and despite the difference in age and position, he wooed her as though it was the most natural thing in the world.

Finally, perhaps moved by his poetic soul and devotedness, she gave him his first unforgettable love experience.

She would always remain etched in his mind.

Noticing his enraptured look Toto said: "What are you thinking about? Don't tell me algebra does that to you."

"No. I won't tell you that" Roberto replied with a sigh, "just copy this equation and let's continue."

Professor Fucile dictated pages and pages of supplementary subjects. He did it at such speed that, afterwards, no one was able to read what they had written. One evening, at the end of his lesson, he approached Roberto who sat on the first row and said, "Take my book and continue to dictate to the end of the chapter." The subject was smelting techniques for the production of Inconel and other special alloys.

As soon as he left everyone began to complain.

"What the fuck we need to know that for?"... "Yeah, we're not going to work in a foundry."... "We have enough to do without casting metal."... "This is the hour for reading or writing home..."

"Proietti" someone called, "It's up to you to go and talk with our captain. Tell him about this rubbish."

"Come on Proietti" insisted Livio, "show us how courageous you are, go see the captain."

"Who, me? You nuts or *somthin'*? He'd chuck me in the brig."

"But you are the head of the class..."

"I'm the class head, not a dick head. I'm not *gonna* go!"

"Don't even ask him" said Roberto with disdain, "He talks big but he's a coward. I bet he already shit his pants."

Roberto requested a meeting with the captain, who listened to his petition, took view of the notes and agreed that, given the load and priority of the other subjects, the smelting techniques could be overlooked.

"I'll talk to your teacher" said the captain at the end of the meeting. Roberto saluted and left satisfied.

The officer must have spoken to Fucile the following day because, from then on, the professor stuck with subjects pertinent to the course.

* * * * *

The company was assembling on the square for the marching session. Students were still arriving from the different classes when Toto noticed an airman with a large gauze patch taped over his nose.

"What happened to him?" he asked a classmate.

"He tried to outdo Von Braun."

"What do you mean?"

"He removed the aluminum capsules from the sleeves of his fight suit to build a mini missile. Then, pretending a sore throat he went to the infirmary and stole several potassium tablets. He scraped some gunpowder from several cartridges, mixed the compound inside the aluminum capsules. Then, when everyone was in bed he snuck to the lavatory, inserted a match for ignition and fired it out of a window. Or at least he thought so. But instead of 'lift off' the missile exploded over the window sill and a shred hit his nose."

"He was lucky it wasn't his eyes."

"Yes, he was. Anyway, the explosion was so loud that it awoke everyone in the radius of twenty dormitories. He spent three days in the infirmary and then, when he got better, he was given five days of prison."

"A poor way to imitate Wernher Von Braun" Toto concluded.

* * * * *

The following day, a fine rain fell from the uniform dark-gray vault of the heavens. Roberto's company was sent down from a lateral stairway at the eastern side of the palace, which gave onto a wide pavement covered by a pensile roof.

"There is no escape from marching due to the weather" lamented one guy.

Warrant officer Iovine was standing by.

"Mark time" he said with the usual tone of annoyance, "doesn't mean that you should take it easy. It means that you should march in place. Do you understand?"

A confused choir of 'yes', 'no' and 'maybe' echoed from the files.

"Lift your damn legs up high" he yelled as he shook his head in disgust, "your thigh must be parallel with the ground!"

They continued up the down the pavement for about an hour, Iovine's commands interspersed with the odd distant rumbling of thunder. Finally, almost hoarse from shouting, he gave the "Diss-miss" command and the company quickly dispersed. There was a dash toward the café and the marble topped bar counter came under assault by the charging cadets shouting: "*Gimme* a sweet bun"; "*Gimme* a pack of cigarettes"; "*Gimme* a coke"; "*Gimme* one of those long biscotti"; "*Gimme* my goddamned change"; "Do you have any stamps?"

Roberto took a notebook from his pocket, sat on a stone bench and prepared to write a letter to Silvia. He struggled to summon her image and recall the tenderness of their encounters, the sweetness of her kisses, the scent of her skin. In the midst of his hard, tough comrades, he did not want those feelings to slip away.

"My dear love" he started, *"I miss you more than I could ever have imagined…"*

- VI -

BREAD-CRUMBS

At the end of the morning classes it had stopped raining and they were taken to parade square. Grouped in battalion strength and famished, they had to listen to the day's journal which concerned new dispositions, oncoming special events and the list of punished cadets.

That last part, as long as one didn't hear his own name, was often amusing.

"Airman 'X'" an officer read on the microphone, "is punished with two days of confinement because, found fishing from the pond, he said to be trying to increment his daily calories intake."… "Senior airman 'Y' is punished with two days of regular cell as caught walking backwards through the gates. He was trying to sneak out by pretending to be entering."… "Airman 'W' is punished with five days rigor, for exhibiting his anatomic parts from the window of his dormitory to unsuspecting female tourists." … "Three days cell to airman 'Z' for using a flower vase in the officer's mass as a Vespasian urinal."

After the reading, the cadets sprinted upstairs like a pack of famished wolves and, standing to attention in the refectory, recited the Aviator's prayer:

> *"God of power, God of glory, who bestow onto us the rainbow of our skies, we ascend towards you, to sing with the roar of our engines, our passion and your glory.*
>
> *We are only men, but we rise towards you in spite of the weight of our bodies, purified of our sins. You God, give us the wings of the eagles, the sight of the eagles, the claws of the eagles wherever*

You shed your light, your love, your splendor, for the honor of our flag and the glory of Italy."

The usual jokers had already changed the last phrase into:

"Oh God – if you're there – give us the beak of the eagles, the claws of the eagles, the stomach of the eagles so that we may shred, chew and digest the goddamned, uneatable food of the academy."

In that racket the harmless change could not be detected. Not even if the day service officer was the notorious lieutenant Cigni.

Cigni was a Tuscan officer who came from the 'specialists' branches and not from the regular officers' courses. He taught electronics to the wireless operators and was held in high consideration because of his knowledge and because, coming from the ranks, one could talk to him, man to man. He was tall, handsome and lean as a whip, expert fencer and an excellent pistol shooter. He sported a pair of thin mustaches a-la-Erroll Flinn and could be considered a fair man.

Unfortunately, when he was in service, and wore that darn blue shoulder band across his uniform, he transformed from Dr. Jekyll to Mister Hyde. Or, as others put it, all he needed was a fiery sword and a dragon under his feet, to be the spitting image of Saint George.

What enraged him most was the battles the cadets used to engage in while eating. They carved out the soft part of the bread, compressed it and rolled it in small balls that they shot to the people of nearby tables.

As soon as lieutenant Cigni caught sight of some projectiles he ran up and down between the tables trying to find the culprit. When he did, it was a sure three days holiday at the Ritz, as the 'regular' cell was called. Because of this obsession, Cigni was soon named *Mollichella*-bread crumb.

One evening an entire bun landed right in the middle of the soup bowl of a cadet who, bathed and scalded all in one shot, yelled in pain. When *Mollichella* heard him and saw the result of that shot, he shouted: "Who did it?"

No one answered.

"Who did it?" he repeated, to no avail.

"You are a bunch of cowards. You should at least have the courage of your actions." Then turned to his aid:

"Sergeant" he said, "take all the occupants of these three tables to Parade Square. On the double!"

When they were all aligned outside, he ordered: "Spread the lines and initiate the decimation."

"The what?" asked the sergeant in astonishment.

"Every nine men you send one to sleep to the plank" lieutenant Cigni explained, "do you understand?"

"Yessir!" One, two, three…nine, out! One, two, three… nine, out! One, two, three… nine, out!"

"All the *lucky* ones" said Cigni in a caustic tone, run upstairs, grab their blanket and march to the *Ritz*. The others can return to their tables and swallow their cold supper."

"Leave behind your belt and shoe laces" said the guard at the cells.
"What for?" a cadet asked.
"Safety requirements. To prevent you from doing something stupid."
"You've got to be kidding… you think *we're gonna* hang ourselves?"
"*Gimme* your belt and strings and don't piss me off. I could be watching the soccer game instead of tending to fools like you."

Toto was among those selected to spend the night in jail. Fortunately, after a long wait, he and other two cadets were sent back to their dormitory because, as often happened when *Mollichella* was in service, they had run out of cells.

He was happy to avoid sleeping on the wooden planks, but as soon as he had reached the dozy stage he heard the loud clip-clop of wooden clogs.

"Goddammit" he exclaimed. He lifted his head and in the pale glow of the tenuous blue night-light, he saw the usual short fellow from next dormitory, a white towel wrapped around his waist returning to bed. Why does he go to the showers just when everyone was trying to fall asleep? He thought. This needs to be fixed.

The morning after in the lavatory, as Toto was shaving near Cicci, he said:

"We've got to do something about that fellow with the red nose who showers after lights out."

"You mean Marcolin" said Vito laughing, "yeah, he is a pain in the ass. We gave him a warning already, but it wasn't enough... we'll find the right cure for him."

That night, when Marcolin returned to his cot in the dark, his roommates had placed several knapsacks in the middle. He stumbled and fell to the floor. "You bastards," he said.

"Keep it up and you'll see what happens to you!"

The following night, Marcolin returned from the showers, his clogs in hand, his feet leaving wet tracks all over the floor. He switched on the light momentarily to ensure that no obstacles were in his way. Those who were not asleep, swore at him and vowed revenge. He continued drying himself and finally went to bed.

The third night the undaunted Marcolin returned from his habitual night shower bare-foot and wet. He opened the door, put his hand on the light switch and a large spark orange and blue illuminated his pale silhouette. He let out a loud scream followed by a string of profanities. Then, he ran out in the corridor, "Bastards!" he yelled, "I'll call the duty officer... I'm *gonna* fix you, you son of bitches."

Vito got up, pushed back and reconnected the electrical wires to the switch and reinstalled the cover. By the time Marcolin and the officer returned, everyone looked sound asleep and snoring. The officer switched on the light and Vito slowly raised his head and exclaimed, "What the hell..."

A few others turned, rubbed their eyes and with a groggy voice inquired about the commotion.

"This airman says you tried to electrocute him" said the officer. "Who did it?"

"What? Are you kidding" A chorus of voices replied. "Not him again... Look at his red nose, he had one too many tonight as well..." "We can't go on like this..."

Marcolin tried to repeat his story, but was outgunned and booed down. The officer, annoyed for having been wakened, looked closely at him, now sniffling and beginning to shake from the cold, he noticed his red nose and yelled:

"You know you shouldn't drink, and what the hell are you doing taking showers after lights out?"

"But, but …" the poor fellow mumbled.

"Take your goddamned blanket and go to the cell. Let's see if five nights in the can will teach you some discipline."

The nigh-time shower routine was never repeated. Vito had found the cure.

Despite the odd accident, the spirit of camaraderie was beginning to replace the diffidence and animosity of the initial days. Friendship and confidence formed among the cadets and nicknames often replaced the real names. Luciano Canali was called 'Long-pole' because he was slim and tall, Vito Falci became 'Cicci' for his roundish shape, Carlo Zenetti, 'Tze-tze' because he was annoying like a fly, Roberto, who every morning exercised in front of the open window was called 'Perpetual Motion.'

"Ehi Roberto" yawned Franco Vanelli, named 'Indolent', "stop agitating so early in the morning, I get tired just looking at you."

At night, just before 'silence', sprawled over their cots, the boys chatted about the day's events, about home, girls, soccer games and even comics.

They noticed that Toto mispronounced the name of several characters; he said Ion for John, Tecas for Texas and Iak for Jack.

Some of the boys laughed to his face, but he never reacted. Being a 'Terrone' from the deep south, he had an inferiority complex compared to northerners, though those who came from the mountains regions were called 'Polentoni'- polenta eaters.

- VII -

THE MAIL

It was the first Sunday in military uniforms and it was mild and sunny. However, those cadets confined to the grounds of the academy, they beheld the alluring call of nature from the narrow window of a dark cell.

For Roberto it was not a sacrifice, as from what he had read or heard about the city, it did not appeal to him. The strange accent of the people, their different eating habits, the unapproachable women, did not make him miss the opportunity of a day out.

His day was filled with the echoes of many recollections of happier times: strolls along the river banks with Silvia, Mauro, and Giovanni, bike rides up the hills of Monte Falcone or the Guerrini upland, swimming near the old mill. And most of all, he missed the feeling of those moments, which now seemed so far and unattainable.

The only thing he longed for now, was to receive mail from home; his umbilical cord with the past.

It was already over a week since his arrival and even knowing the slowness and unpredictability of the Italian mail system, it was a hard and long wait. Silvia promised to write me right away, Roberto thought, did she forget? Patience was not one of his virtues.

On the ninth day, during a marching break, someone said mail was going to be distributed. The platoon broke lines and gathered around the corporal who had climbed over a bench and called out the names. Roberto was impatiently waiting to hear his name called.

When the last letter or card had been distributed, the corporal stepped down from his perch and the group disbanded.

Even today there was nothing from Silvia.

Those who had mail strolled away towards the grassy area to read their mail in peace, particularly if it was from a girlfriend. Others shared their information with friends, showed the pictures from home. One became acquainted with the news of others, with towns or cities far away and conjured up in their minds the pre-military background of the new friend and questions often resulted:

"Is that your girlfriend?"... "Is that your family?"... "Where did you live?"

"Why did you join anyway?" Toto asked 'Tze'tze', "you're from the north, there is work there".

"For reasons probably common to most of us." Carlo paused and looked far away, as though glancing at his old town, at the person he had been until only a few days ago. "I'm from the north alright" he continued, "but there weren't many jobs in my town. Actually I had one, but I didn't like it."

"What did you do?"

"I worked as a secretary for several teachers in the local school. In effect I was a glorified boy-Friday and I was paid as such. In addition, I had a fight with the history teacher who was the lover of the principal. My days were numbered and I had no future there. One day, walking through the town's main square, I noticed the Air Force ad, portraying two smiling men in a blue uniform and a shiny jet plane in the background. I liked their uniform and remembered some pilots and specialists I knew from the nearby airfield. Compared with my situation, that career seemed to guarantee a reasonable economic future." He fell quiet and then asked:

"What about you?"

"Even worse than you as far as work options. I'm from a small, southern agricultural town near Lecce. I didn't want to be a poor sharecropper like my pa. Besides, I've always been fascinated by airplanes." He smiled to himself and then continued, "In fact…"

"Go on, tell me" Carlo encouraged him.

"Well, I was initially rejected" he said, "despite the fact that I sought recommendation from a local officer." He laughed, "Yes, some old relative I visited one day with a pair of capons. He said he would call an influential person in Rome. Don't worry, he told me. But at the medical visit in Caserta I was eliminated because my tonsils were inflamed."

"Really?"

"Yes. Too many of us were competing for so few places. One way or another, nine out of ten had to be eliminated."

"That's true."

"I was heart broken. I already imagined myself in that blue uniform, working on airplanes, travelling…" Toto seemed to be reliving the moment. "I couldn't accept it, and wrote a long letter to the Minister himself, telling him I was going to have my tonsils removed and pleading him to give me another chance."

"And since you're here, it must have worked."

"Fortunately it did. I was allowed another try and here I am."

* * * * *

After two weeks, Roberto finally received mail from Silvia.

Actually, he received several letters at the same time and some of his friends yelled: "Hey Roberto, you are putting too much strain on the Italian postal system. You need a postman just for you." …"Hey Lanzi, tell you girlfriend to send me a card too, will you? I've got nothing in over a week."

He smiled, slipped the mail under his sweater and, with deliberate constraint, walked towards the wooded area and silently disappeared in a quiet, secluded spot. He opened the letter and saw it was over ten days old.

"*My dearest Roberto,*

you just left and I already miss you terribly. And if I miss you this much I can imagine how bad you must feel, far from your Tuscany and all the people you love.

Tomorrow I'll see Mauro and ask him if he has any mail for me. I'm sorry not to be able to receive it at home, but you know how small town parents are. Always afraid of what neighbours think, and since we are not officially engaged, they would never allow it. I dislike these subterfuges, but my father is rather old-fashioned and I wish to avaoid arguments in the family.

I hope your letter is on the way as I need to hear that you love me.

I wish I could be in your arms. I dream of making love to you, my face against your neck, fall asleep brething the scent of your skin.

I know for now we must be content with words, but I count the days that separate us and never seem to pass. Then, I'm sure, when you'll be here, they will fly away and I'll be thinking of your return even before you part.

Tell me if you know the date of your Christmas furlough, as I want to cancel all my commitments and spend all the time with you.

I'll write you again very soon. In the meantime I pray for Christmass to arrive quickly, to see you, to embrace you, to love you.

Your Silvia

Roberto placed the letter in his pocket, his cap on the tall grass, and lay on the ground. Looking through the forked branches of the pine trees, he followed the soft clouds floating in the sky and began to mentally formulate his reply:

"My dearest Silvia, your letter has been like a welcome breath of fresh air..."

- VIII -

THE INFIRMARY

A while later, Toto found Roberto writing to Silvia.
"That's where you are" he exclaimed, "I should have thought you were writing to your girlfriend."
"Yes I am. What's up?"
"Our company was ordered to the medical center" Toto replied, "we'd better move."
When they arrived at the infirmary they found an earlier group already stripped to the waist.
"What's going on?" Roberto asked one of those guys.
"They're giving us some kind of an injection. A very strong flue shot I think."
"It's an anti typhus, anti cholera, anti just about everything" pitched in another fellow, "but mostly anti us."
"Yeah, mostly anti us!" someone concurred, "look at the fucking size of the needle."
It was indeed a frightening size, and the syringe was more like a hand pump.
"So why did we remove our shirts?" someone asked, "Shouldn't it be the pants?"
"No. This type of injection is given in the chest."
"Ouch!"
Some of the people looked worried and a scrawny fellow exclaimed: "Fuck! I'm just skin and bones up there. It's *gonna* kill me."
As they fell into line and got closer to the medical officer they gained a better view of the syringe.

"That's for horses" Roberto whispered to the skinny fellow. He noticed that everyone looked away and missed the fact that although the instrument itself was about ten inches long and one inch in diameter, only about an inch of fluid was administered to each recruit.

"Last time I got a huge syringe like that" said Roberto winking to the medical officer, "I almost died."

The little fellow, visibly shaking in his pants, paled and tried to retreat. The smell of carbolic acid, sweat and fear was starting to affect many people. The medical officer refilled the syringe, disinfected the needle, squeezed out a drop of fluid.

"You are next" he said to the scrawny fellow, then rubbed the area near his left breast with a cotton puff soaked in iodine and raised his arm ready to strike. The legs of the young recruit folded at the knees and he fell to the floor like a marionette whose wires were cut. Roberto and Toto lifted him and placed him on a chair as the laughter of those nearby eased the tension and masked their own fear.

Roberto was next. He calmly looked at the medical officer, unintentionally tensed his pectoral muscles and upon contact the needle snapped. Afterwards, he developed a painful bruise, and the doctor named him 'iron chest'. Good, he thought. The more people think I'm tough, the more they'd leave me alone.

The day after, many people developed a reaction to the injection which included high fever. They were given time off to recoup and Roberto took the opportunity to write his friend.

Dear Mauro,

Thanks for your for delivering mine to Silvia and thanks for your note.

I enjoyed reading the details of your your part-time job.

I'm halfway through basic training now. It is a brutal but 'necessary' hardship, but these damn fools in uniform will not succeed in breaking either my spirit or my bones. I survived the tannery, I will survive this!

It's not the hard work, the marches, or the confinement that I resent. I just fid hard to obey orders or listen to sermons delivered in a lingo which shouldn't even be allowed in the gutter. And certainly should not be called 'Italian.'

Even knowing that it is the duty of these instructors to yell and order us mercilessly about, I find their manners objectionable. But what offends me most is the difference in the quality of clothing and even food, between the officers and the lower ranks. Perhaps, excuse me for saying so, like in feudal times, it's the only way they can distinguish themselves.

Discipline does not bother me. As I do realize that some of our exercises are implemented with the purpose of determining who will and who will not resist the pressure. Why waste money on training those who will not endure? The drill instructors play their part in drumming anyone out before too much time (and money) is squandered on weak or 'unfit' elements. The objective is a homogeneous mindset, based on self-discipline, sacrifice, obedience, endurance and esprit-de-corp.

So, dear Mauro, through significant degrees of mental and physical stress, we learn the fundamental of military rules; the policies, the etiquette, the customs and the eccentricities of our particular branch of the services (the Air Force) which, I'm told, is the best of the three.

Please say hello to Silvia, Adi, and all the others. Tell Giovanni not to be so... stingy with his correspondence and tell all that I miss them and I dream of coming home in a few weeks.

A warm embrace,
Roberto

Having finish his letter, Roberto looked around the dormitory and saw most of his comrades sleeping or reading magazines. He decided to do some reading as well and went to his metal cabinet to get the book he had bought in Rome. It was *'Bonjour Tristesse'* by Francois Sagan, a French author very popular at the time. He read a dozen pages and then, he too fell asleep.

The following day, having gotten over the fever, they were taken to parade square for the reading of the journal. The cadets were more restless than usual and gave signs of boredom and impatience: someone bumped a guy on the line in front, who in turn swung around and punched the presumed disturber.

Another tipped the hat of an airman over his eyes. A cadet at the back pulled the chewing gum out of his mouth, rolled it into a hard ball, threw it at someone in front. Meanwhile Warrant Officer Iovine paced up and down the flank of the company shouting: "Stiiilll!"

As soon as he'd gone by, Cicci pressed his finger against Livio's hands, at the back, in 'at ease' position. Livio tried to grab it and twist it. After several misses, conscious of the spectators and wanting to up the ante, Cicci took a step forward, unzipped his pants, pulled his penis and placed it in Livio's hand. This time Livio did catch it and squeezed it hard. The agonizing cry of pain and laughter obliterated the voice of the officer reading the 'news of the day' .

W/O Iovine ran back and forth yelling: "Who did it?"

No one replied.

"No one will eat" shouted the lieutenant, "until the guilty party comes forward."

Despite the threat, no one advanced.

The company was detained and forced to march for a full hour and had to eat their meal cold.

Even this was esprit-de-corp!

They were getting close to the end of formal training. The disjointed group of individuals of early days, together with the 'esprit-de-corp', had acquired a unified deportment and become a cohesive group. Their posture was straighter, their marching stride smarter and perfectly synchronized. When they stepped on the hard ground, rather than a staccato hail of bullets as it sounded at the beginning, it was now a thundering thump.

The student, the farmer, the tannery worker, were on the way of becoming real soldiers.

- IX -

THE OATH

Only a few days remained before Roberto's group would take the oath.
The actual date had been fixed at the tenth of December, probably because, together with the end of the theoretical course, it also coincided with the festivity of the *Madonna of Loreto*, patron of the Air Force.

Notwithstanding its ceremonial importance, no one regarded it as a solemn promise to the flag, the Country or any other symbolic abstraction. Despite being the peak of the cold war, Italians of that generation joined the Forces only as a means to have a job or a career. They had no illusions of conquests or of 'exporting' democracy or other political ideals to foreign Countries. Hence, for the cadets, the oath was just the day which separated marches and other pointless war games from the more valuable classroom time in the *Sirtori* Airplane zone, removed boring routines from the actual practices of specialized trades. After that day, they would no longer be recruits, but qualified Air Force personnel, subject to lesser discipline and worthy of some respect. It was the end of forced captivity and everyone was champing at the bit in anticipation.

The ominous gates of the guardhouse would be opened and on the other side there would be girls, pizza places, restaurants, uncensored movies and even bordellos.

Everyone felt a bit special, the general attire just that much better; uniforms pressed, shoes shined, caps straightened. Despite the cavalier attitude, when the cadets marched in parade in front of the ceremonial stand, the martial music, the synchronized steps, the pride, would make it a moment that would remain in their minds for the rest of their lives.

On the day that Roberto's group took the oath, it had rained until early morning and the air was brisk and refreshing. By ten o'clock the sun peeked through the clouds and a light mist rose from the southern end of parade-square. When the battalion reached the far end of the *Piazzale*, the captain ordered a turn-about and the thundering step of the men, heard as one, confirmed its perfect execution. The Aviator's march began to play from four large speakers behind the stands and momentarily, in the distance, a uniform grey-blue block began to emerge from the haze. White gloved hands swayed in a syncopated rhythm across the blue coats.

They advanced, and reached the elevated platforms where the school commander, the civil authorities and special guests stood.

Captain Cricchi, who led the battalion, raised his ceremonial sword and shouted:

"Attenti-aaa!"

Another thunder answered his command, soon followed by, "Left!."

Eight hundred feet rose a foot from the ground and came down with a thunderous boom while, in a well synchronized movement, all heads snapped to the left and the gun muzzles were lifted forty five degrees.

It was a happy moment for everyone, but especially for those who had parents, girls or friends watching the parade.

At the end of the ceremony, the cadets who had trained in the hobby shop building airplane models, had their moment of glory. Everyone was asked to move at the edge of the square, while several mini planes were placed at the center. One by one they took to the air and, under the expert hands of those who held the remote controls, the planes made loops, vertical climbs and vertiginous dives to the delight of the crowd. The most impressive was a scale reproduction of a WWII German V1 flying bomb. It was held to the ground by an airman, while another pumped air and propellant into the pulse-engine. At ignition it was released and darted off like a bullet. A third cadet operated the commands and made it perform incredible aerobatics.

Everyone, hand over the ears because of the extreme noise, followed the astonishing maneuvers.

At the end of the show the crowd exploded in a prolonged and well-deserved applause.

- X -

OUT OF THE GATE

Those students who lived in Caserta or in nearby towns, were the lucky ones as they could briefly visit their families. And, if they had made a formal request for an extended leave, called *pernotto*, they could stay home overnight and return before midnight of the following day.

Roberto, Toto and many others who lived far, remained at the academy. Their only comfort was going to be the 'superior' meal promised for that special occasion. And, if they passed inspection, permission to spend a couple of hours downtown.

Rumor had it that *'lasagna al forno'* would be served that day, and remembering the exquisite taste of his *nonna's*, Roberto felt his mouth water.

Unfortunately, when it was served, the 'special' dish was a macaroni slab, held together by a strange concussion of melted cheese, béchamel and overspiced tomato sauce, sprinkled with green pees as hard as bullets.

Roberto shook his head in disgust as his empty stomach promptly shut its door.

Just like the language, during its migration south of the peninsula, the lasagna had undergone an unsavory transformation.

"Aren't you eating?" Toto asked him.

"No, I have a sudden stomach ache."

It wasn't a total lie.

After lunch all cadets were lined up on parade grounds. When the 'break the lines' was ordered, they all ran towards the exit like a heard of crazy buffalos, looking forward to the delights envisioned beyond the gates.

Unfortunately, standing in the middle of the way, a duty officer and his helpers examined the approaching crowd for out of ordinance clothing, irregular hair cut, unshaved faces etcetera.

"Hey you" yelled the officer spotting a transgression, "where do you think you're going with those multicolor socks? It's not carnival you know? You are confined to barracks for three days."

"Airman" he shouted stopping another, "show me your hat. It looks like a seagull with folded wings. What happened to the steel wire? What did you think would keep it straight, fumes from your brain? Consigned three days."

"You! Yes you smart fellow. Why the fancy shoes? Are you going to a disco? Go put your boots on and dance in the dormitory with your comrades."

"Airman, your hair is longer than a woman's. Go have it sheared and try again next week."

All those picked for non-conformance could forget about going to town, as no excuse or prayer could change the verdict of the duty officer. The others, having safely passed inspection, rushed out of the gate and flocked toward the city center. But even then they must behave properly, salute the watch patrol and all the officers they met. Some, either remembering the lesson on military salute, or still scared of the duty officer, quickly brought the right hand to their visor and stood to attention even when meeting a hotel doorman or a uniformed postman.

The ones who had applied for the night out, had to contend with the *Deus ex machina* of the administrative office where leaves, permits, and doctor's visits were issued. Everything in that office revolved around Warrant Officer Busato, a middle- aged, mild mannered man of average height and constitution, with big reddish mustaches a-la-Buffalo-Bill.

Within the academy ground he rode a bicycle and if a cadet happened to pass by, chances were he would be enrolled for some personal duty. He always had something to carry, fix or move; a desk, a locker, a table a box or some other paraphernalia.

Naturally, knowing his importance in relation to permits, no one dared deny him help. He was not a bad fellow, and became even more agreeable with those who used his hobby to their advantage. He was an avid stamp collector, and couldn't resist the temptation to enrich his assortment at student's expense.

Before signing a permit, he held his pen in the air and asked: "Tell me young man, do you have any stamps by any chance?"

That very day, Toto happened to go by his office. W/O Busato saw him and asked the same question.

"As a matter of fact I do" Toto replied, "but they are at home."

"I'll give you a *pernotto* if you go and fetch them."

"But I live near Lecce, about 250 miles from here. It would take me two days just for the train round trip. It's a pity" Toto continued, "because I have even stamps from San Marino, the Vatican and England."

"Well then, what if I give you a short leave of three plus two days?"

"That ought to do it" Toto answered. "At that" he now telling Roberto, "his right mustache started to vibrate. I had the impression that the picture of the '*Black Penny*' flashed into his eyes."

"What picture did you say?"

"The *Black Penny!* The one with the profile of Elisabeth I, the most famous stamp in the world. Obviously you don't collect stamps, but anyway, I got my permit."

"Have a nice trip."

"And you?" Toto asked collecting his rucksack, "what are you going to do?"

"I'll write some letters, maybe go to a movie and take a walk in the park. Go home and have a good time, I'll see you when you return."

Toto's account told Roberto that unless he adjusted to the prevailing modus operandi and played the game, he would never gain any favors. It wasn't going to be easy for him to accept that reality.

After his friend left, Roberto showered, wore a fresh uniform and walked toward the city center, alone. He wasn't in the mood to talk to anybody, nor to be dragged into places he was determined to avoid. He was content to stroll about and acquaint himself with the town. See if beside the Royal Palace and its gardens, there was anything else of interest.

After a while, tired of the multitude of military people he encountered, the constant saluting of officers, and the dreadful sound of the local dialect, he buried himself into a cinema.

When he came out, it was already dark, and the sidewalks were sparsely populated. He breathed the fresh night air, thinking of the movie just seen. It starred Rock Hudson as a colonel of the Strategic Air Command and, during its projection, Roberto dreamed of being that high-ranking officer, instead of a simple student at the beginning of his career. He was convinced he had the capacity, but wondered if, when and how he would reach that distant goal. He was too impatient to think in terms of years. Unfortunately, the present system of promotions was based on seniority much more than merit. Therefore, currently, it could probably take him three years to be sergeant. Then he would have to pass a university test to become an officer.

Meanwhile, he could try to be among the best by the end of the course, in a position to choose a good destination in northern Italy, near Silvia, his friends, his mother.

He kept walking on and dreaming of a brilliant career. If nothing else it helped soften his present grief.

When the sentinel saluted and stamped his foot on the wooden platform, Roberto suddenly realized he had arrived at the gate. From the pinnacle of his dreams, he fell again into the melancholy depth of the real world.

The following Sunday several cadets – Livio and Carlo among them – had planned a trip to Capri. Although Roberto considered the idea, he ultimately decided against it. Nor did he join others who were going down town, but elected to visit the park of the Royal Palace. He had wished to go there since he had seen it in photographs and today was a good opportunity.

He walked towards the back of the Palace and moved fast along the large park avenues. They were bordered by nicely kept meadows, and crossed by numerous paths, scattered with elegant marble statues.

All around, the typical Sunday traffic was coming and going, some afoot and some piled in carriages pulled by horses.

After a while, Roberto sat on a bench and let his mind indulge in pleasant memories. Then, he pulled pen and paper from a side pocket of his jacket and began to write:

Carissima Silvia,

Today, during my free time, I decided to visit the gardens of the Royal Palace. I am still here now, sitting on a stone bench, far away from the thoroughfare, alone with you. I jot down a phrase, then I close my eyes and think about us, about the future.

When I open them again, I meet Diana the hunter, standing at the edge of a fountain, with a quiver over one shoulder, her head turned towards me, seemingly observing my movements. She seems to wonder, just as I do, why on a beautiful day like this, I'm here alone, far away from you.

The bloodhounds at her side sniff the air, a frozen fauna about to awake from a long lethargy.

I listen to the silence, interwoven with the rustle of leaves of camphor trees, of Lebanese cedars, and when a gust of wind blows my way, I can hear the sound of the water jets, like whispers of love. I close my eyes and pretend it's your voice. I write a few more words and then stop to contemplate the distant hills, pretending they are those of Tuscany, dreaming I have returned to your side. But soon, transported by the wind, the air is filled with unknown accents, and behind me, even without turning my head, I can feel the mass of Vanvitelli's Palace. Then

I know I'm still faraway from you and to console myself, I close my eyes again and, in my memory, I return to our sweetest hours of love, to that grassy spot at the water edge of the Arno River.
  What else could I do from here, but live on memories?
  I must go now, before my mood turns into sadness.
  I'll write you soon again. Very soon.

I love you,
Roberto

- XI -

BAPTISM OF THE AIR

On Monday, Roberto's group was taken to *Capodichino* airport near Naples for a short flight.

Since no one had flown before, it was named 'Baptism of the Air' and everyone was enthusiastic about the new experience.

Although still winter, the weather was very warm and during the one-hour trip, the tarpaulin of the military truck was rolled up so people would breath fresh air.

At the airport the truck stopped near a World War II *Savoia-Marchetti SM 82*. The plane must have been parked in the sun for hours as, once on board, with the padded flying gear and the parachute, it felt like entering an oven wearing a straitjacket. Soon Roberto felt sweat stream over his chest and his backbone and his forehead beading with droplets.

At last the plane rolled on a runway and after an interminable run, it finally took off and headed toward the Tyrrhenian Sea. Out of the window, Roberto saw the mainland recede, the sea move towards him. He felt a sensation of nausea and a gush of saliva in his mouth, a prelude to vomiting. Beside the inconvenience it would bring a lot of embarrassment to throw up in front of his colleagues on his very first flight. He desperately tried to resist the urge.

"Look down to the right" someone yelled, "at five o' clock, you can see the island of Capri."

Roberto turned his head slowly. Floating like a gigantic green iceberg in the placid surface of the Tyrrhenian Sea, he saw the beautiful isle. It looked like a big emerald embroidered by the coral roofs of its villas. It sure is beautiful, Roberto thought, and for a moment he was disappointed to have missed visiting it because of his foolish prejudices against the South.

He checked his watch, the flight would have lasted at least another thirty minutes; it would seem an eternity. He swallowed again and hoped he'd overcome the critical moment.

Maybe he was going to make it.

"Eh Roberto" Toto asked cheerfully, "how do you like it?" He seemed undisturbed by the heat, the stinky air and by the deafening noise of that vintage airplane.

"I do" he answered mechanically while unbuttoning his shirt and fanning some air around his face with his hat.

Finally, the plane veered right, drew a large circle in the clear sky and started the descent heading towards the landing strip. Roberto looked out of the window a last time, while the coast ran toward him. It was almost sunset and the horizon was tinted with a violet haze and a strange yellow band. Was that what people called 'Neapolitan yellow?'

Near the coast the sea was rippled by a gentle breeze, as the sunlight hit the beach diagonally outlining soft, low dunes. A small river meandered toward the sea and near its mouth several white boats were moored at a dock.

At last the airplane lowered its flaps and Roberto saw the land run toward him, then felt a bump, and was deafened by the triumphal hurrah that welcomed touch down.

He had made it!

* * * * *

The following morning, all cadets were gathered in the large room of the school general store where some non-military personnel employed by *'Unione Militare'* had readied two long tables covered with merchandise for an itinerant sale: Remington electric razors, Geloso tape recorders, fountain pens, books, rings, banknote holders with the symbol of the academy, which was the legendary Icarus fabricating wings to escape from Crete's labyrinth.

The sale was sponsored by the school and the students could pay their purchases by monthly instalments which would be deducted from their pay. All profits would go to the Aviator's orphans.

After thoroughly examining the merchandise Toto decided to buy the silver ring bearing the symbol of the academy, the note holder and the small Geloso tape recorder to play music while in the hobby shop. Roberto purchased a Remington electric razor, as shaving every morning with the blade razor irritated his skin and sometimes cut his face. He also bought the silver ring, which he wanted to modify in the hobby shop, to wear it on his little finger.

Almost everybody had bought something either to keep or as presents for when they would go home on leave.

Once he finished adjusting his ring, Roberto offered to help the boss of the hobby shop, a civilian of indefinite age, rather plump and jovial, who had lost his left arm during WW II. Although skilful with one arm, he was having problems giving the last touch on a wood airplane model he was preparing for an upcoming exhibition.

He gladly accepted Roberto's help and told him to return any time. "Maybe next time I'll help you with something" he said. Roberto thanked him or the offer and remained a bit longer to write a letter to his friends.

Dear Mauro and Giovanni,

only e few lines to let you know that in a few days we will receive our Christmas leave. It will be a welcome ten days away from military routine. I'm looking forward to being with you and Silvia talking about old times. I promise not to bore you with my new experiences. Now that the worse part is over - at least I hope- I can say that the challenge was worthwhile. Twelve weeks of exercising, and intensive drilling, have produced more camaraderie among us than the many years spent in school.

Talking of school, in the next few days we will have several exams. I am a little apprehensive as I didn't study as much as I should have. I also hope they will not subtract any points for the 'unjust' punishment I received earlier.

Don't tell Silvia yet of my return as I wish to surprise her.

Please let me know what's new with you and all our mutual friends.

I hope you're in good health.
Roberto.

- XII -

THE COLONEL'S MESSAGE

That week ended with a multitude of term exams, written and oral. A few days later all students were summoned to a large hall where several high ranking officers were chatting among themselves. When all students were aligned and stood to attention, a captain went to the low wooden platform, adjusted the microphone and ordered: 'At-ease'.

"I'm going to start a roll-call" he said, "those whose name is called, will step out of ranks and align against the right wall. The others will remain where they are."

Some of the boys started making assumptions. Had they failed the exams? Were they to be punished?

"Maybe it's to tell us the date of our Christmas leave" somebody ventured.

"For that" someone else replied, "there would be no need to split us."

Meanwhile, Toto, Roberto, Franco, Tze-Tze, Pennellone, Patrizio were among those called out. Everyone knew they had scored top marks.

What was it then?

Whispered suppositions travelled from one student to the next while curiosity increased.

Finally the roll call ended and the captain announced the arrival of a colonel, causing expectations to rise even higher. When he appeared, the bustle faded into absolute silence, and when he reached the microphone, it felt as though everyone had stopped breathing.

The air was loaded with expectations.

"On this side" he said pointing to the right, "are the students who got the best results. Results above average, sometimes even above our expectations. These young boys have spent their time at best, studying and even sacrificing their leisure time to achieve higher objectives. I congratulate you and hope you'll have the perseverance to continue on this path."

His eyes scanned the faces of those boys anxiously waiting for a favourable conclusion.

"Ten years ago" he continued, "four short years after the war, our Prime Minister De Gasperi, made the difficult decision to ask for Italy's inclusion into the North Atlantic Alliance. This restored a certain parity to our international standing, only two years after signing a punitive peace agreement. Now, the Italian Air Force has a chance to reinforce this pact by a stronger alignment with Washington removing doubts about Italy's flirtation with neutrality. As part of this commitment" he continued with greater vehemence, "after your return from your Christmas leave, you will be required to do more."

He paused and within the group he had addressed, looks of disbelief were exchanged. "What the hell" someone whispered, "is this the reward for our performance? Just more work?"

"Yes" said the colonel as though reading the minds of the airmen, "In addition to your normal study program, you'll begin a course of English language. Those who pass will have the opportunity to attend advance missile training in the United States of America."

The colonel words were still echoing in the air when a loud hooray thundered in the room. The boys shook hands, congratulated each other, and slapped shoulders.

A few of them had heard of that possibility by parents or relatives employed at the Ministry in Rome, but most often they were considered unreliable rumours that never materialized.

This time they did.

Roberto's frustrations suddenly disappeared. He felt like hugging that colonel who, with simple clear words, helped him regain trust in a system that finally recognized and rewarded the best.

From the tannery to America, he kept repeating to himself. A dream was coming true.

When silence was regained the colonel now frowning, addressed the students on the left side and said: "And here we have the students who didn't work hard enough and failed. I can only tell you that you have disappointed us. Not only you will not go to America, but many will have to repeat the course with no chance to select your final destinations. I hope this unpleasant event will imprint on your mind that destiny is not built by fortune but by your own hands. In the Air Force, rewards and punishments are always at hand, ready to be applied to those who deserve them."

Toto elbowed Roberto who had stopped listening. The news had been like a shot of adrenaline. America was beyond his wildest expectations. He would immediately wright the good news to his mother, to Mauro, Silvia.

Silvia!

At that thought his enthusiasm ebbed. How long would he be away from her? How would she take the prolonged distance? Would this advance or delay the unspoken plans of engagement, family?

One thing at the time, he told himself. There was still the English course to overcome.

Damn!

Many of his friends had studied English in school, while he had studied French. He'll have to work harder than ever if he wanted to succeed.

- XIII -

GOING HOME

The day of the Christmas leave had finally arrived.
The dormitories seemed to overflow with excitement. The boys prepared their knapsacks, amid laughter, chatter and schemes of what they intended to do once they were home. Girlfriend, good food, wine and sleeping late, were things most commonly mentioned.

They descended the large stairways of the Palace in droves like a stampeding herd, and then ran across the square to the train station. While waiting for the train, many dug the stylized silver eagle out of their pockets and placed it on the left breast side of their jackets even though, by regulation, their entitlement to that emblem came only after final exams.

Many would travel up to Naples together, and then take trains to different destinations. It was a voyage full of expectations, particularly for those who, leaving far away, had not ben home since enrolment.

Roberto, Patrizio e Renzo, would travel together up to Pisa. Between Napoli and Roma they spoke enthusiastically about going to America and the experience they would gain. At Rome's Termini station several French girls boarded their wagon and they were promptly invited in their compartment. They conversed, traded compliments and caresses. Near Pisa they exchanged addresses and promised to write each other.

Pisa was the final destination for Patrizio and Renzo. Roberto took the Florence connection and disembarked at San Romano.

He crossed the small waiting room connecting with the small square at the front of the station. The acrid smell of cigarettes brought back school-time memories when he took the train to go to the Technical Institute of

Pisa. And just like then, the old Sequi Bus was in service shuttling between San Romano, Castelvecchio and Santa Chiara.

He had taken it so many times.

Roberto jumped onto the bus and the conductor, whom he recognized immediately, while printing his ticket, looked at him with a vague sign of familiarity.

Perhaps he could not conciliate the serious looking young man in a neat blue uniform with the cheeky youngster of yesteryear. Roberto smiled, placed his knapsack on the rack and sat on the right hand side, near the window. He wanted to fully experience the emotions of his first return and that side afforded him a better view of the places he wished to see. He anticipated the pleasure of seeing his mother, his dearest friends and Silvia.

Particularly Silvia.

What a pain not having a telephone at home, not being able to call her right away. He had ultimately let her know of his arrival from a last letter to Mauro, and had suggested they meet around five in the afternoon in the Market Square of Santa Chiara.

Finally, the bus moved with a jerk. It passed the railroad intersection and over the bridge of the Arno River, Roberto thought of the many times he had crossed it on foot or with his bike. He looked towards the low dam and the ruins of the old Medici mill. The water level was higher than usual and the color of cappuccino, indicating recent and abundant rain. He looked at the high right bank where the ferry-boats used to be moored before the reconstruction of the bridge. Farther down, to the little bay where, in the summer, as a young boy, he swam with his friends. Now, one could no longer swim in those waters. Contamination and a greater consciousness of its consequences, discouraged even the most determined.

At the end of the bridge, dominated by its quadrangular bell-tower and partially surrounded by its ancient walls, the town came into view. Despite the amount of new construction it still had the appearance of a medieval town. Ten years hence, Roberto thought, that panorama, practically unchanged for centuries, will no longer be. Between the destruction of the war and the unstructured rebuilding of the recent 'miraculous' economic boom, Castelvecchio's physiognomy would change forever.

It's already changed, he thought. Yet, in a way, it's still the same. Like a dear friend of whom one recognizes the features.

On impulse he got off at the first scheduled stop, just outside the town's southern walls, before the bus turned towards Via Francesca Nord on its way to Santa Chiara.

He said goodbye to the driver, crossed the street, and went through the archway of Porta Catiana and proceeding toward the center he looked around with renewed curiosity, examining people, shops, places, remembering the particular spots where certain events had occurred. The entranceway where his old piano teacher lived, and remembered the day his lesson was interrupted by a bombing raid, his running away towards his home. The ruins of collapsed building obstructed the way.

Lost and fearful, he had stopped in front of a mountain of debris when, as in apparition, he had seen his dear grandmother, white as a specter, come down from the ruins calling: "Roberto", "Roberto *mio*".

A sad smile crossed his lips; she was dead now, and he could no longer hear her cherished voice.

He turned right, towards the small square fronting the old Badia Church; it was the one his grandmother liked to attend. Inside that church there were the remains of ten soldiers of Castelvecchio , who died during the Great War. Although he had not entered that church in a very long time, he remembered the marble tombs, the white altars, the large antique paintings of saints, the life-size fourteenth century crucifix. He noticed with some disappointment that the cast iron fountain no longer adorned the square, and the carpenter's shop at the far corner was gone.

He smiled.

Once, while his grandmother followed church functions, he slipped away and amused himself by filling his mouth at the little fountain and then spitting it onto the wood shaving fire the carpenter had lit under a small cauldron to melt the glue.

After restarting the fire several times, the man realized the prank and Roberto ran inside the church and joined the singing. The man chased him, but luckily, due to his work attire, he stopped at the door. Fearing he'd be scolded, Roberto recited a silent prayer.

Someone up there must have heard him because next time he turned around, the man had gone.

Near the center of town, in a new outside corner bar, across from the cathedral, some old people sat at round tables leisurely observing passersby. They didn't seem to recognize Roberto, and he felt their stare follow him for a long time.

Actually, he didn't recognize many of them either and, passing by he heard unfamiliar inflections. Perhaps they were the evacuees from the south, moved to Castelvecchio during World War II with the advancing American army. Initially considered temporary 'guests', they had later become a part of the town's mosaic. The older folks still tried, without success, to adopt new, local habits, but were unable to modify their native accents. Their sons instead, fully integrated, were now only distinguishable because of their unusual last names.

The sidewalks, there busy with people coming from or going to the various shops: Gino's bakery, Sabatino's butchery, Daria's grocery shop, the new supermarket. And on a corner Dino's cart with his freshly roasted chestnuts.

Roberto inhaled their warm, sweet smell, mixed with that of incense, wafting from the doors of the nearby church.

Some of the town's history could be read on the walls of its buildings, on the rare and worn out coat-of-arms, on the traces of bullets left over by the war and the still visible damage over the façade of the *Municipio*, or Town Hall. But also from the various doors in solid oak, from the ancient, bronze door Knockers with lions' heads, Muses heads or other mythical figure. In addition, it could be also surmised by the new street names; those of heroes or martyrs of the last conflict.

Roberto could have closed his eyes and perfectly remember the sequence of those doors, facades, palaces, tenements, shops and *'chiassi'*, as they called those unusual dark and somnolent tunnels, that people used as short cuts to reach the center of town. When people went by, they seemed to come alive with the echo of steps bouncing back from the high arches.

There was a certain order in Roberto's recollections, like a memorized musical score whose notes' sequence is impossible to forget.

* * * * *

A young man, of approximately his age, entered a gate bearing a large sign in bold characters, perhaps a shoe manufacturing company. Roberto followed him mentally, and imagined a life that could have been his.

He didn't remember if that company existed when he left town to join the Air Force; so many were born of late.

He thought nostalgically about those old walls, which had seen him play with other kids, run to school or home, ring the bell of an entrance door and then run away and hide behind a corner, explode fire crackers during some holiday, or chase young girls. Now, those same walls, seemed to look at him as he walked at a fast military pace; perhaps they remembered he had learned it from his grandmother, way before he had joined the Forces.

He finally reached Via Francesca; the street where he had lived. This morning the asphalt of the well travelled roadway shined in the sun. Roberto remembered when, after the passage of the war front, truckloads of gravel were poured all over the old unpaved surface, full of pot holes and dust, followed by loads of tar and the acrid smell that rose from the black concoction. Then, gigantic compressors came to smooth down the old provincial road.

Afterwards, the traffic of scooters, cars and trucks increased considerably, and the distance between towns became shorter. But young kids had lost the pleasure of playing in the puddles after a rain.

He hastened his pace and passed by the house of the old *Podestà*, the mayor during fascist times. Fearing for his dubious political past he had enclosed his house and garden with a metal-mesh fence. Behind it, a ferocious black Belgian shepherd barked at every passer-by. Two more houses and finally, behind the luxurious foliage of his garden, his home appeared.

"Mamma" he called passing the gate, "Mamma!" he repeated loudly.

She emerged on the terrace and came down running. She was wearing an apron and she seemed to have aged. They kissed and embraced in the garden, then climbed the stairway and entered the kitchen. He immediately recognized the wholesome scent of his home.

"You are so handsome in a uniform" she said gazing at him, "you are the mirror image of your father."

"Thank you, mother. I'll keep my uniform a while longer to show Mauro and Giovanni, but I'll change into civilian clothes later, to go to Santa Chiara."

"You'll go to see Silvia?"

Those were the words, but her sad smile seemed to say 'you have hardly arrived, and already leave me…'.

"Yes, mother" he mildly replied. "I promised." Then wishing to change topic he said: "It's almost lunch time, can I set the table? What are we going to eat, I smell something that stirs up my appetite."

"I prepared lasagna, just the way you like it."

"Oh, mum, you know how long I've been dreaming of it…?"

* * * * *

"I'll go" said Roberto hearing steps outside. He pocked his head out and exclaimed: "Rascals you anticipated me."

Mauro and Giovanni appeared at the door.

"Come in, come in" said Roberto's mother, "we are finished eating already."

"Military life seem to suit you" said Mauro as Roberto pulled two chairs for them, "you look as fit than ever."

"Really…" added Giovanni.

"You look good as well, guys" said Roberto. "Tell me what's new…"

Patrizia left the room to give them privacy and they talked for over two hours. Then noticing that Roberto had glanced at his watch a couple of times, Mauro smiled and asked:

"You have to go somewhere?"

"Yes. I'll have to go to Santa Chiara. Can we meet tonight?"

"Of course" said Giovanni, "but now you'd better go, I'm sure Silvia is dying to see you."

"I'll be back for supper" said Roberto lowering his voice, "otherwise the old lady won't be too happy with me. Let's meet at the Pepi's Bar at nine."

"Goodbye."

- XIV -

WITH SILVIA

Wearing a pair of jeans, an old leather jacket, and a pair of black moccasins Roberto walked to the bus stop.

In Santa Chiara, the Market Square was full of people.

It was almost five o'clock, soon I'll meet my love, Roberto thought.

Walking up and down the Piazza, old school memories and the more recent ones of the tannery surfaced his mind. The minutes separating him from Silvia felt like hours.

Finally, he saw her cherished elegant figure come out of a side street and his heart began to beat faster.

She is more beautiful than what I remembered, he thought.

They rushed towards one another, briefly embraced and kissed on the cheeks; there might be seen people who knew them and would report to her parents.

"Silvia!" he exclaimed losing himself in her delicate scent.

"Roberto… this seems like a dream."

"To me too. Where should we go?"

"I have my father's car, we could go to the woods on the hills."

"Excellent idea."

"Start on foot, I'll go fetch the car and catch you around the corner."

"I'm gone" said Roberto turning away.

He crossed the street, turned left at the light and continued on the Via del Bosco in a northerly direction. Thinking they might make love, was sufficient to infuse him with euphoria.

Silvia reached him near the Town Hall gardens.

"Hello aviator" she yelled slowing down, "going my way?"

"How did you know that, Blondie?"

"Instinct I suppose."

He got in, slammed the door, caressed the hand over the gear shift and then reached for her thigh.

"If you want us to go in the ditch" she said smiling, "continue what you're doing. But then you'll have to tell my father what happened."

"Okay, okay, I'll stay still another five minutes. But no longer" said Roberto without retracting his hand. "Do you know where to go?"

"I certainly do" she replied slyly.

Surprised, Roberto looked at her and she added: "To the beautiful place we once visited with the school, near the ruins where you abandoned me in Benito's company."

"It's exactly where I wanted to go. But please don't mention Benito, you know I was jealous of him."

"And from what I can see" she said in a laughter, "you still are."

Roberto did not answer, but when she put her hand over his, he said: "I love you, Silvia."

At the top of the hill, they skirted the Bargalli's property, abandoned the paved road and entered the graveled one along the crest of the hill.

"Slow down" said Roberto. "otherwise you'll cover the car with dust and you'll have problems explaining to your father."

"Good idea."

"A bit further there are several paths leading to the thick of the wood. There, take the second to the right."

"You seem to be very familiar with this place."

"I've never taken any girl here, if that's what you imply" said Roberto. "Or anyplace else for that matter. I used to come here with my friends when you girls had three hours of Home Economics. Sometimes we even swam in the small lake behind the villa."

"You certainly can tell a story."

"It's the truth, my dear" said Roberto. And then, "Turn to the left now, there is a clearing. Here it is, stop."

There was no further need for words. They moved to the back of the car, they clutched in a strong embrace and after the first passionate kiss, the desire accumulated during those three long months of distance, burst out of their young bodies. They quickly removed coat and jacket while continuing to kiss, then Silvia pushed her hand between them to unfasten Roberto's belt. He started to unbutton her dress with trembling hands and felt his desire swell inside his body. He lifted her bra and kissed her breasts trying at the same time to remove his trousers.

"The fragrance of your skin is an aphrodisiac" he whispered kissing her neck.

"Yours drives me insane. Love me Roberto."

He lifted himself a little and for a moment observed her semi-naked body under his. With one hand he caressed her silky belly, so smooth and supple; it was soft and warm and made him anticipate the pleasure of his contact with her soft pubic hair. His fingers reached further down and he felt her quiver with pleasure.

"Come inside me."

Even her words excited him.

She received him in her soft nest and began to move slowly.

When she felt close to be totally invaded by pleasure she had a moment of hesitation.

"Don't worry, my love" he said realizing it, "I'll be careful."

He too was close to his orgasm. When he heard her moaning of pleasure and felt her gradually relax, he reluctantly left that warm and pleasant harbor and abandoned himself to his own pleasure. He closed his eyes and moved his head close to Silvia's neck, kissing her again softly, and breathing in unison with her. She caressed his hair, "I wanted you so badly, Roberto, I thought the days would never pass."

"Me too" he said remembering the moments that preceded his sleep in Caserta. When, to sweeten the feeling of doubt and anxiety, abandoned himself to his dreams, evoking the moments of ecstasy spent with her.

Silvia continued to caress him, pressing her body against his. "Tell me about your courses, your new friends, Caserta…" she said pressing her body against his, breathing the scent of their love.

"I think the worst is passed" said Roberto, "it won't be as hard now. There were moments I thought to have made a mistake, and moments in which I missed you so much that I thought of running away and come back to you."

"My poor dear. Did you make new friends?"

"Yes. The one I'm closest to is Toto, a guy from the south, near Lecce." Roberto smiled, "we have little in common, but somehow we have become close friends. But no one can replace Mauro and Giovanni" he continued. "I missed them a lot and when I think of them, Dante's verses to Cavalcanti, come to my mind:

"Guido io vorrei che tu e Lapo ed io… – Guido I would like that you and Lapo and I…"

"I like Mauro a lot" Silvia said, "Giovanni too, but he is a bit too condescending, at times a bit insufferable."

"I know he gives that impression, but I know him well and I don't think he is that way. For me he is like a younger brother."

"What about this Toto? Have you been able to overcome your prejudice about the south."

"Well… I'm afraid some are still there, but it's not intolerance towards the people. It is… how can I put it? It is a dislike of a place that stinks of feudalism, antipathy for coarse dialects that degrade our beautiful language. The customs, so different from ours, give me an alien sensation, disquietude. But then you may say, I am the problem, not them."

"I won't answer that. That's enough. I didn't want a socio-political essay. Other things are more important to me."

"Like what?"

"Like… when will you go to America?"

Roberto sighed deeply. On this matter, his sentiments were mixed in a caldron of contrasting thoughts; excitement and separation, opportunities and distance, departures and returns.

"We don't know the exact date yet" he said. "And then I still need to pass the English exams. It will be months I think. But hopefully they'll give us a few days leave before departing."

"I will miss you terribly" she said leaning towards him.

"Me too, but I'll write you often."

"Will you?"

The last sunrays had just abandoned the high manes of the pine trees and a light mist rose from the damp ground. Birds' chatter filled the silent air. Evening had silently arrived.

"We must go" said Silvia, "or my parents will think I had an accident. Do you want a ride to Castelvecchio?"

"No, thanks. I'll catch the bus in the square and in ten minutes I'll be home."

"Will we see each other tomorrow? I won't have the car though, my father has to go to Florence."

"Then let's meet in Market Square at two we'll think of something."

They drove quietly for most of the way, each enwrapped in their thoughts.

"See you tomorrow then" said Roberto kissing her cheek.

That evening Roberto met with his friends.

He told them about the possibility of going to America for missile's training. Giovanni and Mauro were quite impressed. The latter, always keen on political subjects, said:

"I followed the matter of missiles' placement on television. General De Gaulle has refused to have them in French territory because the Americans wouldn't give him full control."

"True" Roberto replied, "but I think that accepting their deployment in Italy, our position within the Atlantic Alliance will be enhanced."

"As you know I'm a pacifist" said Mauro, "but certain realities cannot be overlooked. Hell, even the left parties haven't opposed the move."

"Yes" Roberto concurred, "and exploiting the American fear of Italian communism, real or inflated, our politicians have carved a preferential relationship with the United States."

"Mauro maybe a pacifist" said Giovanni, "but you, Roberto sound like a cynic."

"Realist" Roberto replied.

* * * * *

The days passed quickly.

On one side there were the hours with Silvia, with friends, with his mother, and the comfort of familiar accents and places, made more precious by the knowledge he would soon leave them behind. On the other side, there was the vision of America, and the unknown adventures and opportunities for the career he envisioned waiting ahead.

At night, when he went to bed, the pleasant day's recollections were mixed with the dreams and conjectures about the future. In the dark silence of his room, he often fell asleep in pursuit of a distant thought and woke up in the morning surprised to be still at home.

As days went by, the only thing he regretted was the little time he spent with his mother. When their eyes met, together with love, they seemed to express uneasiness. He was afraid to betray the thought that her hair, her posture, her slower pace, made him think that she was aging quickly. She, that her son had grown too rapidly and was now propelled towards his own future.

Now that they had come close and become friends, she seemed to want more of his company. Patrizia never complained, but her dignified silence was more eloquent than a thousand words.

The short leave was coming to an end and he would soon return to Caserta.

His company would be split in smaller groups before going to America. But before that, there was the hurdle of the English course and the exams in Rome. After, those who passed, would be issued new uniforms, and the beautiful navy-blue gabardine trench coat, sported by the airmen of previous courses back from America.

These coats made them easily identifiable and many of Roberto's friends approached them to hear their impressions of the New World or to ask the phone numbers of… accessible women. The word was that there were many, mostly married and of easy inclinations. Roberto thought of post-war times, when poor Italian women, pressed by need, had resorted to sleep with American soldiers, in exchange for food or cigarettes to resell in the black market. In those days it was called prostitution. Now, from what he could deduce, sleeping with strangers, seemed to be a much more acceptable practice.

* * * * *

On the day of departure Roberto went to Santa Chiara to say goodbye to Silvia, and at the moment of his leaving she shed a few tears. How many more goodbyes would there be in their relationship?

In the afternoon he saw his friends and promised to write them very soon. Then he donned his blue uniform and after kissing his mother, he left the house and walked to the bus stop. He was waiting at the stop of the Fallen Soldier Square when his old school friend Walter stopped his scooter to shake hands and ask him questions.

"How do you like your military life?... How long is your course?... Do you miss your family, your friends?"

He seemed genuinely interested and Roberto gladly answered him.

Then Walter said: "I found employment at a bank in a nearby town. Benito works in a bank as well" he continued, "but he is at BCI, in Florence."

Roberto nodded but did not make any comment; soon after the bus arrived and they said goodbye. Roberto thought about his old school pal Benito, their squandered friendship, and his pursuit of Silvia. He hated to admit it, but he still felt the sting of jealousy. What if during his long time away Benito would start wooing Silvia again? Roberto trusted her, but long absences could be dangerous.

He was soon on the train for yet another voyage south. His fears were sweeten by the thought that, perhaps, at the end of the course he'd go to America.

- XV -

THE ENGLISH LESSONS

A new cycle began at the school.
Marches, military indoctrination, algebra and physics were behind, but a new harder phase started. Now, as Polyvalent Jet Engine Mechanics, in addition to theory, there began actual work on engines, airframe and hydraulic systems.

In the morning, the students were taken to the Aircrafts Area where, beside the classrooms where the theory was taught, there were hangars with several jet engines, multiple electronic panels, and vintage fighter airplanes.

Towards the end of the first week, the airmen selected for the English language course were gathered in a large auditorium where they were told of the new program. A captain explained that the three to four weekly hours dedicated to the learning of the new language had to be 'carved out' from the free time, and confirmed that the final exams would be held in Rome.

Those who passed would be sent to America.

The Missile courses would begin in San Antonio, Texas and then continue at the NASA base of Huntsville, Alabama. During these courses, the participants would receive two salaries, one from the Italian Air Force Ministry, the other issued by NATO and the American Air Force.

On the following Monday, a middle age woman, accompanied by a lieutenant was introduced to the class as the language teacher. She had ragged looks, had no books or attaché case. As soon as her military escort left, she let herself drop on the armchair behind the desk and drew a long sigh.

"I've never taught military personnel" she said between long yawns, "therefore I haven't yet decided what method to follow. I suppose I'll improvise."

"Does teaching men in uniform require a particular teaching method?" Roberto asked.

The teacher looked at him as though awakening from a bad dream and after a long pause she said, "Honestly, I don't know."

Roberto couldn't hide his disappointment, paused a moment and then asked:

"When are we going to have our text book?"

"I'll order them when I decide which one to use."

"Should we take notes then?"

"If you wish."

It only took a couple of lessons for the students to realize that their teacher was lazy, uninterested and her language skills inadequate. Especially for them who needed to acquire a good working grasp of the language, quickly.

The additional proof of her unfitness came when Toto, having taped a BBC transmission on his recently acquired recorder, replayed it to the teacher in class. As expected, the teacher didn't understand a single word.

"There are only three months to the date of the exams" said Toto, "and only four hours a week to learn this language. How on earth are we going to do it?"

"We are fucked!" someone replied.

"We'll never make it with that bitch" said Renzo.

"I think I should talk to our captain again" said Roberto.

"She is the lover of a colonel" someone said trying to talk him out of it, "you'll get into trouble."

"I don't care" Roberto snapped. "Do you want to play it safe and fail or do you want to take a risk and give yourself a chance?"

He asked for a meeting with the company commander who asked him:

"Haven't I seen you before?"

"Yes sir. I came to tell you about the metal smelting notes."

"Oh yes, I remember. And what is it this time?"

He listened to Roberto's explanation.

"But" he then commented, "how do you know your teacher is inadequate if, as you say, you haven't studied English before?"

Roberto told him of the BBC recording and added: "Captain sir, I have studied Latin and French and I know this is not the way to learn a language. Besides, after four lessons she hasn't yet given us a text book. At this pace we won't be able to pass any test."

"I see."

"Sir" Roberto concluded: "whatever your decision, I do thank you for listening to our plea. We are genuinely concerned about making a good show with the Americans."

"Is that all?" the captain asked his lips curling with a wily smile.

"Do we have any other concern you mean?"

The captain nodded.

"Of course we do, sir" Roberto answered, "It would be a pity missing the opportunity to go to America because of inadequate language preparation."

"You can go now" said the captain getting up, "I'll see what I can do."

Roberto saluted and returned to his classroom.

"How did it go?" Everyone was around him.

"I'm not sure, but he listened to our concerns. At least we know we've done all we could…"

* * * * *

- XVI -

THE NEW TEACHER

The following Monday, as they entered the classroom the student noticed an English textbook sitting on their desk.

At eight o-clock sharp, a man about fifty, with a dark three-piece suit, black mustache a-la-Charles-Chaplin and a black umbrella entered the room. He seemed to have just stepped off a double decker in Soho.

"My name is Antonio Serra. I'm your new English professor from the University of Naples" he declared in a clear, strong voice. "I've been given the impossible task to teach you the rudiments of the English language in less than fifty hours. That's what we spend in a month of study at the university just to cover the grammar."

He stared around the class with vulpine eyes. Then continued: "It's a desperate case and ninety per cent of you will surely fail". He assumed an amused smile.

"Too bad, so sad! as the British would say. It's the other ten per cent that interest me and I will go at their speed."

The sigh of relief of a few good students was drowned in the mumbling complaint of the mass.

"And now" he said as he sat at his desk and opened his book, I will read you from page fourteen and by Wednesday you shall memorize the story and be ready to answer my questions.

"Jack lives in a pretty house surrounded by a lovely garden. In the middle of the garden, there is a fountain…"

* * * * *

Once the English course was finished, the cadets who had passed, were told to get ready to go to Rome for the final exams. They would stay there three days and lodge at the *Romagnoli* barracks, near the Air Force Ministry.

They were accompanied by two officers and the military chaplain, Don Dante, who told them:

"There might be an opportunity to attend mass at the Vatican. Perhaps even have a private audience with the pope."

Some were exultant, others couldn't have cared less. Renzo was one of the latter.

"Big fucking deal" he said, "I'd rather have an audience with my dick!"

"You blasphemous Tuscan" replied one of Don Dante's darlings, "Malaparte was right to call you 'Cursed Tuscans'."

"Fuck you" Renzo yelled back, "fuck the priest, fuck the Vatican and if you piss me off, I'll even include someone higher up."

"Enough you guys" sang a choir of voices.

Finally the controversy came to an end.

* * * * *

As they boarded the military bus, the Eternal City seemed to be awakening. San Peter's dome was glowing under the warm spring sun.

The exams were held in a large amphitheater at the American Embassy and, as the cadets entered the auditorium, they stared with awe at the electronic apparatus. At each desk there were buttons, speakers, earphones and other unknown gadgets. They were never told the exams would be conducted that way and had never used those devices.

An American instructor said something to the bewildered students, but between his strange accent and the cigar between his teeth, few people understood they were to sit and start the exam. Some did and the other soon followed, but every one was slow in wearing the headsets, finding the 'ON' button, adjusting the volume.

When they did, the story had already started.

Eventually some understood that it had to do with two people called Mary and Sebastian. The person who had recorded it had a strange accent, someone said it was Texan. A wave of dismay crossed the auditorium. At the end of the story the students had to respond to questions asked in the same lingo.

- XVII -

THE SHOOTING RANGE

They returned to Caserta.
Several days would go by before they would know the results of the exams, but given the circumstances the boys had no illusions. Meanwhile they continued to fulfill all the requirements of the course and a few days later several companies were loaded into lorries and taken to an isolated location of the countryside used as a shooting range.

It was a hilly site, suitable to exercise and acquire the rudiments of warfare shooting hand automatic guns, fifty-caliber machine guns, and throwing hand grenades.

The *Moschetti Automatici Beretta* - MAB submachine guns distributed, seemed in better shape than those used for parades. They were heavier too, since today the long magazines were filled with bullets. Several non-commission officers in charge of training and supervision were barking like angry dogs.

"Don't point the goddamn thing that way" a sergeant was yelling, "the fucking thing is loaded."

"Be careful with that MAB and lower it to the ground" shouted another, "you're *gonna* kill somebody..."

"Don't pull that lever, you've dropped your magazine. If you loose it you're *gonna* have to use your balls to shoot!"

After the initial excitement, a little discipline was acquired and, a few cadets at the time began firing. A few showers of bullets standing up, then, laying flat on the ground, single shots directed at far away target. One of the NCOs was keeping score. After, everyone had a turn at the heavy machine guns placed on rocky spots on the ground and aimed at a distant ravine. Two men at a time lay flat on their bellies, one doing the firing, the other, easing the cartridge belt out of the metal casing and waiting for his turn at shooting. The noise was unbearable and several people shoved pieces of Kleenex in their ears. Clouds of dust and bits of stone were flying on the almost vertical wall of the gradient hit by the bullets.

Around mid morning they took a rest, sat down on the patchy grass of the incline and swallowed the skimpy sandwich distributed by the draftees. Roberto sat with Toto and Mario who gulped down his bun with just two bites.

"To quench my appetite" said the big man, "I'd need six of these."

"No kidding," Roberto replied.

Mario was one of the taller and probably stronger cadet of the battalion.

"Next will be the hand grenades" said Toto. "I wonder if they'd be the same as my grandfather used during the Great War on the *Carso* line. He told me they had to rub the phosphorous side over a rough stone before throwing them."

"I hope we've got better stuff" said Mario, "but we'll soon see."

Roberto didn't comment. He had turned his head away and was observing the parched landscape, rocky and irregular. It wouldn't be good for any kind of gardening or crop growing, he thought. In the distance, in a slightly more even part of the terrain, he could see a small orange grove; he discerned two or three persons busy picking the fruits. He squinted and covered his eyes from the blinding sun and noticed they were loading them on two large baskets hanging on the back of a donkey.

"Come on guys, wake up and let's finish with this... *exert-cize*," yelled a staff corporal. Come and get your grenades, and don't touch the safety pin until told. Else we'll have to scrape you out of the ground with a spoon."

Three or four warrant officers stood beside a crate of hand grenades shaped like pine cones. They called six or seven men at a time.

"Pull the pin only when ready to throw. And for God sake, throw *it* – the grenade, not the pin – as far as you can. See if you can hit that soft earthy spot down valley, so we won't get stone splinters."

Roberto, Toto and Mario stood in line. A small airman – an air frame specialist, was just ahead of them and, as he tried to pull the pin, the grenade slipped from his hands and dropped to the ground.

"BOOOM!" Mario roared behind him. Many people laughed, but the sergeant beside him, who had seen the scene and thought the safety had been removed, became white as a sheet, his hands rose to his face and those near him heard a wet popping sound. Soon afterwards, they smelled something that didn't have anything to do with cordite; the poor fellow had literally shit in his pants.

When the laughing ceased and calm was restored, Toto threw his grenade. He shook his head in disgust, all that effort for nothing; it was a dud. Then was Roberto's turn. He looked at the stone wall down valley. On the other side there was a narrow mountain path that winded its way from the orange grove and beyond, up towards the shooting range and past. It wasn't considered a problem, as no one had been able to land his grenade even close to that wall. Roberto took a few steps and threw with all his strength; it was a good throw, it exploded near the wall, but he didn't hit it either.

Mario was next. He looked down to the sergeant and asked:

"How do you want me to throw it?"

"What! Are you deft? I said as far as you can."

Roberto followed the pantomime and noticed that an old man and the donkey with the basket of oranges had left the grove and seemed to be coming in their direction.

"Are you sure?" Mario insisted.

"No. Wait a while, I go ask the fucking department of Defense in Rome."

Several people laughed.

Mario didn't. He had probably noticed the man and the donkey as well, because he asked again "Tell me when I can throw."

"Through it now goddamn it, not next Christmas!"

Even if the sergeant had seen the old man and the donkey he knew they were far beyond reach and clear of danger.

Mario looked at Roberto, they exchanged a shrug, then he pulled the pin, raised his long powerful arms and threw it. The grenade arched high in the sky, over a tree and beyond the 'unreachable' wall, just as the old man and the donkey were approaching. When the sergeant realized it, he put his hands on his head and closed his eyes.

There was going to be a slaughter!

BOOM!

The grenade exploded and bits of metal and rocks smashed against the wall or flew up in the air. A cloud of dust rose from the ground. After what seemed an eternity, man and donkey, scared but apparently unhurt, were seen running, falling and tumbling downhill. The entire content of the two large baskets of oranges was dumped, spread around and rolled all over the incline.

"Let's go fetch them!" someone yelled.

It was taken as a command and the entire platoon ran down, climbed the short wall and continued down hill, catching as many oranges as possible. Relieved that the old man was unhurt, the sergeant didn't oppose the run. He just sat down on the ground, wiped his forehead with a white handkerchief and slowly regained his color.

The day after the shooting, Patrizio, Poli and another airman were in the arched roof section of the toilets. They used to go there to sing mountain jingles as they had discovered the resonance there was so good as to make a trio sound like the Wien choir.

"Yesterday was a good day" Patrizio said during a pause while rubbing his belly, "but I shouldn't have eaten fifteen oranges."

"Why not?" Poli asked.

"Too much acid. My poor ass burned like hell when I took my morning dump!"

- XVIII -

THE ENGLISH EXAMS

Finally Roberto's group was preparing to go to Rome. They would stay at the *Romagnoli* barracs near the Air Force Ministry. Two officers including the military chaplain would accompany them.

"There may be an opportunity to attend mass in the Vatican" he said, "and perhaps even have a private group audience with the pope."

Some were exultant, others couldn't have cared less. Renzo reviled the thought.

"Big fucking deal" he said, "I'd rather have an audience with my dick."

"You are a blasphemous Tuscan," replied one of Don Dante's darlings, "Malaparte was right to call you 'Cursed Tuscans'."

"Fuck you" Renzo replied, "fuck you, fuck the priest, fuck the Vatican and if you piss me off I'll include even someone higher up."

"Enough you guys" sang a choir of voices.

Finally the controversy came to an end.

* * * * *

The exams were held in the large amphitheater of the American embassy. As they entered the auditorium the students stared with awe at the electronic apparatus, the numerous buttons, speakers earphones and other gadgets at each desk. They were never told the exam would be conducted that way and did not know how to use those devices.

An American instructor, said something to the bewildered students, but between his accent and the cigar between his teeth, few people understood they were to sit and start the exam. Some did and others followed, but were slow at wearing the headsets, finding the 'ON' switch and the volume button. By the time they did, the story had already begun. The person who had recorded it had a strange accent, someone said it was Texan.

A wave of dismay crossed the auditorium. At the end of the story the students had to respond to questions asked in the same accent, probably by the same man.

"I didn't understand whether Sebastian opened or closed his goddamned bedroom door" mumbled Livio.

"And what about fucking Mary" said Renzo, "did she eat the fucking *weiner snitzels*, or did she shove them up her ass."

"I thought they said sausages…" suggested Franco.

A few words were understood, but the general sense of the story was lost. Most people shook their heads and abandoned the assignment.

The second test was about grammar.

Confident with that part, Roberto proceeded very quickly to fill the pages. When he finished he looked at the clock, and noticing he still had half an hour, decided to revisit "Mary and Sebastian". The questions had a multiple choice answers. Four to be exact, a, b, c and d. Thinking they would be tabulated by an automatic device, he filled the incomplete answers at random, relying on the twenty five per cent chance to get it right.

During their return trip to Caserta, the boys commented on the stupidity of that exercise.

"Can you imagine" said Livio, "sending us to those exams unprepared and unfamiliar with the equipment."

"Bastards!" said Renzo, "and with the twang and inflection of that fucking Texan."

"And you don't know the rest" said a cadet from Rome.

"Tell us then" they replied.

"I'm told that the officers scheduled to go to the States, take a year long course at the American Embassy and with that very equipment."

They were already upset and and sure the test had been a failure and this last information did nothing to lift their spirits.

What would happen now?

* * * * *

A week later an airman from Roberto's group was in the administration office waiting for a permit. A few officers stood around talking and the airman kept back not wishing to intrude.

"We must do something about the English course" said a captain reading what appeared to be a cablegram. "This is from Rome. Of one hundred and three students that took the exam, only two passed. The others will have to repeat the course."

The airman sneaked out of the office, returned to the class and repeated the news.

"Did they say who the two were?"

"No. But I gave some cigarettes to a recruit who works in that office. He promised to let me know."

Everyone wondered who the two might be.

The day after the airman came in waving a scrap of paper. "The suspense is over" he announced. Two names were scribbled on it: "Lanzi and Maestri."

It was unofficial, but it was credible.

Two days later it became official. All but Lanzi and Maestri were to repeat the course.

This time, a crash course of four weeks and eleven hours a day study.

Being excluded from the course, Roberto and Patrizio Maestri were delighted with the prospect of free time and made plans to visit Naples and perhaps Pompei and Ercolanum. They made formal request for a permit and when they were called to the administration office they could almost taste the fruit of their reward. Since Warrant Officer Busato was away, they were addressed by his superior.

"You two" said lieutenant Fiorito, "have been exonerated from repeating the English course."

At those words Roberto didn't even mind that Fiorito had punished him (unjustly he thought) in his early days at the academy, and stood there, repressing a smile, ready to collect his permit.

"While your friends will be busy all day repeating the course" the lieutenant continued, "no permits, can be issued. Due to the shortage of personnel, you'll have to double up on all services."

Roberto felt as though someone had punched him in the stomach. Echoes of early disappointments surfaced his mind, submerging every positive feeling he had derived from the news of his test results in Rome.

Quickly dismissed, the two stopped in the corridor to vent their anger.

"So this is the fucking reward for passing the exams" Patrizio shouted kicking the wall. "In this joint is more profitable to be an ass than a good student."

Roberto couldn't even articulate his rage, he took his hat off, twisted it, slammed it to the floor and then stamped on it. "Goddamned bastards" he hissed.

They were given all kind of tasks: guard duty on Saturdays and Sundays, receiving new recruits, dressing them, doubling up as marching instructors and yell to the newcomers as Warrant Officer Iovine had done with them.

Att…tention!' 'Right… turn, right!' 'Left-right,' 'Left-right,' 'Platoon halt!' 'At… ease."

One morning, during marching exercise, Roberto watched as Patrizio purposely led his group through a large puddle and twice ordered 'about front' right in the middle of it. Water splashed all over the woolen pants of the recruits, making them damp and smelly.

"Thanks the Lord for new recruits" Patrizio said, "now they too will have a taste of marches, sweat, and abuses."

It wasn't the end of it!

One day, warrant officer Busato called them to the mess hall with a 'new' task. His coppery-brown mustaches vibrated with excitement; it wasn't a good sign. He took them to one side of the room filled with hundreds of aluminum water pitchers, all lined up against the far wall.

"What are we supposed to do with these?" Roberto asked.

"Too many are disappearing lately. You are to hand-paint a four digits number over all of them starting from one thousand. They will be assigned to each table and everyone will be responsible for its own. If one disappears, we'll know who's responsible. I'll give you brushes and paint."

"But Warrant Officer, it will take us a month…"

"Well… in view of this, I'll dispense you from all other services and…" he caressed his mustaches and concluded, "do a good job and make me look good with the captain and, at its completion, I'll give you five days leave."

"But…" said Patrizio still unconvinced.

"Do we have your word?" Roberto asked.

"You do."

When Busato left, Patrizio looked at Roberto in dismay, "What the hell are you smirking about? We're *gonna* grow white hair before we're finished."

"White hair my ass, we'll do it in two days."

"You are crazy. How?"

"Go get the paint" said Roberto with a glint in his eyes "and meet me here in an hour. Get us big painting brushes too, four to five inches wide."

"How can we paint small numbers with big brushes?"

"Trust me Pat. You'll see."

When they met again, several cans of black paint were lined up near the water jugs and Patrizio was looking incredulously at the two wide brushes.

Roberto held a pack of folders under his arms.

"What the hell is that?"

Roberto spread a collection of stenciled flexible sheets, some with the number one hundred others with numbers one to nine, plus one with zero.

"I'll be dammed… how did you do that?"

"The boss of the hobby shop owed me a favor" Roberto replied, "he let me use the stencil machine and gave me also some masking tape. This is how we should organize the work…"

Three days later, Roberto and Patrizio sat in a train compartment on their way north. They were still laughing thinking of W/O Busato's face when, only two days after being given the job, they went to tell him it was finished.

- XIX -

HOME AGAIN

After a full day in Castelvecchio, Roberto was finally able to contact Silvia.
They met the following day in Santa Chiara and after a short embrace she asked:

"Why didn't you tell me you were coming?"

"It's a long story. Let's say I didn't know it myself until the last minute. There was no time to advise you."

"The important thing is that you're here now" she said. "I'll see how I can carve out time for us. Now though I must go, I have to take my mother to the doctor."

"Is she sick?"

"No. Just a routine visit, but it's in Empoli. I'm taking her there by car."

"What about tomorrow?"

"Tomorrow is Saturday" she said as to herself. "Yes, that will be fine. Shall I come to Castelvecchio?"

"Why not? Come to my house in the early afternoon" said Roberto on impulse, "my mother knows about us."

"Are you sure?"

"Otherwise I wouldn't ask you."

When Roberto told his mother she didn't seem too enthusiastic about the inevitable encounter. "You should have met somewhere else" she said, "you know how small town people are. People talk and you are not even engaged with the girl. So why compromise her?"

"Mother" he said resentfully, "even in small towns like ours things are changing. Besides, she is an old school friend."

"Those things don't change as fast as you think. Moreover, what about your career?"

Roberto did not reply. He did see the logic of his mother's objections. Going to someone's house, and being formally introduced to a parent, was more than just a casual visit. Also, with his upcoming departure to America and the time it would take for him to acquire a firm position... what was he to do?

Roberto and Patrizia had a quiet lunch. It was clear that, if from different angles, they were thinking about Silvia's visit, but didn't want to argue.

When the bell rang Roberto dashed to open the gate. He recalled the distant day she had stopped in front of his garden and his jealousy had made him behave in a way that kept them apart for a long time.

"Come" he said kissing her, "my mother is upstairs."

"Mamma" he said entering the living room, "this is Silvia."

"Good afternoon Mrs. Lanzi, I'm pleased to meet you."

"Thanks Silvia. You are more beautiful that I remember." Than smiling, "I saw you from my window long time ago, when you stopped to talk to my son."

Roberto wondered why his mother had said 'my son' rather than Roberto. Was it to say she had a prior claim to him?

"I have not had my coffee yet, would you like a cup?"

"No Thank you Mrs. Lanzi."

"In that case, I'll prepare one for me." She left the room and closed the door behind her.

Roberto heaved a sigh of relief. "Sit Silvia" he said pointing the armchair.

He sat on the sofa facing her, and perhaps in an effort to keep his eyes away from her striking legs, he told her the story of the aluminum pitchers.

"You should have seen the face of the Warrant Officer, when after only two days we told him we had finished the job…"

"Roberto" she said. Her tone indicating she wanted to change subject. "I've been thinking…" She paused, either to find the right words or the courage to continue.

"Tell me" he encouraged her.

"How long are you here for?"

"Only three more days."

"Why don't you come and meet my parents before you go? That way you could write me at home, it would be easier for both of us..."

Roberto was caught by surprise. A man's visit to a girl's parents was equivalent to an official declaration, a public commitment. What would he answer her father if asked how he planned to raise the family? Or where he, and consequently his daughter, would be stationed? And if he asked about children...?

"I know it would be easier, Silvia, but it is premature."

"What do you mean?"

"I'm still at the school. I'd be glad to talk to your parents when my future is a bit more defined. Perhaps when I come back from America..." Roberto took Silvia's hand, "You knew the situation when I joined and I thought you were prepared to wait for me."

"I was" she said. "I still am, but... I'm twenty years old, Roberto. My parents wonder what I'm waiting for."

The conversation lasted a bit longer with Roberto reiterating his position. The Silvia said she must go.

"Will I see you again before you return to Caserta?"

"I'm not sure. I'll let you know."

Patricia saw from her son's face that something had gone badly. She did not ask any questions but her concerned look seemed to say: 'I told you it wasn't a good idea.'

Silvia met Roberto at the train station, only minutes before his departure.

"Forgive me" she said wiping her tears, "I didn't have the courage to meet you earlier. I was afraid we'd have an argument just before you left. But I couldn't let you go without coming to see you off. I'll write you soon, Roberto, goodbye."

"Goodbye Silvia" he said holding her tight in his arms, "perhaps in writing we will understand each other better."

He loved Silvia but, in addition to the reasons he had stated aloud, there was something else. Especially now on the verge of going to America, an inner longing to remain free a bit longer, unencumbered by a wife, children and other responsibilities.

Perhaps this is ambivalence, he thought, but that's what I feel.

- XX -

GENERATIONAL GAPS

While his group was repeating the English exam in Rome, Roberto, back from the short leave, marched his platoon in Caserta and dreamt of America. After a long while he lead his company to a shaded area and said:
"We made good progress today" checked his watch and then shouted: "Diss-miss!"
The recruits broke the lines and rushed toward the P.X. to buy cigarettes, soft drinks, sweets.
He walked toward a grassy mound and sat down on the soft green blanket. His eyes were closed, his face turned to the sun. He was wondering whether his situation with Silvia was compromised by his refusal to meet her parents.
"Do you mind if I sit here?" a voice intruded.
He opened his eyes, recognized the old jet engines' instructor and said: "Good morning sergeant. I don't mind at all."
"I'm on my break and strolled to this quiet spot to smoke a cigarette."
The sergeant bent his knees with some effort and let himself fall to the ground with a groan.
"Goddamned war souvenirs" he said rubbing his right leg, "still bother me after so many years." Roberto kept silent and he added "Especially in winter."
"Where did you serve?"
"You name it kid. But the worst was in Africa."
"My father was there too" said Roberto.
"Where exactly?"

"Tobruk to El Alamein and then... all the way back."

"He made it, then?"

"No. He died near Bizerte just days before the end of that campaign."

"I'm sorry to hear it" said the sergeant in a sincere tone. "How come you don't wear the orphans of war star?"

Roberto chuckled. "I'm too stupid or too proud. I want to see how I'll do on my own merits. I didn't like the idea of passing ahead of others on account of my father's death."

"You're a good kid" said the sergeant nodding, "some people would wear one even if their father was still alive."

"Is that where you were wounded?" Roberto asked after a quiet moment, "In El Alamein, I mean, or after that bloody rout?"

"Right there" said the sergeant smiling sadly. Then looking at Roberto expression: "I know, you young people don't think much of our generation. It's easy for you to dismiss it. To remember only that we let the Country slip into fascism, the war, the whole mess."

Roberto did not reply. The sergeant shifted his position and continued, "I should know. I have a son about your age, and we often argue about it. We failed, but we also paid for our foolishness, and we still do. Look at me; I'm still a sergeant after 20 years of service, plus a war and several wounds. You young guys will outrank us in four, five years of service. Some of you will make it all the way up through the ranks, even to general for Christ sake!"

"I know what you're saying, but we suffer the consequences for the actions of our fathers, for their bad reputation. 'Thanks' to them we are called *'spaghetti e mandolini'*. We are the 'funny' people who sing, eat and dress well, who march in parade with the best of them, but lose every war."

"Don't feel too bad about it son. *Japs* and Germans might have fought harder than us, but they are not perfect either; look at some of the *'nice'* things they did. Some of you young guys are too idealistic to grasp the reality of things. It's good, don't get me wrong, but life is not all ideals."

Roberto couldn't disagree much with that statement.

There was a long silence, and then, his eyes lost in empty space, the old veteran said:

"I remember it as if it happened yesterday. For days we lay at the bottom of our trenches, waiting for supplies we knew would not come. We lay there like animals, or sat in a dug-out, watching the arching trajectories over our heads, listening to the whistling shells, the explosions. The sky above us was laced with tracers and smoke tracks like a loose woven canvass, while we held our breath, hoping they'd explode somewhere else, that we'd survive the onslaught.

When the British finally came, we did our best to defend ourselves with what we had left and died or surrendered at our posts. It's just a miracle that I did neither. I was wounded before we were overpowered and I was carted to the rear lines."

He fell silent. Then, nodding at his inner thoughts, concluded: "I hope you young people will never have to live through such madness."

If not in real battles, Roberto answered in his mind, he too had suffered the horrors of war, lived for months in German held territory, awakened at night by *SS* incursions, strafed by Americans planes, feared the pillage and rape by Moroccan troops... But could he really blame his father's generation for all the suffering and misdeeds of their time? And, would he have behaved much differently had he been in their shoes? It was easy for him to wish that fathers should have fought harder, died in greater number in order for their children to now feel prouder. It was easy for a young man reading Homer, Virgil and Caesar, to idealize the exploits of men and armies. Death is not so bad when sung in beautiful verses and when heroes, after their death, rise to the Olympus and become semi-gods.

Simple mortals, unfortunately, end up buried under six feet of mud.

The sergeant took another drag from his cigarette.

"I have to return to my duties" he said burying his butt between two buffs of grass, and struggled to get up. Roberto jumped to his feet and helped him.

"Thanks a lot for the chat, sergeant" he said respectfully. "I hope I didn't spoil your day by forcing you to remember those sad events."

"Don't worry, son... I don't mind talking about them. It reminds me that even after disasters like those, life still goes on."

* * * * *

Later that day Roberto heard that Renzo, the blasphemous but likable Tuscan, had been excluded from the courses in the USA.

"Why?" he asked.

"Because during the ritual background investigations they found that a distant uncle belonged to the communist party."

"Maybe his family didn't tip the postman" Luciano remarked.

"What do you mean?"

"Some of these checks are not… as deep or 'scientific' as one would think. In my case, the *carabinieri* only asked the postman, and since we give him treats at Christmas, Easter and other holidays, he told them our family was apolitical, we all went to Mass and gave to the church."

"And is it so?"

"Are you kidding? Half my relatives belong to the communist party and hate priests like the devil."

"Interesting" Roberto remarked, "poor Renzo, goodbye America for him."

"Talking about America" Luciano continued, "I hear the furlough allowed before going is only two days. We'll have to spend them entirely in Rome for outfitting."

"Shit" Roberto exclaimed, "my hope to go to Tuscany are wiped out." His reconciliation with Silvia would have to be done by mail.

Another set back.

He could do nothing about it.

- XXI -

LEAVING FOR THE USA

Mid November.

The first group of specialists left for Rome on their way to America. They were followed a few days later by another small group and then another. Since among them there were none of the people who best qualified during the course, many wondered the method chosen for the priority.

Falling again prey of his expectations, Roberto was growing impatient and disappointed.

"Don't worry buddy" Luciano told him, "our turn will come."

"And so will Christmas, Long-pole. You'd better talk to your postman again, he is letting us down."

"It won't help."

"Why?"

"Don't you see? They are sending first all those with 'connections' at the Ministry. They are all from Rome."

"The usual 'justice'" Roberto exclaimed. He was embittered.

"Yes, and you'd better get used to it."

Roberto made an eloquent gesture. A silent phrase that his friends understood to mean: "I don't know if I can."

* * * * *

Finally, on December 18th, Roberto's group received the departure's order.

There was twelve of them, counting NCOs and warrant officers. They gathered in Rome and received the new equipment including the famous elegant blue gabardine trench coat.

Roberto wrote a letter to Silvia and to his mother, told them of his disappointment for lacking the time to go see them, and promised to write again soon, probably from New York. Silvia had only written a postcard to him since his last visit to Castelvecchio, and he wondered about her state of mind.

On the day of departure, the group took a bus for Ciampino Airport to board Alitalia flight AZ 900 to New York. As they crossed the town, Roberto remembered the distillery his father had built in that very place in 1937 and the pictures of the grand opening attended by Mussolini and a host of Fascist hierarchs. Everybody wore a ceremonial uniforms except his father who, refusing to wear the fascist attire, attended the event in his usual work clothes. Roberto wondered if the complex was still there or if, like others, had been destroyed by the war.

"Our airplane" said a pretty hostess, "will make a brief stop in Shannon, Ireland for refueling. Then, after a flight of about 19 hours, another stop in Boston and finally will proceed for our final destination, New York."

Roberto's mind conjured up many iconic landmarks of the city, seen in movies or magazines: the Empire State Building, Rockefeller's Centre, Time Square, the silhouette of the Brooklyn Bridge. He wondered if the real city would confirm his imaginary notion of it, or if the collection of images assembled by his fervent mind would betray him... as they usually did.

Like most or all of his young comrades Roberto had never flied in a civilian airplane. Their only experience had been the short experimental flight while at the school, in Caserta. Though as part of the Atlantic Alliance, Italian pilots flew American Jet fighters, the flight had been in an old, pre-war SM 82 *Savoia Marchetti* propeller plane over the island of Capri and a stretch of the coast of Amalfi. Being hot and clammy, he had not enjoyed the ride and made it barely back to the ground without loosing his stomach.

This time though, with a modern and comfortable airplane, he would probably enjoy the flight.

Upon departing, Roberto experienced the sadness of leaving Silvia and his mother for an extended time. However, he was compensated with the anticipation of the new adventure: America!

In those post-war days of meager earnings and limited opportunities, America still conjured up images of opulence, stateliness, wealth. No other Country had skyscrapers, suspended bridges that spanned across huge rivers or straights, its wealth and military might. It would be a unique opportunity to see New York, Washington, San Antonio and other cities. To be trained in the files of the most powerful Country in the world.

A young sergeant who had been there before for previous courses on jet planes was conversing with two older Warrant Officers.

"I'm glad Italy got the missile's program" he was saying, "now for sure we'll be under the umbrella of America's security."

"And what else is good about it?" one of the NCO asked.

"The two salaries" replied the sergeant. "One which accrues in Italy and we collect at our return, the other, which is five times as much, that we get in the States."

"Now you're talking" said the W/O who had asked the question, "never mind the American umbrella, just give me American money."

There was a short laugh and then the W/O who had not spoken yet, said:

"The one thing that worries me is the goddamn language. It doesn't seem to stick in my old skull." He was a mild mannered tall, lean man with an unhealthy gray complexion and large bags under his eyes.

"So, how did you pass the exams?" the young sergeant asked.

"I've got friends in the right places."

"That helps, but you're *gonna* find it difficult in the States, the system is different there."

"We shall see" the W/O answered philosophically, "it may look that way, but as they say 'the more things change, the more they are the same'... and not only in Italy." He lit another cigarette and inhaled the smoke so voluptuously that his very life seemed to depend on that mouthful of air.

"Did you hear him?" Toto asked Roberto, "if we make that much money I'll save it and send it home and tell my Pa to buy me a small parcel of land."

Roberto didn't comment about the value of land in Leverano. He didn't want to offend his friend and said instead:

"Yes, I heard about the money. And it also occurs to me that as the senior NCO of our group, he will be our 'leader'. I hope we won't be judged by his standards."

* * * * *

"It's a Douglas DC-7 powered by four Pratt & Whitney radial engines" said Toto as he climbed the ramp to the plane. "3200 HP each" he added.

They sat in the comfortable seats and adjusted their belt, their seat, the air vents.

"Do you think they hire them for their I.Q.?" said Patrizio sneaking a glance at the smartly dressed Alitalia hostesses in attractive short skirts sauntering around the cabin.

The growing roar of the engines announced departure, and their eyes were glued to the small oval windows, trying to catch whatever sight of Rome they could. It was soon dark and every now and then one of the engines crackled and long red flames were seen coming out of the exhaust stack. The lady sitting near Toto, probably on her first flight experience, began to cry and leaned on his shoulder.

Perhaps, since he wore an air force uniform, she might have thought his 'experience' would give her comfort.

Once gained altitude, dinner was served; the food was very good. Those were the days that flying was still a privilege reserved to and afforded by few and the airlines treated their passengers as rare commodities.

"If this is how they take care of people in economy" said Toto, "I'd like to know what they serve in first class…"

"Caviar and champagne" said Pat from across the isle, "and after supper the hostess seats on your lap and serves you dessert."

"You wish" Said Roberto.

He closed his eyes momentarily and opened them again when he heard the announcement for all passengers to secure their belt, straighten their seats and get ready for the scheduled stop in Shannon, Ireland, the preannounced refueling before the long transatlantic crossing.

For most of the young Airmen, that was their first arrival in a foreign land. Everyone took advantage of the stop to visit the local Duty Free Shop and other stores to check out or buy exotic merchandize. Different forms, unknown objects, souvenirs, things one would not have seen in Italy. Some people had mentioned Aran knitwear, trinity knot rings, Celtic knot bracelets, and small objects in Mullingar pewter. Deciding whether it was worth it or not to acquire a certain thing was complicated by the calculation of the exchange rate. Is it so convenient to buy anything? Some of the Warrant Officers wondered. They tried to calculate the exchange and engaged in long discussions even for items of minimal value. Suddenly for them, the priority seemed to be 'buy only if it is a deal'.

"It's an obsession" Pat commented, "There is an abyss between that generation and ours. What difference does fifty fucking lire make? If you like the damn thing, buy it."

After about an hour all passengers were called aboard. They wee going to start the flight over the Atlantic which would last the rest of the night.

"This plane is good" said Roberto sitting and buckling the seat belt, "comfortable and not too noisy."

"By the time we return from the States" said Toto who loved the subject, "there might be commercial jet planes on this route."

"That would be fantastic!" said Roberto.

"After all" Toto continued, "the Russians have already offered a regularly scheduled jet service with a Tupolev TU-104, between Moscow and other cities in the Soviet Union. The British used jet passenger planes even before them.

While Toto continued his dissertation on his favorite subject, Roberto remembered having read that the Russians, having been the first to draw from the pool of German scientists, involved in the development of missiles, were more advanced than the American in that field.

A small sliver of moon peeked from above the right wing of the plane, out of a dark blue starred sky. Silvia, Roberto thought, look at that moon and our glance will meet.

"Ehi, look at that thing coming our way" said Toto giving him the elbow.

Roberto opened his eyes and saw a tall man coming from the first class section. He had long, wavy gray hair and wore a black cape with a bright red inner lining, held near the neck, by a flashy broach and a golden chain. Many people looked at him in wonder and finally someone said:

"It's John Barrymore Junior, the famous actor."

"He looks like Dracula to me" Roberto whispered leaning towards Toto, "what does he want in this section anyway?"

"Maybe he's looking for a long neck to suck on…"

"I hope it's yours. Good night."

Two hours before landing in Boston the lights were turned on and breakfast was served. It was another pleasant gastronomic experience. The quality of food and the flavor of the cappuccino far outstripped that of the mess hall.

Just before landing the purser announced that a blizzard was hitting the area and everyone should take a blanket before disembarking and crossing the open space to the transit lounge.

After refueling and boarding other passengers, they returned to their seats and one hour later, they landed in New York. The city was blanketed by a heavy snowfall and little was visible on approach.

The Airport was called Fiorello La Guardia, after the Italian who had been the Major of New York city for three consecutive times and served at the infamous Ellis Island. He also fought to allow women to vote and for the abolition of child labor. During his twelve years at City Hall, he had gained the reputation of a honest and efficient man.

They moved to the carousel and collected their gear. The senior NCO dug out several folders from one of his bags and said, "Someone from the American Air Force is supposed to meet us at the exit."

He had hardly pronounced those words that a young staff sergeant approached him and saluted. "Are you the group from Italy?" he asked politely, "please follow me, our bus is just outside."

When it was evident by his embarrassed silence that the Italian NCO had not understood a word, Roberto said, "Yes, we are. We'll follow you right away." Then he related the message in Italian to his superior.

On the bus the American sergeant checked their travel documents, then departed. They drove the unusually semi-deserted streets of New York in the single lane plowed by heavier vehicles and noticed that several cars had slid sideways and had been abandoned. A few people walked the sidewalks, their heads wrapped in scarves, advancing painstakingly over the knee-deep snow. Some of them had strangely colored things over their ears.

"I'd rather freeze my ears" said Toto, "than look that funny."

"We're going to Fort Hamilton" said the sergeant towards Roberto sitting right behind him, it's in Brooklyn."

"Thank you."

Roberto followed some of the street signs: Ditmar Blvd., then Astoria Blvd., and as the buss climbed a ramp he read "Brooklyn Queens Expressway East."

Finally a familiar name, 'Brooklyn!'

He had heard that name many times, in books, the radio or in movies. He knew it derived from *Breukelen*, the name of the Dutch village of the original settlers. Now, it had become one of the most populated districts of New York.

"Lots of Italian live in Brooklyn" said the sergeant, "it's a nice middle class neighborhood, with strong family presence."

"We've heard about it." Roberto answered.

On the one hand he appreciated the friendly manner of this American. But on the other, he feared being associated with the mostly destitute and illiterate early immigrants, from poor southern regions of Italy.

"I'm from Florence" he said defensively, "the birthplace of the Renaissance." He mentally recited the dozens of first magnitude artists, writers, scientists, the Tuscan city had produced.

The sergeant nodded. Roberto had no way of knowing if he had understood.

Finally the bus stopped in front of a gated area. The sign above the gate read:

"WELCOME TO U.S. ARMY GARRISON FORT HAMILTON."

"We're just across from the Verrazzano narrows" said the sergeant, "at the south end of the borough. Further down is Brooklyn Bridge."

Roberto made a mental note to check the words 'narrows' and 'borough', but understood they were related to the district.

After a short ride among well lined barracks and other ordinary, but well kept buildings, the bus stopped.

"Here we are" said the sergeant, "inside you'll be assigned your rooms for the night. Depending on the weather, tomorrow or the day after you'll continue your journey."

- XXII -

THE BIG APPLE

Toto, Patrizio and Roberto, had an early supper at one of the mess halls on the base.

Afterwards, despite the cold wind and the snow, they decided to venture into downtown Manhattan.

"We're here for a short time. We shouldn't throw away the opportunity."

"We should take the subway" said sergeant Moroni who had joined them uninvited.

"We'll take a short tour" he added, "and return early to the base. We've got to catch some sleep, tomorrow it will be a long day."

The other three glanced at each other, pretending they were in agreement with the sergeant.

The subway car was crowded, but after a couple of stops some people got off and the sergeant snagged an empty seat. Several people got on and stood in front of the sergeant. Toto, nodded to Patrizio and Roberto and at the next stop quickly jumped out of the subway car leaving sergeant Moroni behind. They climbed the two ramps of stairs and as they surfaced to ground level, a glittering flood of neon signs, incandescent and florescent lighting, greeted them.

Flocks of people rushed by on the wide sidewalk. There were shops, theaters and cinemas, the face of their massive overhanging showing in capital letters the title of the featured show. On one of them, Roberto noticed the title "Love is a many splendored thing" with William Holden and Jennifer Jones. The speedy pace of people surprised him. They walked looking straight ahead; it made one think they were afraid to meet other people's gaze. They seemed hypnotized like a flock of bees running towards the apiary. Many men wore Frank Sinatra style hats and funny ear mufflers so strange in color that clashed with almost everything else they wore. In a shop windows, they noticed they were called ear muffs and sold for ninety-nine cents. After a random stroll, they tried to ask some passer-by how far the Empire State Building was, but no one stopped or gave them an answer.

Finally, they asked a policeman, who looked at their uniforms and said "*Idaliani foste*?" Then he gave them directions.

Walking toward the famous skyscraper, they were distracted by a loud music, which came from an open door. It was a strange dancing hall, crowded with pretty young girls who asked for twenty dollars for a dance.

"A dance? And then what?" Patrizio asked.

"Then nothing" one girl replied. "Or perhaps…"

"On account of the 'perhaps'" suggested Patrizio, "I would say we stay a while."

"We're just soldiers" Roberto told one of the girls, "can't we have a discount?"

"Just because you're cute" she said smiling.

They remained there over two hours.

* * * * *

"What the hell happened to you?" sergeant Moroni asked at breakfast.

"That's what we'd like to know" the three promptly answered, "at one of the stops we looked up and you were gone. We spent half the night finding our way back."

He seemed doubtful, but did not reply.

The weather had improved, the snow was melting and the temperature was bearable. Since there were no engagements, the day was spent sightseeing. Every one had different priorities and Toto, Patrizio and Roberto joined again to follow their own itinerary.

They stopped to watch ice skaters at Rockefeller Center, they toured Long Island, climbed the Statue of Liberty and the Empire State Building. They walked for hours on city sidewalks, now cleared of snow, stopping for a quick bite and a drink. They returned to Fort Hamilton at suppertime.

Though admiring the wide avenues, the tall skyscrapers, the big cars… Roberto was a bit confused by the aloofness of the people, the disproportionate plastic signage that scared the buildings, the frenetic pace of the traffic. Too many movies of the Big Apple, had given him unreasonable expectations.

He had yet to mail the letter written to Silvia during the flight and the one written to his mother, a letter full of enthusiasm and plans for the future, prominent among them, saving money to fix the house at his return. Then, though still confused about his feelings toward the city, he decided to write his impressions to his friends.

Dear Mauro and Giovanni,

I'm writing you from New York, or as they call it here, 'The Big Apple', hence I must talk about modern time pyramids we call skyscrapers. Immense vertical shapes, too large for the size of man, too cold for his spiritual needs.

Though they rise to challenge the sky next to each other, I perceive them as isolated entities, thinly but effectively separated by sharp slices of cold space and murderous traffic.

Perhaps it's because, being from Tuscany, I'm accustomed to a different scale and sense of order. Perhaps my aesthetics need the sense of security I derive from old architecture: softer lines, warmer colors, balance. I dislike concrete, it has no color, age or character. It contrasts nothing and matches only grey skies, empty streets and hollow souls.

But I don't want you to believe that I didn't like New York at all. In fact I did, but I must digest the reasons and will tell you about them in my next letter.

Dear friends, I will write again in the near future and as soon as I have a semi-permanent address, I'll send it to you so you can tell me of your progress at the university and of life in general.

A warm embrace,
Roberto

- XXIII -

SAN ANTONIO – LACKLAND A.F.B.

They left New York for San Antonio, with a brief stop-over and plane change in Dallas.

It felt like landing in a different country.

People wore lighter clothing due to warmer weather, but also more informal ones. Many wore cowboy boots, large hats and colorful shirts. Instead of ties, they wore leather strings with metal or bone pendants called 'bolos'. The shops sold goods and souvenirs reflecting the different culture of the region. Together with Navaho jewelry with turquoise stones set on silver, there were colorful belts with enormous buckles, ten gallon hats, cowboys' checkered shirts, cowboy boots, spurs, saddles and other horse paraphernalia. Country music was piped in all shops and common areas. In some place, a long horn trophy hung from the fascia of the store.

There was less than an hour before the next flight and they rushed to various shop to purchase souvenirs and postcards to send back home, then returned to their gate to embark for San Antonio. They were boarding at ground level and the DC Electra airplane was stationed about 40 meters away from the gate. Many Americans were still smoking, and a single ground crew member was ready at the gate to check the boarding passes. When boarding was announced, the smokers promptly extinguished their cigarettes in a large ashtray or threw them to the ground even though they had just lit them.

"Look at them" said Toto, "those buts are longer then our full size cigarettes. In my town there would people who'd pick them up and smoke them or crash the tobacco into their pipes."

The flight to San Antonio was short and eventless. Except for an obviously drunk American woman who wanted to take Toto home with her.

Another USAF sergeant was waiting for them at the airport.

"This is what I call service!" Toto exclaimed.

They picked up their gear and were directed to a waiting bus.

They had travelled about fifteen minutes when someone said, "Look over there, on the left. I see the outline of a city, it must be San Antonio."

Roberto turned his head and in the distance, as though in a haze of fine rosy dust, he saw the silhouette of several tall buildings cut against the far horizon. Obviously the city center, he thought. He couldn't see enough to formulate an opinion and wondered how long it would to be before he could visit it.

The pamphlet received upon boarding the bus spoke of its well-known Chinese garden, the canals travelled by light boats, and of the legendary Alamo. 'The fort of Davy Crocket and Jim Bowie's fame, conquered and destroyed by the Mexican army commanded by *Generalismo* Santa Anna. Eventually, the pamphlet continued, after the uprising, general Houston gathered sufficient troops to the rescue and defeated the Mexicans near San Jiacinto, and now this part of Texas belongs to the United States of America.'

Pat must have been thinking along the same lines because he asked, "Roberto, did you ever see the television mini series about David Crockett?"

"Yes I did. I remember a scene with Ernest Borgnine who fights with the actor impersonating Jim Bowie, just to prove his valor. And the final assault, when the Mexican play *El Deguello*, or the assault without quarter."

"The what?"

"*El Deguello*. Literally 'The cut throat'. It means that every one, even prisoners would be slaughtered."

"I wonder how much is myth and how much is truth."

"What we know is that rather than frighten or discourage them, the massacre strengthened the determination of the Texans to fight and defeat Santa Anna."

"Maybe we'll learn more when we visit the sight" said Toto.

"Maybe. Let me see if this booklet says anything about Lackland Air Force Base."

He read it was named after Brigadier General Frank Lackland, and was commonly known as LAFB. At the beginning of the Korean War it rapidly grew and the temporary facilities were expanded to include over one hundred new dormitories. In addition to basic preparation, several training squadrons were accommodated at Lackland or in the nearby Air Bases of Kelly and Randolph.

"Look here," said Pat elbowing Roberto and showing his pamphlet, "it also says the base houses a bunch of interesting airplanes. Some vintage and some brand new, including a B 25 Mitchel, a B17 Flying Fortress, F-4 Phantom, SR-71 Blackbird, C-121 Constellation, even a B- 52 Stratofortress and…"

Toto raised his eyes from the pamphlet, "Boy, would I like to see them…"

"You'll have your chance. Some are operated by Air Force veterans and with a small fee you can go inside."

"Really? Where did you read that?"

"Over here," said Roberto placing his index finger over a small note at the bottom of the page.

They kept on reading and talking and forty five minutes later they entered the base through the main gate. They immediately noticed platoons of American recruits in fatigue uniforms, shaven to the skin, marching by in the wide inner lanes of the base. Military Training Instructors or MTI, with uniforms which seemed starched and pressed right to their bodies and the wide brimmed campaign hats, low and straight down almost to their eyebrows, walked watchfully at their side.

About sixty feet from an intersection, one MTI, yelled a command that was shouted back in a sing-song way by the entire platoon. A single man immediately detached from the squad and ran ahead. He placed himself at the center of the intersection at ninety degrees to the marchers and spread his legs and arms wide. He remained in that position until the entire platoon had passed by. Then, after another command by the MTI, echoed again by the soldiers', he ran back and rejoined his platoon.

What on earth did those recruits chant? What was that maneuver about? The Italians, faces glued to the bus windows, were mesmerized. Among other things, they couldn't understand why there were four stop signs at the intersection.

"Why do they need four? Wouldn't two stop signs be sufficient?" someone said in Italian.

"There is no bloody traffic interfering with the marching" said another.

"Besides, with this flatness and the good visibility, you can spot a vehicle miles away. What was all that commotion about?"

Everyone now was adding his own commentary.

"What's the matter?" The bus driver asked hearing loud comments and laughs.

After being told, he said: "It's part of the discipline given to the recruits. The phrases shouted are: 'Road guard out and road guard in' to indicate when the man in charge of safety is to leave the platoon and then reenter it."

It was still very strange for the Italians.

They continued over a large road surrounded by well aligned barracks of recent construction. Narrow concrete pathways branched out from the street, cut through the immaculate lawns and ran to the four steps stairways of the barracks.

Along the way they met several platoons of female recruits Women Air Force or WAF and some of the airmen shouted compliments and catcalls to the amusement of the women and the contempt of the driver who shook his head.

"Italians!" he said, "it never fails."

Finally the driver stopped at barracks 2075 and said: "This is your destination."

The inside consisted of a pleasant foyer with a glossy wooden floor, a few arm- chairs, two small tables, two lamps and a telephone. The telephone was presently used by an Italian airman first class seemingly conversing with an American girl. A wide corridor led to eight small but comfortable bedrooms accommodating two persons, their bed separated by a long, narrow table and two chairs. A reading lamp sat in the middle of the table. Against the far wall, two metal cabinets with wire hangers and four drawers for clothes and other personal effects.

"Pretty damned good" Roberto exclaimed, "I wish we had these in Caserta."

The Italian sergeant permanently stationed at the base came to greet the new group. After a short welcoming speech, he showed them the rest of the facilities; the laundry room, the showers and, through the window, he pointed to the closest cafeteria. "The rest," he concluded, "you'll learn from those who arrived here before you. Any questions?"

"Yes," said Roberto, "what are we supposed to do the rest of the day?"

"Settle down, fix your room, have supper and then ask 'the veterans' what kind of activities there are within the base. Tomorrow you'll be issued passes and I.Ds then, classes will begin."

As soon as they learned of their arrival, Carlo and Franco, who had arrived with a previous group, came to visit.

"Lackland is about twenty minutes from town center" said Carlo. "We're allowed to go on week ends and we can use the military shuttle busses."

"Many recreational facilities are within walking distance from here" pitched in Franco, "skating rinks, dance halls, gymnasiums, swimming pools, library and a general store, called P.X.."

"What can you buy at the P.X.?" Toto asked

"Records, cigarettes and nice blue shirts, all quite inexpensive" replied Franco. "And for your information" he concluded slyly, "there are lots of women around the base and down town. They are mostly Mexican. However, the easiest to get into bed are the white wives of military personnel."

"They are easy" Carlo concurred, "and the reputation of Latin lovers doesn't hurt us at all."

"What about the courses?" Roberto asked, "have you started missile subjects?"

"Yes. And they are easy enough" replied Carlo. "The usual multiple answers and all. That leaves lot of free time to go around."

"And the food?" Pat inquired.

"Excellent" said Carlo patting his belly, "I've already gained a few pounds." He then checked his watch and concluded, "You've got time for a quick shower if you want to refresh yourselves. Supper here is at eighteen hundred hours."

"Are you going to call us or do we meet at the cafeteria?"

"We'll meet there. We'll exchange more news then."

After a hot shower Roberto and Toto changed into a fresh gear and walked to the Cafeteria.

They arrived to the door before an American colonel. They duly saluted and stepped aside to give him priority.

"In this Country" he said with a good-natured smile, "if you are ahead of anyone, even a high ranking officer, you go first."

The two were astonished. They looked at each other and thanked him.

Accustomed as they were in Italy, to respect differences in rank in all places and circumstances, Roberto and Toto were truly and positively surprised. They told Carlo during supper.

"It happened to me too" he confirmed, "not only, but as you can see they eat in the same cafeteria and the identical food as the lowest ranks."

They talked of many other things, but Roberto's mind was stuck for a while on that 'equality'. He thought of the arrogance and injustice of the Italian system in creating a class distinction even at dinner table. After all, he thought, it's almost always the low ranks that must face the hardest tasks, and the greatest risks.

Why feed them badly or make them feel inferior?

The following day the small group received their IDs and then went to class where a young civilian teacher began the course with relatively easy notions based mostly on missiles' terminology and safety procedures. During the latter section, he said: "Certain words, we call 'false friends'. "These are similar to Italian words, but mean different things in English. *Flammable* and *inflammable*, for instance, mean the same thing in English."

Before dismissing the class, he said an exam would be given at the end of the week to test the level of understanding of each person.

"What did he say?" the old warrant officer asked when the teacher left. "I didn't *understood nothing*."

Roberto and Toto looked at each other remembering his comments at Ciampino Airport, and shook their heads in astonishment.

At the end of the week, as scheduled, the teacher dictated an extract from the textbook. All students were supposed to write it down on a sheet of paper and then consign it to him before leaving class.

It was relatively easy to follow except for the frequent interruptions of W.O. Napolitano who asked in a whispering voice: "What did he say?" "I didn't get *nothing*."

The instructor pretended not to hear and completed his reading. "And now" he then said looking at the class, as we say in America T.G.I.F. It's the acronym of 'Thanks God is Friday'. It's the weekend and you spend it however you like. As long as, Monday morning, you'll be here at eight sharp, sober and ready to start another five days of hard work."

Many ran immediately downtown in search of easy adventures. Roberto and Toto, who shared a sober behavior and wanted to save money for the future, decided to remain at the base. They visited the P.X. mentioned by Franco, and were positively surprised by the large variety of merchandize: clothing, records, records players, photographic equipment and hundreds of other items. Being also surprised by the low cost, they made a short mental list of what they would buy after payday.

"Can you imagine?" Roberto asked Toto, 'If we had at our bases in Italy this type of abundance?"

They walked around the P.X. another while and then they decided to go to a movie. In addition to the entertainment, they reasoned, it would help improve their language skills.

Later Toto, to satisfy his passion for aircrafts, purchased some inexpensive plastic models and in the evening, he passed the time assembling them. Roberto spent some of his free time writing letters. He realized that, lately, with all the excitement and new things to digest, he had spent very little time thinking about Silvia. Was he beginning to forget her? Impossible, he thought, but he certainly felt a certain detachment.

Later, hearing that the foreign students, in view of the oncoming Air Force Judo championship had formed its own class, he decided to join it.

Most mornings saw the Italian group going towards the cafeteria, after a late night out, walking sleepily, while shoving shirts inside their pants or buckling their belts. By contrast, the group of German airmen, in their impeccable uniforms, marched under the guide of a leader, towards the mess hall as though in a parade.

"They must have discipline in their DNA" someone commented.

"Whatever it is, that behavior certainly behooves men in uniform."

As soon as Roberto's group arrived in the classroom the instructor distributed the corrected tests. Sergeant Moroni and the two master sergeants had barely taken passing marks, while W.O. Napolitano received a mark so low that the teacher did not even want to divulge it. Later, when he read some of his translations, the hilarity of the class was hard to contain. Roberto and Toto received ninety eight out of one hundred. The teacher said it was the highest mark ever received.

"Colonel Terini, commander of the Italian students office in Lackland" said the teacher addressing the two, "will surely call you for commendations."

- XXIV -

HASTENED RETURN

"Lanzi" sergeant Moroni called from the corridor, "colonel Terini would like to see you immediately in his office."
"I'll be there in a moment. But about Marciano?"
"The colonel didn't say anything about Toto. He only asked for you."
Roberto straightened his tie and hurried towards the office of his commander in good spirit; he was going to be congratulated for his good performance. Perhaps, Toto was already there. He was happy, and then as his dear grandmother used to say: 'He who starts well, is half way there'.
He climbed the four steps, entered the office and saluted. The colonel was with W.O. Napolitano, resting against the edge of his desk, his arms crossed over his chest, his face unsmiling.
After returning the salute, the colonel picked up a sheet of paper from his desk and gave it to Roberto.
It was a telegram: "Require presence in Italy of Airman First class Roberto Lanzi for matter of extreme urgency." He read it twice without understanding.
Then, he looked up at the colonel "What does it mean? he asked, "who needs me so badly that I have to return to Italy?"
"I have no idea, son. But there is a flight out in a couple of hours and I've arranged for a car to take you to the airport. Someone will meet you there with tickets."
Roberto was shocked. Instead of being congratulated for his good performance he was sent back to Italy. What had happened? Had someone discovered some distant relative to be communist? Was something wrong with his mother? How could it be? He had left her in perfect health.

Besides, he had never seen her sick a day in her life. No, he was sure, it must be something else, but what? Why weren't they able to tell him more?

"Go on son" said the colonel, "I'll recommend you for special citation and make sure we bring you back in time for the next course. Don't worry" he repeated putting his hand on Roberto's shoulder, "I'll advise the Ministry and you'll return to America as soon as 'whatever' you have to attend to in Italy is looked after."

Roberto could not fathom the reason for that strange telegram from the Air Force Command in Rome. Now more than ever, he wished they had a telephone at home or knew somebody's number to call and ascertain the problem. But if the Air Force couldn't, how could he?

Soon after, he boarded a military airplane directed to Dallas. The flight was so turbulent that made him think the God of winds Aeolus had taken a dislike to that DC4 and was determined to make it crash. The plane bounced in the choppy air like a plastic toy and three or four times, Roberto truly believed his day of reckoning had come. He thought of Silvia and his mother and imagined them reading the Ministry's report:

"We regret to notify you of the sudden death of First Airman Roberto Lanzi ..."

At last, after an amount of time that had seemed unending, the airplane stabilized, prepared to land, bounced over a Dallas runway, taxied along the tarmac and finally stopped.

An hour later Roberto continued for New York with a larger commercial plane.

He was landing again in the big city and this time there was no snow.

This time though, rather than the stirring anticipation of his first arrival, his sole companion was the dreadful feeling of loss which he could neither justify nor discount.

He retrieved his backpack and exited the airport. He was alone and stood there at the edge of the sidewalk for a while, observing the traffic of cars, busses and taxis, not knowing exactly what to do. Finally a yellow taxi stopped in front of him, the driver lowered the window and shouted *"Ehi Paisa'*, you *needda* ride?"

"I do, but I don't know how much it cost"

"Where you *goin'?*"

"Fort Hamilton."

"It cost you *nothin'*. They'll pay for it."

"Are you sure?"

"Sure I'm sure, I pick up *yous guys all da time*. Come on *guaglio' monta su-get in.*"

Roberto felt relieved and got into the cab. "Are you Italian?" He asked.

"Sort of. My folks *was Eietalian*. They came from near Napoli many moons ago. *What'you* doing in here?"

Roberto explained that he was in the States for technical courses and now was returning home.

At Fort Hamilton he signed a receipt for the cab driver, thanked him and went to the reception office where was assigned a bed for the night and told to hurry up if he wanted to take advantage of the cafeteria.

After supper, with many unanswered questions in his head and pains in his heart, Roberto felt unable to sleep. He remembered the sergeant's comments upon his first arrival and walked to the southeastern edge of the grounds, near the narrows. He stopped at the water edge and stood there in contemplation, fighting the premonition that didn't want to abandon him. The silence of the night was broken only by the distant car traffic over the Brooklyn Bridge and the odd foghorn of boats gliding through the Hudson.

He watched the other side of the city and then its likeness on the water, an upside-down image reflected in the mirror laid between the two banks. He saw the picture shuttered by a passing boat, the buildings shake, their lights spread in the broken water surface, tremble like fallen leaves, and the reflection sink in the foamy wake. And then, after a while, the waters stilled again and the city, like a mirage, reappears luminous as though painted on a wet wall. He hung there for a long time, fascinated by its reappearance, looking at the two cities, the real and the imaginary one, come together again, joined at their roots.

At the next passage of a boat, the image broke again, he walked back trying to calm the uneasiness.

Finally he went to bed.

All Alitalia flights were fully booked and, since he was only allowed to fly with the Italian flag airline, he had to wait two days to embark on a flight to Rome.

It was going to be a long and painful voyage as he was tortured by the haunting questions burning inside him. They were hours fraught with anxiety. The only consolation was that his sudden return would give him the opportunity to see Silvia and his friends earlier than anticipated. He was longing for her.

He held fast to this thought and as the lights of the airplane dimmed, he pushed back his seat and closed his eyes. The drone of the engines now reduced to an even purr, he evoked the tender moments he had spent with Silvia during his Christmas furlough. He remembered how the sadness of their looming separation, the concern for the future, had all disappeared in her tender embrace. His troubled mind calmed down even before they made love; soothed, secure, restored. And after, how she held him in her warm embrace, for a long time. He had felt like a weightless bird, soaring in the invisible current of the winds. Like a sailor, who has travelled over rough seas, rattled and shaken, finally enters the calm waters of a protective harbor.

Ah! How he longed for her embrace! For her kisses. He wanted to caress her, make love to her again, feel her eagerness, and drown in the delicacy of her flesh. Then sleep. And like Leoncavallo's shepherd "*...e nel sonno l'oblio trovar!* –... find oblivion in the quiescence of sleep!"

He remembered the sweet sounds which escaped from her lips, they were like musical notes. And her hands, clasped around his neck, his shoulder, moving and searching for every inch of skin yet unexplored, while still inviting him further into her flesh.

Sweet eternal moments!

And then he thought of Mauro and Giovanni, of the things he would tell them about his short yet remarkable experience in America. But even his most enjoyable thoughts were marred by the uncertainty that lay ahead.

What is wrong? He kept wondering.

He was finally in Rome, but even while waiting for his rucksack, he experienced a sense of loss.

He went to the Ministry where, due to the colonel recommendations, he expected to be immediately recognized and helped, told what had happened.

However, despite the promises of colonel Terini in San Antonio, no one seemed to even know of his return; let alone its reasons. After wandering like a lost soul through several offices, a snappish captain told him not to waste his time. "*Primo Aviere* Roberto Lanzi is in America" he said looking at him, "don't bother me with silly stories."

"And what do you think I am? A ghost?" he answered as ire was mounting inside him.

"Don't use that insolent, sarcastic tone or I'll throw you in jail!"

"Well sir, can you then tell me who I am, if not Roberto Lanzi?"

The captain did not answer. Roberto was incensed. He took a step forward and would have grabbed that captain by the neck had not a superior officer heard the conversation and intervened. He read Roberto's telegram and assisted him in getting a week furlough to go home.

"Go, check what is wrong, son. We don't seem to have any information here. We will straighten this mess out and relocate you. Obviously" he unceremoniously concluded, "someone has fucked-up your paper-work."

* * * * *

The strange foreboding persisted during the short train ride home.

It was already dark when he got off the train in San Romano. He thought of the happier time when, returning from his tests in Caserta, he had found Silvia waiting for him.

The last bus had left and he took the narrow path along the river and walked by the old distillery, indulging in thoughts of the past to tear himself away from the ominous premonition which grew with every step. The silent shadows of the abandoned buildings loomed in the night like eerie ghosts. His father, his mother had spent their time there, in an activity that no longer existed. He crossed the place where he had found a shiny object that turned out to be a heavy grenade. He could have died, had an oncoming person not torn it out of his hands and thrown it into the river. And then, out of the veil of the night, he began to discern the silhouette of the bridge. He thought of the night during its reconstruction, when he had crossed the river over twelve inch wide planks, after missing three consecutive trains in Pisa and the last boat crossing. With his bike on a shoulder, he walked over the shaky planks, eighty feet above the water, with nothing but desperation in his heart. Step by careful step he made it to the other end. Even before he put his bike down, cut like an apparition against the dark shroud of the night, he had seen the ghostlike shape of his old grandmother, her silvery hair shining in the moon light. She must have been there for hours.

How could she even think that he would attempt the crossing?

He could still hear her scolding while they walked home. And feel the thrashing his mother gave him upon arrival; it was almost three 'clock at night and the two women had feared for his life.

Poor *nonna*, she loved him so much...

He reached the point where his grandmother had met him and had to refrain from running home to discover what was waiting for him. He walked at a fast pace, but how long were the last one hundred yards... As he reached the proximity of the house, he noticed that all windows and Persian shutters were closed. He arrived at the gate and yanked on its iron scrolls, but despite his energetic jerks, it did not yield. Thinking it was stuck he put his rucksack on the ground and grabbed it with both hands. But on the point of yanking it again, his hand clasped a cold block of metal and he saw a thick chain padlock.

"Mother!" he cried, "Mother!" each time underlining her name with another more violent jerk on the gate.

He had climbed over that gate many times before, but he was held back numbed, not by the physical obstacle, but by the ominous significance of that chain. Never before, not even in wartime, had there been a padlock on that gate.

Could there be a simple, reassuring explanation? The anxiety of the previous days seemed embodied in that cold metal chunk shining before his eyes.

"Mother!" he cried once more.

"Roberto, is that you?"

He turned towards the voice and in the pale glow of the moon, he recognized his neighbors who, summoned by the clamor had come out in the garden.

"Good evening Mister and Misses Giani. Ciao Lucia. Yes, it's me."

They came into the street and shook hands. Then, after a long moment of uneasy silence, Mr. Giani spoke.

"We locked the gate to keep people away from the property."

Then, reading the confusion and bewilderment in Roberto's face, he added, "Didn't you get our telegram?"

"No. I only got one from Rome. But it didn't explain…"

"We sent one too. We didn't know how to get in touch, so we went to the *carabinieri* who telegraphed the Ministry in Rome."

Roberto hesitated.

There was only another question, but before he summoned the courage to pose it, Lucia said: "Roberto, we buried your mother two days ago. Sorry you couldn't make it to the funeral."

The simple finality of those simple words made him feel numb. Then, mixed with the deep sorrow of the next moment, he discerned, almost with horror, a feeble sense of relief. 'She is gone', he thought 'yet fate and circumstances have spared me the agonizing moments of her departure.'

He had been saved from the inevitable, trite burial rites, the religious arrangements, the morbid ceremonies. He was spared the torture of listening to the expression of sympathy of strangers who hardly knew her… or him.

"We found a tomb not far from that of your dear *nonna*" said Nina Giani, "we thought she would have liked that."

"Thank you," Roberto finally said. "Not only I didn't receive your telegram, but I didn't even know she had fallen ill. She was healthy when I left. In a way though" he added in a quivering voice, "I felt it inside."

"Why are we talking in the middle of the street?" said Lucia's mother, "Let's go to our place. There is no need for you to go *there* tonight."

He gladly accepted the offer. Maybe tomorrow, in the daylight, he would have been better able to visit his place and confront reality.

He drank tea, and sat on a leather ottoman across from Lucia. She questioned him about his recent experiences in the Air Force, including his short spell in America. That night, everyone avoided any talk about Patrizia's sudden death.

After a while, Mr. and Mrs. Giani went to bed and he and Lucia were left alone. They continued talking about his first impressions of New York, San Antonio, the different military set up and some cultural nuances.

Lucia told him of a recent trip to London, organized by the school. She had visited the Egyptian Museum, Westminster Cathedral and other famous sights. Also, that a girl of her group, noticing they were made of silver, had stolen tea spoons from the hotel.

Finally, realizing it was quite late, Lucia showed Roberto to his room.

After switching off his lights he lay in the dark thinking of the husband and wife games played with Lucia as children. She had put an end to them prior to her first communion. He surprised himself wondering if she was still a virgin. And, though knowing it to be just a defense mechanism, to avoid dealing with his mother's death, he felt guilty to be drifting into thoughts such as those. He hoped that sleep would catch him by surprise and postpone the inevitable; at least until tomorrow.

Then, the thought of Silvia came alive again. She doesn't even suspect that I'm near, he thought. I'll try to see her tomorrow or the day after. He adjusted his pillow and turned on his side. Then, tired and gratified by the anticipation, he fell asleep.

In the morning, while having breakfast with the Gianis, Roberto approached the topic of his mother's death: "How did she die?" he asked in a firm voice.

"She had an aneurism in the brain during the night" said Mrs. Giani, "that's what the doctor told us. In the morning the mailman rang the bell to deliver your letter from America. He rang many times, but got no answer. He knew your mother was always at home in the morning. Always waiting for your mail. So, suspecting something wrong he came to us and…" there was a moment of hesitation, "… the rest you know."

She then spoke of the people who had helped with the burial arrangements and Roberto made mental notes to thank them.

An hour later he was inside his house.

Everything was in perfect order as though his mother had been expecting him. He dropped his rucksack in his room, took a quick shower, changed into a pair of jeans and a light sweater and went downtown to attend to the things needing his attention. He settled a few bills he had found on the kitchen table, then stopped at the clergy house and paid the priest for the services. Lastly, he looked for a woman called Vera, who, Mrs. Gianis told him, had washed and dressed his dead mother. He found her near the church. After offering her condolences, she meekly asked if she could have some of Mrs. Lanzis' clothes instead of money. She was almost as tall as his mother had been, and about the same build.

"Come in the afternoon" Roberto said "I'll be back home by then."
"Thanks a lot Roberto. I can use some clothes and she was always so elegant..."
She came around three o'clock and Roberto took her to the armoire in the spare room. "Take whatever you want" he told her as he opened its door. He was glad for the opportunity, he knew Vera to be very poor and, in a way, her request and comment were a tribute to his mother's taste. She chose some clothes and then, not daring asking for more, Roberto noticed her eyes caress his mother's old fur coat.
"You can take it, Vera" he said, "I'll be happy to know that you wear it."
"You are as generous as your grandmother was" she said while tears filled her eyes. "Your mother must have been too" she quickly added, "but I didn't know her as well."

The worst seemed to be behind.
Now Roberto wished to be alone. He didn't have the strength yet to face his friends or even Silvia.
A strange feeling persisted.
He tried to analyze it. He had confronted his sad and unexpected news with manly dignity and propriety. He had satisfied the most immediate duties... what is it then?
Suddenly, he realized with much surprise that throughout the trials of the last several days, and despite his affection for his mother – the person who had given him life – he had not shed a single tear!
It's not possible, he thought. It's not right.
He was shocked!
He looked around as though, written on the blank walls, or in a silent object his eyes rested on, he would find the answer. He lifted his rucksack from the floor and went to his room, all done up and ready as though he had never left. He tossed it over the bench, removed his jacket and placed it over the chair. He returned to the kitchen and began to unpack the few things he had bought to prepare a frugal meal. Suddenly, an impulse stronger than his conscious will, took him away from the

kitchen. He felt his legs and feet move over the ceramic tiles of the foyer though commanded by remote control. He stopped in front of a closed door, raised his hand to the handle and pushed it open, gently, as if afraid to waken someone inside. From the doorway, his eyes met a large, empty bed with the white blanket crocheted by his grandmother, the large feather filled pillows his mother propped herself with while reading, her night table with the old Tiffany lamp and on the white marble top, two or three books. After some hesitation he walked in and found himself in front of the Victorian mirror. And there, where he had so often encountered her smile, he only met his image.

Suddenly, he felt very lonely... lost!

Unconsciously he raised his hand to the flat, cold surface of the mirror, as if to feel the invisible traces of her presence. It was as though that gesture had touched a hidden button inside him and a flood of warm tears poured from his eyes. His body shook with silent sobs. "Oh, mother!" he finally cried as warm, salty tears fell without restraint.

"I did love you and miss you so very much!"

For an instant, the empty house resounded with the echo of his grief. A short while later, all was silent again.

- XXV -

HODIE MIHI CRAS TIBI

Later, he went over the papers the Gianis had left for him. He found the letter he had written during his initial flight and posted in New York; it was still unopened.

He remembered his words; he had written about his desire and resolution to save all his money, to make improvements to the house, order a telephone, plant more fruit trees in the orchard.

She never read it. He wished she had!

He took his jacket and briskly walked towards the center, but turned right before entering under the bell tower. He had taken that route so many times with his *nonna*, skirting the medieval walls to then turn in the road of the woods and Monte Falcone. Under the large Plane-trees he recalled the time he had come with his mother from the Banchini farm, to see the first American soldiers who had finally crossed the Arno River. She had shown such strength during the war. He felt his eyes prickling with tears, but he held them back, stopped, and then, decided to walk to the place he had thought of avoiding.

He had to wait crossing to the other side of the road, but many cars were dashing by. He shook his head. Even in this remote country town, cars accelerated, rather then slowed down at the approach of a pedestrian crosswalk. It was as though the 'zebra' stripes painted on the asphalt signaled the start of a race. It would have been very strange, he thought shaking his head, were it not in Italy, where every one, even while driving a modest Fiat 500, imagined driving a Ferrari.

Finally, after yet another vehicle sped by, he was able to go across and above the entrance, he noticed the old Latin sign:

"HODIE MIHI CRAS TIBI – Today to me, tomorrow to you."
A fitting message for a cemetery, he thought.
Yes, eventually every one dies.

As soon as he crossed the iron-gate, he was greeted by the smell of decaying flowers, mingled with wax and unspoken sorrow. An air heavy and tired seemed to weigh over the white marble headstones like a winter blanket. Even more despairing were those stones heralding the names, dates, and infantile rhymes obtained in a moment of anguish:

"You left us suddenly,
Your love well known,
You left us memories,
We're glad to own."

Fleeting words, for bodies, minds and spirits now reduced to inert matter. Inadequate symbols for the pain caused by their passing!

Death, Roberto thought, hidden inside every one of us, from the moment we start breathing; we are born, we live, we die! We all share the same fate, and yet, when the final curtain falls, we are so surprised, unprepared.

He listened to the silence; it seemed a primordial quietude. And then, the cry of a bird, the whisper of the wind, a step over the stones, spoke of a life that endured.

Yes, he thought looking up in wonderment, our planet continues unperturbed its own journey.

Roberto walked slowly, wrapped in his own thoughts. And then, almost without knowing it, he was in front of her headstone!

He stopped.

On the other side of that cold white marble rested the vestiges of Patrizia Lanzi; his mother! Her name, a date, a small oval picture, were all that remained. He found himself unprepared for the feelings which suddenly seized him and tried to fight the gut wrenching emotional wave that rose so unexpectedly.

It was a futile effort. His throat was knotted and tears pressed behind his eyes.

'Dear mother, we didn't love each other much. We weren't even friends, until after grandmother's death and the last months of your existence. Then, and only then, when I had finally gained a more mature perspective, I began to understand you and gave you a real chance. But I soon parted, and the opportunity was lost and I even missed your funeral. In a way mother, I was glad of that. Glad I could still remember you as you were in life, like the last time I saw you, the night I left, and you wore a once fashionable time-worn jacket.

You kissed me with controlled affection, almost afraid to betray a new sense of tenderness. Or as though we were to rejoin but a few days later. "I'm proud of you son" you told me while we stood on the terrace, "my own son going to America. And all on his own merits! Your father would have been proud too."

You then let me go but you remained on that terrace until I disappeared beyond the edges of the garden - *nonna's* garden - like you did when father parted, many years before. I can imagine you afterwards, sitting on your chair, gazing into space. or on an open book which you could no longer read. Trying to follow me in your fantasy, on that airplane, crossing the ocean and then in another continent.

Only now I can imagine what it cost you to let me go.

Thank you, mother.

While I was there, playing soldier and carving out my destiny, you left this world, during a silent night. As though thinking you were a burden for me in life and wanting to spare me in death. You left suddenly, as though you had exhausted your reasons for living. As though you felt you had already played your last, useful role:

'Arevoir mon enfant' I hear you whispering. 'Goodbye Cucciolo."

You were gone.

He shook his head in self-mocking jest; no need to shield emotions from people who might see him, he thought letting the tears flow down his face. Before walking away, he took a last look at that small photo glued to the cold marble, to see one last time the beautiful face, the tender smile, the slender figure wrapped in that pure silk dress with floral designs. Perhaps the same she wore that distant day at the farm, during an aerial bombardment when Otto, the German officer, stopped to talk to her.

"*You grande Kapitalist*" he exclaimed in his flowed Italian, "*dressing like tis during wvar.*"

"No" she answered with laughter, "what should I save it for? I could be dead tomorrow."

As if to underline her words, the earth trembled and loud explosions were heard. Moments later, huge stacks of smoke climbed towards the limpid sky in the direction of Castelvecchio. The Americans, unloading their bombs from way above the safety limits, had missed again the bridge over the Arno River and hit the village instead, a couple of kilometers away. Five blocks of the old town were destroyed, thirty three people – mostly women and children – killed to be 'liberated'.

"*You hav not fear?*" said the German officer to Patrizia who had continued to wash her hair at the outside tub.

"What's the point?" she said nodding at the smoke, "when one doesn't even know where death comes from?" She smiled, uncovering her spotless white teeth, "And then" she continued, "on a sunny day like this, even fear of death seems to quickly vanish from the air."

She turned around and began to sing, just as the sirens began to scream, announcing with the usual delay, the already past aerial raid.

Captain Otto Bredis looked at her again; he appeared to want to say something else. Then, after a long instant, he whispered: "*Aufviedersen*" put his hat on, clicked his heels and left.

* * * * *

The humming noise of the speeding cars over the gray asphalt of the street outside broke into Roberto's thoughts. He never even knew the name of that street; some called it the Cemetery Street, others Street of the Woods. It didn't really matter, everyone knew it by either name.

It was, up to recent times, an unassuming country road, dusty and full of pot holes which filled with murky water when it rained. It was mainly used by the local farmers, with straw hats and sun-burned, leathery skin, who drove their heavy wooden carts pulled by solemn, *Chianine* cows which had graced the Tuscan landscape since before Etruscan times. Except, on that distant summer day, when Roberto and his mother had come to see the arrival of the first American troops who had finally crossed the Arno River.

That day, it was full of soldiers with fresh uniforms, shiny weapons, and smooth, shaven faces. As though instead of a war, they were going to a dance. Their smiles a welcome relief, after being subject to the dour expression of the Germans. He also saw the first black soldiers and marveled at the contrast of their white teeth with the dark complexion.

Tears were flowing over Patrizia's face and he, too young and naïve to understand, asked her why.

"Because I'm happy that our ordeal is over" she said. "I cry from joy!"

Roberto did not understand.

He had never conceived that one could cry by emotions other than pain or sorrow; especially his mother.

He walked on, then, turning to the left found himself in front of his grandmother's tomb.

"My dear, dear *nonna*" he whispered. He bent down to straighten a bunch of flowers someone had placed on the tomb. "I love you *nonna*."

He remained there for a long time, thinking how much he would have liked for her to hear him.

Finally he left the cemetery and returned home. It was getting darker, but he didn't switch the lights on. He went to his room pushed the Persian shutters open and closed the windows. He stood there, with his head resting against the cold glass pane, his arms crossed over his chest, looking at the sad winter landscape beyond the garden. It seemed to be enveloped by the same shroud of sadness he bore in his heart.

He felt alone, yet, he did not long for company; not even Silvia's.

Finally, wanting to escape even his own thoughts, he went to bed.

- XXVI -

WITH MAURO

"I know you probably don't want to talk about your mother" said Mauro in the morning, "so I'll just give you my condolences and leave it at that."

He gave Roberto a long bear hug then continued: "Tell me about your impression of New York. I got your letter but I wonder if you changed your opinion."

Roberto returned the hug and noticed that Mauro had gained some weight, but did not comment.

"Mauro, it's an amazing city, with plenty beautiful things, architectural marvels, great universities, bridges spanning over wide rivers and straights, daring designs. However, I didn't feel at home; too big, too fast, and too... baffling."

"I'm not sure I understand."

"After standing in awe in front of the Empire State Building, I found myself thinking 'so what?' Even as I appreciated some of the many positive attributes, part of me was obsessed by questions like: why would I want to live one hundred floors above ground and stare at hundreds or thousand roofs and smoke stacks? Or walk in streets that resemble canyons? Or stroll a sidewalk, to be suddenly stampeded by an underground avalanche of people getting out of a subway and rushing past you as though you did not exist?"

"But what about the Metropolitan Opera House, the remarkable museums, Broadway, the beautiful stores...?"

"They are all there of course, but for me. I perceive them as out of context."

"What do you mean?"

"I find no pleasure in an exhibit of Renaissance painters in Manhattan, or a travelling display of Egyptian mummies in Brooklyn, or the beautiful Tiffany store on Fifth Avenue, when just three doors over there is, a so called 'novelty store', with switch-blade knives, army surplus and fake human feces on view in the dusty display windows."

"But even in the streets or alleys of Venice you may find dogs' excrements on the ground; but this doesn't take away all the charm of the city."

"I know Mauro, but I can only tell you how I felt. You often told me that I always saw the glass half empty." He paused and then continued:

"There is no feeling of permanence. There is always something knocked down and something going up. One building just completed and next to it an abyss, where another one will be erected. There is something to be said for visiting Siena and finding its Piazza del Palio the same as it was hundreds of years ago."

"And what about the other places?" Mauro asked.

"I found the south more like the America I pictured in my mind. Less striking buildings, but for me more distinctively American."

"Did your friends see New York the same way as you did?"

"No Mauro. Most everyone else liked it very much and enjoyed the sights.

Somehow, I had the same stupid reaction as when I was stationed in Caserta; so unexpectedly foreign to me, I even deprived myself of visiting interesting places such as Sorrento, Ischia or the islands of Capri."

"Ah, Roberto, as I told you once, you should learn to enjoy some of the more common aspects of life. Take things at face value sometimes, don't always try to analyze and dig into the essence of things…"

"You're right. But what can I do? That's me."

"I know. Anyway my friend, even if it's not a happy occasion that brought you back, I'm glad to see you. How long are you staying?"

"Four more days. I only got a week leave and I must go back to Caserta to check on my status. I'd like to return to the States with the next available course."

"Four days? Then perhaps you'll see Giovanni as well. His sister told me he'll be back from college tomorrow."

"Good."

"Have you seen Silvia yet?"

"No." said Roberto frowning.

Mauro looked at him quizzically, but he didn't ask any question. It was just as well. Roberto didn't know what else to say; it was too difficult to put his complex feelings into words. Now, with his mother gone, he felt even more reluctant to be tied up to a relationship. He needed more time to sort things up.

"I might though," he added after a moment, "but I don't know when."

They left each other with the promise of getting together before the departure. Roberto spent the next two days compiling the necessary documents related to his mother's death and storing the remainder of her clothing in the attic. He left some money with the Gianis and arranged for them to pay the electrical and the water bills until his return. He also gave them the house keys and told them to let it be known that it was for rent.

- XXVII -

BACK TO CASERTA

He was leaving without seeing Silvia, without even contacting her. 'Why?' He was asking himself as the train left the station and began to run towards the future. He didn't know why, but he needed freedom. But was it really worth bearing that emptiness in his heart for the sake of feeling relieved from cares and responsibilities? How long would it last? Which sentiment would prevail at the end?

Would he chose to love - or liberty?

During the trip Roberto continued to be tormented by doubts and also felt the growing conviction that, perhaps, he had made a mistake. He had asked Mauro to explain to her that, overwhelmed by the duties and responsibilities following his mother's death, he had run out of time, but would soon write. Obviously he owed her at least an explanation.

But would she take it?

Rethinking the matter, he became convinced that he had acted improperly. He should have met her and explained his feelings face to face. But how could he have reached the same conclusion looking into her eyes? He really needed a separation to understand himself, and what he truly wanted.

He arrived at Caserta as the sun was setting behind the palace.

Strange, how old things and places could look different when viewed from a new perspective. The academy no longer felt like a temporary prison, the training instructors no longer threatening, the waiting for his new assignment, bearable.

Some of the old teachers and tutors congratulated him for going to America. Some of the young cadets noticed the blue gabardine trench coat, issued only to airman serving abroad, stopped him to ask about the women, the riches, and the experiences of America.

His company commander, knowing of his vicissitudes exempted him from daily duties.

"Very soon" he told him, "a new group of airmen will depart for America. You'll go with them and probably you'll be able to rejoin your initial group."

Even Father Mariano looked for him to extend his condolences.

The following day, he went to visit the judo instructor at the gym and practiced with him. Then he had a cold showed and, with a block of paper under his arm, he went to a secluded part of the park to write Silvia.

As he walked he was thinking about his future. The acquisition of an important foreign language and the technical skills would undoubtedly enhance his prospects. The stain of the tannery worker faded away, a new Roberto would emerge, in tune with the one he always felt himself to be.

He still loved Silvia and there were moments in which he considered his behavior very selfish, and there were others, in which he was convinced he had been honest. Only time and experience would ultimately give a clear answer to his doubts. For now however, the desire of freedom seemed to rule his heart.

He sat on a stone and began to write.

Cara Silvia:

By now Mauro must have told you.

I don't know if you will understand (or forgive me) for having left without even saying goodbye.

I was ten years old when, leaving for Africa, my father picked me up and said: "Now you are the man of the house!" and since then, I've lived my life in function of other people's needs, often, suppressing mine.

My mother sudden death allows me, for once, to choose how to live my life as I wish, without thinking of others first.

Truthfully, as I write these words, I'm not sure of their full significance and perhaps, since I'm not an extravagant person,

I will never do anything I wouldn't have done before her death. In spite of that, I felt the need to be alone.

Soon I will leave for America and I will be away for several months, perhaps even one year. Time will help us understand if we are destined to find each other again, or it will separate us forever.

Cara Silvia, I miss you terribly, but I want you to be free to make your own decisions.

I'll write you again, but I don't know what or when.

Forgive me,
Roberto

W/O Busato caressed his waxed mustaches. "In the next few days your new group will assemble here" he said, "then, two days in Rome for outfitting and a new jump over the pond. I'm *gonna* ask you for a small favor…"

"I know" said Roberto smiling, "I'll bring you back some stamps for your collection."

"Oh, so you know of my little hobby, do you? Who told you?"

"You did, warrant officer, don't you remember?"

Busato creased his forehead and Roberto continued, "I'll be glad to send you some as long as you don't ask me to paint another thousand carafes."

"One of these days you've got to tell me how you did it so fast. Never mind, here are your travel documents."

- XXIII -

RETURN TO LACKLAND

Finally Roberto was returning to the United States. Despite nurturing some doubts about certain aspects of military life and realizing he had over idealized it, during the moments of calm, he looked at his future with confidence.

He met with the new group in Rome where tickets and travel documents were issued. Since he was the only one who had made the same journey before, he was virtually the group leader.

This time New York enjoyed beautiful springtime weather and feeling responsible for how the new comers would experience the city, Roberto made himself into a guide for his companions and found the occasion gratifying. His friend Mauro was right; he should take life face value and enjoy every opportunity.

Freed from images created by his imagination, this time the Big Apple appeared under a new, more positive light. With his group, he visited the Rockefeller Center, the Empire State Building, Saint Patrick's Cathedral and walked Fifth Avenue as though for the first time. A few days later, they boarded a Braniff International Airways jet. It was its maiden flight to San Antonio, so they drank champagne and were treated as though they owned the plane. It was an excellent 'welcome back'.

* * * * *

In Lackland Roberto rejoined his initial group.

His friends were happy to see him again, gave him their notes and helped him to quickly reintegrate with the program. Some of the teachers helped him too and dedicated some of their free time to matters they considered essential.

After two weeks of intense study, he caught up with the others.

The following advanced English course was taught by Manuela Sanchez, a civilian teacher hired by the USAF. Thanks to the languages specialization acquired in England, France and at Harvard University, she understood the particular help needed by students of different nations.

"As Italians" she told them, "you must watch the pronunciation of words such as milk, miss, kiss, because you tend to pronounce it as though written with double 'e'. Also words with 'th' which you don't have in your language."

She was on her early thirties, and her olive complexion and very dark hair, revealed her Mexican origin. She had studied at the Santa Rosa University in Texas and then specialized at several universities around the globe. Given her multiple interests and wide travel experiences, Roberto was attracted to her. It seemed to be reciprocal and during the lessons, despite her professional behavior, it was difficult to conceal their empathy. During breaks, she stopped going to the teacher's room and sat on the grass beside Roberto, talking about Italy, arts, history. Their conversation held an interesting range. Sometimes, captivated by the unusual perspectives of the young man, she invited him home.

For Roberto, those weekends were enjoyable and stimulating and the fact that she was beautiful made the company even more pleasant. So far though, the relationship had remained a platonic one.

One day, during a coffee brake, captain Quadra walked to them, dug a pack of cigarettes out of his pocket and offered one to Manuela who, on alternative days, also thought his class.

"Miss Sanchez" he said in a mocking tone, "if you like the company of Italians, I'm available. Not only I'm Italian, but I'm also a pilot."

"Thank you captain" she answered refuting the cigarette, "I'll keep it in mind."

Fortunately the bell rang and the further potential embarrassment was avoided as everyone returned to class.

* * * * *

A few days later it was announced that the national USAF Judo championship would soon be held at the base. Keen to participate, Roberto enrolled and joined the 'Foreign Students Team' that included several Japanese aviators of very high standing. He was glad to have the chance to improve his skills and understand the 'inalienable spirit' or *Fudoshin* they applied to this discipline. However, the frequent training sessions left very little time or energy for other distractions. This included Manuela, but both knew it to be a temporary situation.

When the competition started some of Roberto's friends attended and urged him to fight hard. Sometimes even Manuela came, and since the majority were Americans, he was surprised to see her applaud when he won a bout.

He had eliminated several adversaries including two black belts, and the last fight was against a brown belt. He had seen him advance through the tournament and knew his favorite throw to be the *tomoe-nage* or circle throw. Disliking the fall it produced, Roberto was particularly attentive to its approach, a frontal push by the adversary. Roberto had never been thrown that way.

The fight started in a predictable manner, with Roberto even pushing his opponent to make him believe he'd be an easy target for that throw. Sergeant Argano yelled twice from the stands: "Lanzi be careful and stop pushing." Annoyed by the interference, Roberto yelled back in Italian: "I know what I'm doing", which, had the referee understood, would have been sufficient for disqualification.

The bout continued, and with the following push from Roberto, predictably, the American brown belt let himself fall on his back ready to throw him over. Expecting the move, Roberto crouched and pressed his opponent down on the *tatami* ready to immobilize him. Then, in a moment of overconfidence, he looked up towards the stands as if to say to Argano: "Didn't I tell you?"

It was just enough distraction for the American to adjust his feet against Roberto's stomach and, with a pull, make him tumble over his head.

"*Ippon*" shouted the referee; Roberto had lost his bout.

Embarrassed and mad to himself, he quickly got up and bowed to the victor. He left the *tatami*, avoiding to look up the stands. How could I be so careless, he thought.

Despite his loss, the tournament was an unqualified success for the Foreign Students' team who, thanks particularly to Onichi Obata of the Japanese contingent, had won most of the prizes.

A stupid act of arrogance had led Roberto to loose his last bout, depriving him to receive, in addition to the team trophy, even the individual one.

Fortunately that evening Manuela was not in the arena.

ATC JUDO CHAMPS—Colonel Berthold Nowotny, personnel director, congratulates Warhawk coach Earl Onishi following the awarding of the command team championship trophy. Team members are: (L to R) Giancarlo Gariella, Kinya Takaseya, Richard Iacovocci, Junichi Obata, Onishi, Renato Argano, Daniel Schiff and Yuki Hachiya.

* * * * *

The following day, while going to classes, Roberto saw in the distance, someone resembling Patrizio, with two gigantic M.P.s at his sides, one holding the caliber 22 Pat had recently bought. When they saw W/O Napolitano the three stopped.

"What happen?" he asked.

Pat explained in Italian that he had gone in the open fields behind the barracks to shoot at field mice. The two M.P.s had arrived in their jeep, taken Patrizio and the carbine and told him it was forbidden.

"Enough with the *Eytalian*" said one of the M.P.s, and continuing in English he explained to Napolitano that he had to confiscate the weapon.

"O.K., O.K." Napolitano answered.

"And there is also a fine to pay."

"O.K., O.K." he repeated.

"And you should put this airman in jail for a week."

"O.K."

"Just a minute" said Pat to Napolitano, "did you understand what they said?"

"No" he answered in his dialect, "I understood fuck all."

"So why you kept on saying O.K.?"

"*Cause I donno whatta say.*"

Fortunately an Italian officer attached to the liaison office intervened, said he would guard the carbine and cancel permits to the offender.

Roberto walked to his class with Pat shaking his head about Napolitano.

* * * * *

"Congratulation Roberto" said Manuela upon seeing him. "Now that you're famous I hope you won't forget your friends."

"What are you talking about?"

"This is what I mean" she said flashing the base newspaper "Talespinner" with a large photo of the winning team.

"Don't pull my leg" he replied. "Last night I lost my fight."

"But the team won. We should go out tonight and celebrate."

"Sorry Manuela. Tonight I can't. I promised my teammate to go with them. Tomorrow maybe."

"See what I mean? You've already forgotten me."

Roberto tried to explain that he couldn't break his promise, but Manuela seemed unconvinced.

"Time to start our lesson" she said curtly. Then turned around and walked to her desk.

That evening, Roberto and sergeant Argano took the base shuttle and twenty five minutes later they got off at the corner of Hildebrand and Broadway, downtown San Antonio, not far from the Alamo. The five Japanese Judokas came with Lieutenant Tehuki Kano's car. Tehuki was a fierce looking Ju-Jitsu expert, built like a tank. They all met at a restaurant which, in addition to conventional food, offered also fish, rice, sashimi and other dishes suitable to their diet.

After ordering, Onishi dug out a pack of photos his friends had taken during the competition. There were some of Argano and Roberto as well, as they fought their opponents. They would be cherished mementos of that singular event.

The conversation proceeded with some difficulty as the Japanese, and especially Lieutenant Tehuki, had a limited knowledge of the English language. However, with smiles of approval, and body language, they tried to congratulate one another for the victories and the trophies. Pointing at Onishi and slapping his back in praise, they all agreed, he should have been given the overall trophy as well. Everyone that is, except Tehuki, who didn't seem to understand a single word. His subordinates were intimidated by the strange and muscular exemplar, and their deference could not completely hide their antipathy for him. It was difficult to understand whether it was because he was an officer, or because, being an expert in Ju-jitsu, he did not appreciate the '*fudoshin*' or spirit of Judo.

Despite his lack of Judo experience, it had been interesting to see how he had eliminated many of his opponents without using conventional throws. At times, a wild shout combined with the unbalancing of his adversary, had been sufficient for him to throw his opponent to the mat or even off it.

At a certain point he pointed to the empty water carafe and, since no one paid attention to him, he got up and left the table. Tehuki saw him stop in front of the water fountain against the far wall and noticed an overweight red faced policeman watch him closely. A few feet away another white policeman kept an eye on the scene and bounced his nightstick on the palm of his hand. Tehuki bent towards the fountain and the policeman closer to him yelled: You fucking Jap, can't you read? This is for niggers only."

Tehuki turned around, smiled like an imbecile, and bent his head again towards the water. The policeman grabbed his shoulder and tried to pull him back, but a kick in the crouch and a karate chop to the neck, sent him to the floor. The other policeman took a step forward, raised his arm to hit Tehuli with the stick, while groping towards his pistol with the other hand.

The action had been so fast that Roberto was barely able to to shake Onishi's arm and point out to the scene. Onishi smiled as Tehuki yelled his ferocious battle cry, 'Ahiiiii" that made the twenty or so clients in the restaurant jump in the air. He hit the policeman to the solar plexus, catapulting him over a table and onto the floor like a sack of potatoes.

Argano pulled Roberto by the arm and indicated to the others they'd better leave. Argano threw twenty dollars on the table – they hadn't ordered food yet – and ran out of the place as sirens were heard in the distance, pulling with them poor Tehuki who probably thought the aggression had something to do with Pearl Harbor.

They turned around the corner, ran three or four blocks then separated, the Japanese went to their car and probably returned to the base.

Roberto and Argano stopped at a small place where, judging from the smell, the barbecued hamburgers and the grilled onions promised to be more enjoyable than the sashimi.

"that was a close one…" said Argano as they sat at a corner table. He then looked Roberto straight in the eye.

"Yes sergeant, what else?"

"About the other evening, Roberto. I hope you don't mind me telling you. You are an excellent judoka, however, you can be even better remembering one important Judo saying: 'When you're thinking you're good enough, you're just starting to decline.'"

"I know sergeant, and I'm sorry I behaved like that. It hurts me to know I lost that bout on account of stupidity."

"I hope you learned from it."

The day after, Roberto's group was told that after the visit of an Italian attaché from Washington they would depart for the next destination.

- XXIX -

THE MILITARY ATTACHÉ

The 'big shot' turned out to be the Italian military attaché in Washington, coming for an official visit to Lackland AFB.

A squad of airmen of all categories dressed in official uniform, including the *'Forrestal'* hat and woollen tie, were aligned on the square not far from the colonel's office. Two officers and three Non Commissioned Officers (NCO) chatted and smoked in the shade of a nearby building, while the airmen were kept under the fierce midday Texan sun, as though they were tobacco leaves out to dry.

After about half an hour waiting, impatience started mounting. In the stifling heat, the shirt collars, tightened by that inappropriate woollen tie, started to soak with sweat that poured from foreheads and necks. Many airmen, tired even in the 'at ease position' began lifting their hat and wiped the sweat from their foreheads and necks with a handkerchief. One of them asked the captain permission to go drink a sip of water, but his request was denied. Another one asked when the guest would arrive.

"I don't have a crystal ball" he was answered, "your guess is as good as mine."

"It's over one damned hour we are roasting under the sun" said Carlo.

"If I knew I'd be out here this long" cut in Pat, "I would have spread myself with olive oil, so I'd fry better."

"Shut up!" Barked the captain.

A few 'fuck yous' could be deciphered out of the buzz that rose from the files.

One and a half hours had now elapsed since they were marched to that darn spot in the sun. Minutes later two airmen, drained, fell to the ground.

Others feigned sickness and sat on the ground. Everybody wondered what the reason was for the long, senseless wait under the fierce Texan sun.

"If the *fucking* attaché had not yet arrived at the base, why were we lined up so early?"

Roberto remembered that during a lesson on Military Culture they were told: "A military squad should not be exposed or kept for a long time in a position which causes stress or discomfort." He wandered if their officers had ever studied such a subject, or if it that theory did not apply to their case.

Finally, when the mood of the squad was on the edge of insubordination, they heard someone approaching the square. Colonel Terini, captain Quadra and an elderly gentleman wearing a military uniform and a blue band slung over one shoulder appeared from around the corner. The older man was the long waited attaché. He staggered along and seemed to have a hard time walking at the same pace as the others. The colonel stood close to him to offer support.

"Atten...tion!" ordered captain Quadra approaching the squad.

Everybody came to attention and the three newcomers joined the other officers and NCOs in the shade of the building.

"At ease!"

The attaché went to the microphone, held the pole with his right hand, but more than to adjust its height, and began:

"I'm glad to have the opportunity to meet an example of our best Italian youth here in Texas" he said. "Your commanding officer told me that you represent the best of our Country and your performance on missile training, is excellent." He stopped. He seemed to be searching for words on the faces of the young men staring at him.

He cleared his throat, then forcing a smile, concluded:

"As you have done with your courses, I urge you to distinguish yourself with Texan women as well. Show them the hot blood that flows in the veins of all Italians."

Then, he nodded to captain Quadra, who seemed surprised at the brevity of the speech and, receiving the elbow of colonel Terini shouted:

"Att...tention"!

When the "At ease" was ordered again, the group of officers disappeared behind the barracks and at the "Break up lines" a chorus of imprecations and curses rose from the squad.

"The bloody drunk" burst out somebody, "kept us burning under midday sun, just to tell us to fuck for the honour of our Country…"

The comments were even worse when it was learned that while the boys were kept baking in the sun, the attaché had spent a couple of hours in the colonel's office sipping *'Southern Comfort'*, rising from his chair only when every drop had been drained from the bottle.

Hurrah for Italy!

- XXX -

REDSTONE ARSENAL

"Before you leave Lacklamd" said colonel Terini in his farewell speech, "I'd like to congratulate you for the excellent results of your tests and for your overall performance."

He went on for the next ten minutes with the perfunctory words of the moment, as Roberto and Toto exchanged looks and elbowed each other to underline the points which they did not consider genuine, or at least applicable to the entire group. The fiasco at the Department of Defense in Rome, did not allow for Roberto to be very generous in the assessment of the colonel and, together with the poor performance of the attaché they were the beginning of a broader disillusionment.

Fortunately, after a few more closing comments, the colonel introduced an American civilian instructor for the ensuing more relevant information.

"The theory you leaned in Lackland" he began, "will be applied at your next destination of Redstone Arsenal, the Army complex located near the town of Huntsville, in the north east corner of Alabama. It's a small, quiet city of about 100,000 people, a good portion of them being in the military. As you look at this area map" he said turning to the wall and placing his pointer over the area, "you can see the Tennessee River at Redstone's southern corner. You'll also note that other interesting metropolitan areas are relatively near. If you're interested in seeing more of America, you can go visit them during long weekends.

Among these, "he continued moving his pointer over the different locations, "there is Birmingham, the capital of Alabama, Atlanta, in the state of Georgia, Chattanooga, Nashville and Memphis in Tennessee." He paused, letting his audience absorb those details. "Redstone Arsenal comprises over 38,000 acres of land and was named for the reddish soil of that area. The base was built in 1941, with the original purpose of fabricating conventional, as well as chemical ammunition during WW II and, at its peak it employed almost 20,000 people. By the late 1940s though, employment had fallen to a few hundred and many of its buildings were empty. In 1950, because of the large amount of available space, the easy access by road, rail and water, the Army chose it as the ideal place for the consolidation of recently formed missile programs. The rest" he said placing the pointer on the desk, "you will soon learn first hand.

Good luck and good bye!"

* * * * *

Most of the people elected to go by train. Toto and Roberto joined sergeants Argano, Moretti and Napolitano who would travel by car.

"I'm glad this is not a Fiat" said Toto upon getting in the car, "or else we'd be like sardines."

It wasn't very comfortable though as the air conditioning did not work. But what could they expect from a car bought for 200 dollars?

"We'll keep our windows open" said Argano. "Besides, since we will travel in civilian clothes, we can wear shorts and T-shirts."

Their travel itinerary would bring them to some interesting places: Galveston, La Fayette, Baton Rouge, and New Orleans, where they planned to stop to visit the French quarter, taste its Cajun food and cross the Mississippi River on a paddle-wheel boat.

They arrived in Huntsville seven days later, and joined the group that had travelled by train. They sat down at the reception hall and began to exchange stories about their experiences and opinions about the voyage.

"We had some strange episodes on our way, but over all, the trip was good" said Toto.

"Like what?"

"We decided to spend the first night in Galveston" he continued. "After supper, having spent many hours in the car, we decided to go for a walk. Since it was dark, we remained near our Motel. Suddenly, the bright lights of two cars burst out of the darkness and someone shouted: Raise your hands!"

"Who the hell were they?" Luciano asked.

"Once they came out from the shadows, we saw they were policemen. Who are you? They asked. Where do you come from? Where are you going? Roberto gets mad and yells back 'which of your fucking questions do you want us to answer first?'"

"Oh boy, and then what?"

"It took us about twenty minutes to explain, show them our I.D. cards, our travel orders and convince them we were neither illegal Mexicans, nor Cubans. Argano was incensed and afterwards exclaimed: "I haven't seen a scene like that since fascism."

"Then" pitched in Roberto, "there were the scenes with our great leader."

"Napolitano?"

"Who else? We had just left Texas and stopped for a steak, the waiter asked us what we wanted to drink, before we could answer he replied 'beer'. She looked at him strangely and exclaimed 'What?' Beer he repeated. Then, since she didn't seem to understand, I wrote it on a paper napkin and showed it to her. Oh, 'beer' she exclaimed, you cant, this is a dry state."

"Dry state?" repeated Napolitano, *"Dontah warry, soon you getta someh rain. Meantime breengha da beer."*

When we explained the matter, he reverted to his Neapolitan dialect and yelled: "I can I possibly eat a steak and drink Coca Cola?"

"Then" Toto continued, "he wanted to stop at a Hotel showing a 'No Vacancy' sign, thinking it meant the owner were not in holidays. "And finally" Toto concluded, "he caused a farmer to shoot at as."

"Why?"

"We lost our way and stopped when we saw a sign that read 'Trespassers will be prosecuted.' Napoletano ordered Argano to continue, believing it meant *'proseguire'* – Italian for 'keep on going'"

"It must have been quite a trip" Luciano commented.

"Yes" said Roberto, "but now tell us something about the facilities here."

"The logistic facilities aren't as good as those at Lackland" he said, "here, instead of two men per room, about thirty people are billeted in older, open barracks. They resemble the typical ones seen in vintage war movies about new recruits, marines and military. You can almost see the stereotype master sergeant – Burt Lancaster with 'fifty' smiling teeth - barging in for inspection at dawn, stand in the middle of the floor and, hands over his hips, bark orders and instructions."

"Fortunately though," interrupted Cicci, "they know we are here to study missiles and not to be subjected to discipline like new recruits. But you know what's humiliating? These very barracks were considered substandard by the German commander who refused them outright. But when the American showed them to our big chiefs, they said they were very good for us!"

"Goddamned bastard. I'd like to see the quarters they chose for themselves."

"And then people wonder why we don't respect our superiors" Luciano added.

It was evident that life at this base was going to be more… 'communal' than it had been in Lackland. Also, that Huntsville offered less amenities and forms of entertainment than San Antonio. Perhaps, as the civilian instructor had suggested, some of the free time should be used to visit other cities.

* * * * *

The following morning, they were assembled in a conference room for the official welcome to the base and to receive pertinent information.

The speaker however, a captain in the American Air Force, embarked on an unexpected subject.

"Recently, we have witnessed several accidents" he said, "some of which turned out to be lethal. They have befallen 'white' soldiers who, venturing down town, were found in the company of 'black' girls. Accidents aside, remember that, although the police is harsher with blacks, under those circumstances no one is safe."

Those who were not familiar with the Tehuki Kano's incident in the cafeteria of San Antonio, found the news a bit shocking.

"To conclude" the captain said, "I strongly recommend that you do not indulge in these extra-racial contacts and, whether in uniform or civilian clothes, when visiting the downtown area, you stay away from certain districts and venues."

Given the times and the self-portrayed image the Americans liked to give their nation, this was a surprising reminder that 'equality' in the law-books didn't translate to tolerance in the streets.

The officer looked around the table and, apparently thinking he had made his point, picked up a folder and said: "And now to our main topics."

He went on to describe the early days of the NASA Marshall Space Flight Center in Huntsville Alabama and the impact of German born physicist Wernher Von Braun and his 'team' in the development of the 'activity' at the base. "Some of you may have read that as early as 1930, Doctor Von Braun was involved in the German Rocket Society, *Verein fur Raumschiffart* or VFR and that, at about the same time, he began working on ballistic missiles for the German Army. You will certainly know," he said glancing at the attentive faces around the table, "that with his team, he was responsible for developing the first ballistic missile, the V-2 during the last phases of WW II."

"Of course!" many replied in unison.

"At the secret base of Peenemunde, near the Baltic coast" said Roberto.

"Think of Redstone Arsenal as our Peenemunde" said the captain smiling "what else do you know?"

"I've read" said Roberto, "that Von Braun engineered the surrender to the Americans of several hundred of his top scientists, along with plans and test equipment."

"Correct," said the captain "and, since we were vying with the Russians for the Germans' technical know-how and advancement in rocketry and guided missiles, we brought them to the United States. Originally at Fort Bliss, Texas, and launched the first generation of American made rockets from White Sands, New Mexico. Later, Von Braun and his team were moved to Huntsville where they have already finished many projects, including the powerful Jupiter ballistic missile. This" he said, "is the very missile which you are here to study and learn to maintain and launch."

Although the captain didn't mention it, it was an open secret and everyone on the Italian team knew they were working on other important projects, including the powerful Saturn V launch vehicle, which the Americans hoped would one day propel their first men into space.

"To his credit," concluded the captain, "though involved in missiles weaponry, Von Braun was and is the most prominent spokesman for the usage of rockets for peaceful space exploration."

"Lastly" said the captain closing the folder. "I wish to congratulate your group for having achieved the highest marks of the course in San Antonio. I hope you'll continue to meet with success here in Huntsville. And one recommendation." He smiled and then bringing his speech to a close, said: "If you happen to see Mr. Von Braun or any of the German scientists around the base, do not approach them or ask for autographs. For one thing, they are heavily guarded and for another they wish to be left alone. Thank you gentlemen and… good luck with your work!"

"Obviously" said Cicci, "when the American officer was out of sight, "when convenient, the Americans are ready to overlook the massive usage of slave labor and the collaboration with the Nazis at Peenemunde and other facilities."

"Sure," replied Roberto, "Haven't you heard what they say about their protected Central American dictators?"

"It might be a bastard" chipped in Toto, "but he is *our* bastard!"

"Perhaps Von Braun was O.K." said Roberto, "but I wonder if they say the same thing about the scientists who joined the Russians."

* * * * *

That afternoon, they were sent to the base photographic studio. Pictures were taken and new passes and I.D. cards issued. They had to be worn at all times on the outside left pocket of the shirt. Then they were taken to an auditorium where heavy digital locks were distributed. They were to be used on the lockers where 'Top Secret' missile manuals were to be stored after classes. An instructor in civilian clothes, talking from behind a teleprompter, began coaching them on how to set the individual codes on the combination locks. The explanation was long and tedious and when he finally said "Don't lock them until I tell you the next thing" it was too late and most had already done it. The locks were now unusable. To the annoyance of the instructor, a new set had to be issued and the process repeated. Finally, they were given the large technical manuals, with a blue hard cover.

The 'Top Secret' wording stamped above the titles, made everyone feel quite important.

The second day, after the theory session, they started doing work on actual ground equipment and Toto seemed to be in heaven. They all followed the explanations, but some were not as enthusiastic as he was.

It was approaching lunch time and Roberto, wishing to wash his hands, followed the sign to the main latrines and when he got there, he was surprised and embarrassed. The place was as large as a football field, with six circular basins in the middle and sets of foot operated sprinkling taps radiating from their center. There were two rows of latrines of twenty or more at the far walls. They had no door and, while entering or washing one's hands, one was invariably treated to the view of several men, in various postures and expressions, busy unloading their daily burdens; privacy did not apply in here!

A man, his legs crossed, comfortably resting against the short side panel of a latrine, conversing with the man seated on the pot, red faced for the effort. "So Billy" he was saying between puffs from his pipe, "are you *gonna* work on the propulsion system when you're done?"

Roberto thought of *Ostia Antica*, the ancient port of Imperial Rome. There too he had seen open latrines, but those were over two thousand years ago, had mosaic floors and a constant flow of water to wash away human wastage.

"Embarrassing" exclaimed Toto.

"Haven't you heard?" replied Cicci, "beggars and soldiers can't be choosers."

Weekend at last!

Toto, Roberto and Luciano decided to have a stroll downtown, and a piece of lemon pie, which they had learned to appreciate in San Antonio.

Huntsville's main square was full of people. A tall wooden platform had been built at the center with, at the back, a 'Redstone' missile, a direct derivative of the famous German V2.

"What's that apparatus for?" Luciano asked a policeman.

"They'll project for the first time a film about Von Braun."

"What is it called?"

"'I aim at the stars'. You can watch it if you wish" said the policeman, "it will start in a few minutes."

Given the subject they decided to stay.

At the end of the film, Mr. Von Braun himself came to the stage and, with extreme lucidity, and almost prophetically, he spoke of man's future special conquests.

"This will be something to write home about" said Toto. "Who would have thought in Caserta, one day we'd be near such a scientist."

"I agree" said Luciano, "but now let's go for the pie."

- XXXI -

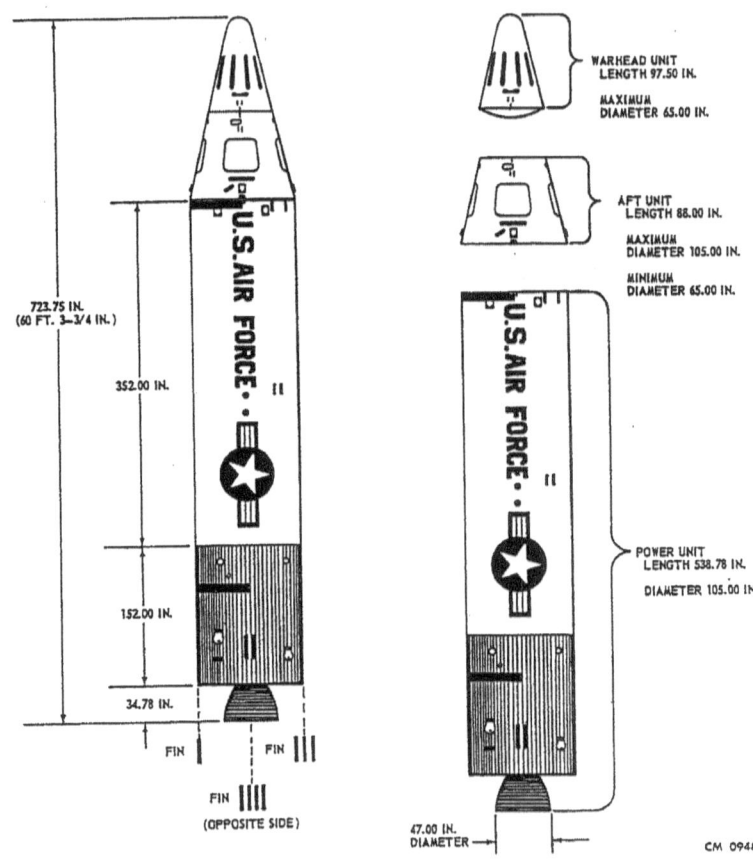

Visione prospettica delle dimensioni nelle tre parti e indicazione delle quattro *Fin* (fonte Salvatore Marciante).

MISSILES' LESSON

"Weapon system familiarization" was written on the blackboard when the students entered the classroom.

Today's instructor was a middle aged civilian engineer with a fresh crew-cut. He wore a short sleeve starched white shirt and navy blue pants held by a nice black leather belt with a chrome-plated buckle. The vinyl case on the left pocket of his shirt contained various pens and below it, his identification badge with name and photograph read: Joe Taylor. It soon translated in Italian by the students *'Giuseppe il Sarto'*.

He had a pleasant voice and gentle manners and after introducing himself, he started talking about missile Ground Support Equipment or GSE. Toto asked how many pieces of this equipment were needed for missile support.

"Normally, the number of GSE varies with the type of missile. The army's 'Corporal' missile, for instance, has different needs than the 'Redstone'. And the 'Jupiter' missile, which is the one we are studying, needs approximately forty five unit of GSE, not counting the Launch Control Trailer or LCT which is the brain of the entire weapon system. Twenty trailers and self-propelling vehicles in the launch area are connected to the missile. Among which, the fuel trailer, the liquid oxygen or LOX trailer, the hydraulic power and the ground power units, etc. etc."

"Are they all used in the launch operation, or do some have an auxiliary function?" Roberto asked. "In other words, are they all directly involved during the minus fifteen count down?"

"It's a good question. The answer is no. Some of them don't have a direct function during launching, but they are all necessary at some stage or other, to add safety, quickness and flexibility to the system."

A slide show of the various equipment followed, and then there was time for questions and answers.

Although Roberto kept up with the program, his real interest lay ahead. He tried to imagine the actual bases in Italy, their locations and, most of all their distance from Tuscany.

The following day another instructor spoke about the pneumatic and hydraulic systems, stressing the fact that extreme caution had to be used when working on high pressure lines and equipment.

Weeks of intense lessons followed by several multiple choice tests, culminating in a final test. Toto and Roberto did very well and most of the other students passed with good marks. There was only one major, but predictable disappointment, as group leader W/O Napolitano, despite the help of his colleagues, failed miserably.

The practical part of the training was carried out on mock-ups and system panels located in a larger room. Roberto noticed that, in front of all those gadgets, Toto behaved as though he was going to heaven.

* * * * *

The words on the blackboard were: "Launcher and Missile."

"Today" said Mr. Taylor looking at his notes, "we'll cover some components of the missile system which are important for the launch operation. Namely, the mating ring, the launch pad, the flame deflector, the electrical cable junction box, the theodolite and the pneumatic system control panel." Then he dimmed the room lights and projected on a white screen several slides illustrating the components he had mentioned.

"The launch pad has a mating ring which is electrically rotated for missile azimuth alignment. The flame deflector is the solid steel pyramid located in the middle of the launch platform and its purpose is to deflect the engine flames when the missile is fired." He changed to another slide and said: "The theodolite is an electro-optical device which deflects a light beam to a prism on the rotating ring to achieve a precise azimuth alignment."

Although everybody was furnished with text-books, they diligently jotted down many notes to later ask the instructor to clarify points not well understood.

- XXXII -

THE RODEO

One day, as they stood in the corridor talking among themselves, a lean, blond American fellow stopped by.

"*Siete Italiani* – Are you Italian?" he asked.

They answered yes and he continued: "I love your language and I would like to practice it."

"For your work?" they asked.

"No, no. I work here as a civilian for the company that makes Teleprompters" he said. "You must have seen it in front of many instructors during your lessons. From the front it looks like clear glass, but from behind one can see the writing. Anyway" he said almost apologetically, "that's what I do now, but my real passion is opera and eventually I would like to go to Italy to continue my studies. That's why I need to practice."

"What role do you sing?"

"Tenor roles. But I have no illusion; there are so many good singers in Italy…"

They continued talking until the bell rang and the class was resumed.

The next day they met him again. "By the way" he said smiling, "My Name is Ray Hagen. *Raimondo* as you would say."

Roberto and Toto introduced themselves, while the others continued their discussion about women, money and food. Shortly, the bell rang again, but before leaving Ray said: "have you guys ever seen a Rodeo.

"Not me" the two answered in unison.

"If you would like to go, tonight there is one at the outskirts of Huntsville. I could pick you up at six thirty and bring you back before midnight. I know the rules."

"What do you think, Toto?" Roberto asked.

"Why not?" his friend replied.

After supper Roberto changed in civilian clothes and seeing his friend still in uniform said: "Well? Aren't you coming?"

"No. To tell you the truth I don't feel like going. I want to finish reading this Aeronautical magazine and…"

"And" Roberto interrupted, "you could have told me before, perhaps I would have said no as well."

"Sorry!"

Roberto got out of the barrack and a few moments later Ray appeared. He was driving a silver Mercedes Benz 320 SL and when he saw Roberto alone he asked about his friend.

"He didn't feel too well" he said, "perhaps another time."

They drove for about twenty minutes, conversing in English as well as Italian.

"I can tell you are from Tuscany," Ray said, "my previous teacher was a Florentine. You guys enunciate your words so clearly."

"We are a bit fanatical about our language" Roberto replied. "Contrary to other regions of Italy we don't have a dialect, so we don't get confused."

"Do you like opera?"

"Yes, I do, but I am not a connoisseur. Maybe one day."

They arrived at the area where the rodeo was held and Ray insisted in paying for the tickets. "I invited you, so please let me take this."

They sat on the bleachers and after a while the speakers announced the beginning of the show. The spectacle seemed a frenetic succession of cowboys trying to ride mad bulls holding only with one hand, being tossed in the air like puppets until they fell to the ground, while other cowboys, dressed as clowns tried to distract the mad beast and save the rider.

Two hours later, Roberto was visibly bored and Ray said: "Would you like to go?"

"Yes, If you don't mind. This thing is way too long for me."

They left and returned to the base with the understanding they would meet again to take advantage of each other's proficiency in their languages and perhaps, to listen to some opera.

"That would be great," said Roberto upon parting, "thanks a lot for the evening."

This, Roberto thought, might be a good opportunity to learn something about America.

* * * * *

The following weekend Ray and Roberto met again. This time they went for a drive in the surrounding countryside and at supper-time Ray suggested a charming restaurant in down town Huntsville.

As they entered, Roberto noticed the waiters in formal black uniform, the walls covered with mahogany wood panels and the heavy carpet gave the impression to be walking on clouds. There were many green plants.

It was more elegant than Roberto expected and upon being seated he pulled Ray's sleeve and said: "Are you sure? It looks expensive."

"It's not too bad, believe me. Besides, I know the owner and I get a discount."

Roberto looked at the shiny Steinway Gran Piano that sat on a corner.

"That's a beautiful instrument" said Ray following his stare.

They were given a table not far from the piano and Roberto noticed they were treated with familiarity and as though expected. While ordering their food several other people arrived and were seated nearby. They had barely started to eat when an elegant man in his forties walked by and said hello to Ray, who nodded in reply. Then he sat behind the piano and began to play. After a couple of tunes Roberto recognized the opening notes of a famous Neapolitan song.

To his surprise, Ray stood up and said: "Help me with the words." He began to sing *"O sole mio"* with a full tenor voice. From a corner, a well dressed man, perhaps the owner or the manager, smiled with pleasure. Roberto was amazed at Ray's beautiful voice and felt a bit self conscious now that everyone was looking at them. At the end of the song there was long applause. Ray gestured his thanks and was obliged to sing again. This time, *Che gelide manine*, from Puccini's *La Boheme*. Again beautifully sang and applauded.

"You have a very good voice" said Roberto with sincere enthusiasm, "you should make it a career."

"Thanks, I'm glad you liked it."

After supper, Roberto insisted he take care of the bill. "You'll either let me pay" he said, "or I'll refuse any further invitation."

Ray was right, it wasn't bad at all.

As they drove back to the base, Ray said: "Can I ask you a political question?"

"Certainly."

"What do Italians think of the cold war?"

"We don't think much about it."

"But you must have an opinion…"

"We certainly do."

"What is it?"

"The communists think it has been caused by American imperialism, everybody else that it is magnified by American weapons manufacturers."

"Either way" said Ray laughing, "we Americans come out the worse."

"You said it."

* * * * *

The following day Roberto received a letter from Silvia.

His heart was beating fast, and although still unsure of what he ultimately wanted, he hoped the letter did not spell the end. He finally opened the envelope and stared at the neat handwriting he knew so well.

He began to read it.

My dear Roberto:

I received your new address from Mauro, but I don't know if or where this letter will reach you. I want to be truthful with you. That is why I waited a long time before replying to you.

Your behavior hurt me a lot. And I still grieve over it. I would have thought that your mother's death, for which I am deeply sorry, would have made you want to be near me. Instead, you kept me away, and didn't want to share your pain. Two people in love do not reject each other in sad moments. If anything, the opposite.

You left without even giving me the chance to see you. I was dying to see you. Didn't you know? From the first days I've know you. I told you 'I love you' every and each way I know how. Do you want me to say it again? Shout it to you? I could do it, but I will not beg. I have never done that for anyone, and I won't do it for you. I am not asking anything of you. It's very simple; you either love me, or you don't. I don't even want to cry any longer, although it would help to loosen the knot stuck in my throat.

I don't know if to admire you for the strength of your decision, or to hate you for having valued my love so little. To have utterly disregarded feelings which I believed were important to both of us.

I cannot tell you that I don't love you anymore. But you should be careful with your cruel sincerity, because the worse lies are those we tell ourselves. They can cause the death of the part of us that aspire to higher things.

My dear Roberto, I can only let you follow your destiny and find yourself, knowing that I still love you.

Sincerely,
Silvia

Roberto read the letter several times, trying to assess his emotions, and whether this was the prelude of a reconciliation or the epilogue. He would have liked to write her back right away. Tell her that he already knew he had made an error, that he still loved her. He still wanted to experience what his desire for 'freedom' really meant.

But something held him back. He should wait a bit longer to be certain. But God, how hard it was…

- XXXIII -

THE SIMULATED LAUNCH

"Today," said the instructor, "we will perform a simulated launch test. Some of the procedures, like the first and second stage separation, the firing of the engine and other operations, obviously will be virtual."

He checked to see if everyone was following then added: "They will be by-passed electronically to signal their completion to continue the procedure. Others, like the fuel transfer, the engine gimbals, the gyroscopes orientation, will be actual. During the intermediate section the jet engine specialist will be required to climb above the engine and check for leaks, the proper movements of the gimbals etc." He hesitated and then continued: "Captain Quadra insisted that chief Warrant officer Napolitano coordinate the procedure from the launch trailer."

Roberto, Toto and Luciano looked at each other in astonishment; 'how could he do it?' their glance said, 'if he failed every test and can't even understand simple commands…?'

Luciano winked at Roberto, "I'll watch over him" he whispered. "Listen to me."

"I'll go," said Roberto to Toto, "If something wrong happens, abort and shut the fucking system off."

"Don't worry. I'll watch out for you."

"Help me up. The goddamned deflection pyramid is slippery and sharp as a spear."

They began the count down and the fuel transfer was complete. During the pressurization of the tanks Roberto noticed a spray of hydraulic oil raining from above.

"Leak noted" he said calmly adjusting his head-set. "Put the system on hold, we'll resume the count-down when assessment is complete."

"O.K. to complete" said Napoletano.

"Noooooh!" Roberto and Luciano yelled in unison.

Too late.

A hydraulic pressure of over 3,000 PSI was applied to the system. A flexible metal line snapped open and lashed around the engine housing like a whip, while a spray of viscous fluid spewed all over. Roberto ducked, but a couple of smaller lines were sliced like butter and he was instantly blinded by the fluid. When the main hose hit his legs from behind, he lost his footing and fell. During the few instants duration of his plunge, he thought of Silvia, and whether he would see her again. Thinking of the pointed steel pyramid below, he prepared to mitigate the fall with his arms and coiled his head forward, as he had learned in Judo.

He lost consciousness on impact.

When he awoke, he was lying on a bed in a very dark place and soft music piped in from somewhere. He thought he was having a dream. He tried to move but felt a stabbing pain in his head and his left arm. He touched his arm and felt a thick bandage. His eyes were itchy and when he raised his right hand to rub them, he felt his head completely bandaged as well. He remembered the high-pressure fluid hitting his face, his fall, and a frightening sudden thought crossed his mind; did he injure his eyes? He had to know!

"Hello!" He called, "is anybody here?" There was no answer. He tried to get up, but a sharp stab in his head convinced him to stay down. "Hello" he called again. He was suddenly overcome by panic; what if he was going to be blind? What would happen to his career? His life? Silvia?

"Hello. Can't anybody hear me?"

"Yes, I can certainly hear you" said a pleasant female voice. "With all the drugs we gave you, I didn't think you'd be awake yet."

"Where am I? Who are you? Why are my eyes covered?"

"One question at a time" said the voice in a cheerful tone. "You are at Santa Rosa Hospital, I am your nurse and I'm going to take care of you. You suffered a bad concussion and a gash at the back of your head and…"

"What about my eyes? They are very itchy."

"Since we had to stitch you and bandaged you, we covered your eyes as well so you wouldn't rub them and irritate them further."

"Are they O.K.?" he asked dreading the answer.

The short silence that followed seemed an eternity. "We don't know yet. The doctor might be able to tell you tomorrow morning. By the way, my name is Catherine, You can call me Cathy."

"Thanks Cathy. I'm Roberto. Roberto Lanzi…"

"I know who you are. I got your records when they brought you here this morning."

"What time is it?"

"It's eight o'clock in the evening. If you feel like having a bite I can call for some food."

"Yes, I could eat but… how will I manage…?"

"I'll raise your bed, I'll prop you up and then feed you. How does that sound?"

"Convenient, but a bit embarrassing, I haven't been spoon-fed in a long time, you know? By the way, how long am I to remain in the hospital?"

"I'm not your doctor." Then after a brief silence, "please don't quote me, but I think you'll be here one week or longer."

"Have any of my friends been here?"

"A whole battalion of them. They said they'll return tomorrow. Meanwhile, I'll be your sole companion… day and night" she added in a teasing voice.

"Thank you, Catherine."

She left and Roberto began to think again about the wrong command that Warrant officer Napolitano had given. Because of it, he could have been killed. If he had, who would the Air Force notify? Who would claim his body? He saw his lifeless corpse back in Castelvecchio. Perhaps the Gianis would have taken a tomb beside that of his mother or his grandmother… He shook himself from those morbid thoughts, after all, he wasn't dead yet.

But what about his eyes. He wished it was morning already to hear the doctor's verdict. Now, he couldn't even read Silvia's mail, let alone reply to her. What a damn affair!

He was preoccupied with these thoughts when Catherine's cheery voice announced: "Dinner is served, *Signor*."

"Good! Tell me when I should open my mouth."

"In just a moment."

He heard the sound of a tray being placed on the night table and the clicking of the bed mechanism beginning to raise his bed.

"Tell me when you are comfortable" she said.

"I'm fine now" he said after a moment. He adjusted his position and felt the bed sheet slide down. He touched his chest and realized he was naked. He pulled the sheet upwards and Catherine burst into laughter, "Don't do that on my account," she said, "I don't mind the view."

He smiled and felt his face redden. She sat on the edge of the bed, so close to him that he could smell her fragrance. "I like your perfume" he said, "What is that you're wearing?"

"Chanel number five."

"It blends beautifully with your body scent." He was surprised at his boldness.

"I'm glad you like it, and now open your mouth, you will regain your strength in no time at all."

He had begun to chew on a piece of meat when she asked: "Do you mind if I switch the radio on? There is a nice program this time of the night."

He raised his hand and finished chewing, "By all means" he said, "since I can't talk while eating it will keep you company."

He heard her fidget with the radio on his night table and search, then stop. It seemed the type of music he liked as well.

"Open up again" she said giving him a spoon full of mashed potatoes. He must have made a face because she giggled and asked, "A bit insipid?"

"Yes," he admitted, "I'm sorry, I didn't mean to be ungrateful."

"It's all right, Roberto, I'm not so fond of this food either. Maybe when you're well I'll treat you to a nice supper out. There are a couple of *Eye-talian* restaurants in Huntsville."

"Italian" he corrected her. "Well, if you make me better soon, I should be the one to treat you." He immediately regretted having said it. Her voice was nice, her smell alluring, but what if she was an ugly duckling? He wouldn't he want to go out with her. Maybe he'd give her a book or some flowers.

"It's a deal!" She said, "but now finish this. Then I'll give you a couple of pills and you should have a long sleep."

He raised his hand to indicate he wanted to say something. He swallowed his last bite and then asked: "Is this Doris Day singing?"

"Yes. Do you like her?"

"Very much. I bought her latest LP, but I don't know this song. What is it called?"

"Bewitched, bothered and bewildered."

"I don't understand what it means..."

"Bewitch means to fascinate. To be very desirable to somebody, as to be under his spell. Like what you're doing to me" she giggled, "but don't worry I'm neither 'bothered or confused' by it. On the contrary…"

"You are teasing me" he said smiling. "You take advantage of me because I'm blind folded."

"I haven't taken advantage of you, *yet*" she said with laughter in her voice, "now take these pills."

"What are they for?"

"To alleviate the soreness and to help you sleep."

"I feel fine. I don't need them." 'Perhaps she's an old, fat boar and she wants to have her way with me while I am asleep, he thought.

"Now, now. Be a good boy and take them." She gave him two pills and a glass of what smelled like orange juice." She lowered his bed.

"Now try to have a rest, I'll come and check on you in a couple of hours."

She switched the radio off. Then he heard the click of the light switch and the soft thud of the door. She was gone.

He turned on his side and spit the pills on his hand. Then reached out for the radio. He switched it on again and listened to the music for a while, then fell asleep.

- XXXIV -

CATHERINE

"Good morning" said a male voice, "I'm Doctor Schmidt. I and head nurse Foster will check your wound, replace the dressing and then someone will bring you breakfast."

"Thank you doctor."

The nurse started to unwrap the bandages and when she finished Roberto tried to open his eyes, but they were sticky. "Keep them closed a while longer, dear, I'll wash them out in a moment." Then she said: "Here you are doctor."

"Not too bad," he said placing his hand on Roberto's forehead. "You heal fast. The nurse will medicate the wound … we had to stitch it a bit, but it's under your hair and it won't leave any visible mark. In about four days I'll remove the stitches."

"Thanks doctor. But what about my eyes?" Roberto asked as his heart raced.

"They are badly irritated by the chemicals. We flushed them out and now we will reapply some ointment. I want you to wear your blindfold for another few days, then we'll see."

"Are they permanently damaged?"

"We won't know for sure for another few days. The high pressure of the fluid and its toxicity irritated them badly, but we don't know if the cornea was damaged. We will know in a couple of days."

They left and another nurse brought him breakfast and helped him eat. She had an older voice and Roberto wondered if Catherine would come again later, but refrained from asking. When she left, he remained for a while listening to the noises beyond his door: a toneless conversation in the corridor, the faint closing of a door, the smothered rumble of a truck's engine. Being blindfolded seemed to heighten all other senses. He shook himself. It was certainly not a good trade for his eyesight.

He switched the radio on. It played some of the hits of the day: "That's Amore" by Dean Martin; "I Believe" by Frankie Laine; "Stranger in Paradise" by Tony Bennet and others songs by Perry Como, Eddy Fisher and Nat King Cole. He really loved American music. It seemed more… progressive and had better orchestration than the popular music back home.

Home! Silvia!

He would be in a state of anxiety until the condition of his eyes was determined.

The radio announcer commented about the T.V. night show, hosted by Walter Cronkite. He also mentioned that Marilyn Monroe was the first centerfold and cover girl of Playboy magazine. "And talking about sexy matters," said the announcer changing tone, "Doctor Gregory Pinkus has co-invented the first oral contraceptive for women. 'The Pill' as it is beginning to be known, by preventing ovulation, will allow women to chose weather or not become pregnant when having sex. Margaret Sanger, the life long advocate of women's rights, who raised 150,000 dollars for the project, will be vindicated. To repeat one of the memorable quotes of the birth control pioneer, 'Against the State, against the Church, against the silence of the medical profession, against the whole machinery of the dead institutions of the past, today's woman arises!'"

Wouldn't it be fantastic, Roberto thought, to have sex without the fear of unwanted birth. But who knows what the damn Vatican would say about it?

At lunch time his friends came to visit and after a few inquiries and reassurance about his health.

"You lucky dog," Luciano said, "have you had the chance to look at the nurse who took care of you on arrival?"

"Not yet. I heard her voice, but I couldn't see her with this goddamned gear on my face. Why? Is she good looking?"

"Very, very good looking."

"And she seemed to enjoy undressing and washing you," added Toto. "If I were you I'd stay a while longer. Who knows…"

"Roberto smiled, then asked: "By the way, how did the simulated launch go? Did you continue?"

"No. We aborted it and Napolitano got his ass chewed by the American supervisor for not understanding and making a mess of it. He might be sent home."

"He shouldn't be here to start with," said Roberto. "However, I'm sorry for him… even if he is an idiot."

The others agreed wholeheartedly.

"Cicci says hello" said Toto. "He wanted to come too, but was detained."

"What has he done this time?"

"He came back late as usual last night and since his brakes don't work he tried to stop against the heavy fence in front of the barracks," said Toto.

"Yeah" added Luciano, "but he misjudged his speed, broke through the fence and smashed against the barracks."

"Cicci will never change," said Roberto, "tell him not to exaggerate."

They shook hands. "We'll return tomorrow in the evening," they said, "we trust you'll behave with the nurses."

* * * * *

"Luciano couldn't come" said Toto upon arrival, "and I can only stay a short time, we have a test tomorrow and I have to do some studying. I brought you a letter."

"Thanks Toto. You are a real friend. Is it from Silvia?"

"No. it's from your friend Mauro."

"Would you read it to me?"

"Sure."

Roberto swallowed his disappointment. He heard the crackling of the crisp paper envelope being torn open, "is there a chair in the room?" he asked.

"Yes. Let me move it closer to the bed."

He began to read.

Dear Roberto:

Yesterday was Sunday. Giovanni and I took advantage of the good whether and took a walk along our usual route over the right bank of the Arno. We reminisced about old times and wished you were here with us.

In the afternoon I went to the Sirenetta dance club with Adriana and saw a few friends including Silvia. She was with some friends from Santa Chiara and seemed to enjoy her dancing. We spoke for a while and exchanged information about your whereabouts and progress in America. She said she will write to you soon and tell you…

Roberto did not hear the end. Like a road block in front of him, the vision of Silvia's dancing at the Sirenetta had stopped him on his tracks. He was suddenly taken over by a fit of jealousy and could see no further.

Why?

He had refused to go out with his friend in quest of girls, he had deflected Manuela's attentions, he had pursued his studies and embraced the Judo Tournament to avoid other form of pastime that may lead him into temptations… and she went dancing?

The silence in the room was finally interrupted by Toto asking, "Do you want me to reply to Mauro?"

"No, Toto. Thanks, it won't be necessary. Hopefully I'll be able to do it myself soon."

"Here is your letter," said Toto "We'll be back as soon as we can. Be well"

As soon as he left, Roberto brought the letter close to his nostrils, but he could not detect any hint of perfume to remind him of Silvia.

* * * * *

After several hours and a couple of visits from nurse Foster, finally, during the early evening news he heard Catherine's cheery voice:

"Hello soldier! Or should I say aviator? How do you feel today?"

"Fit as a fiddle and ready to go," he joked.

"Where did you learn that expression?"

"I don't remember. I heard it somewhere and though violins are fragile instruments … I thought I'd use it."

"Are you ready for your sponge bath?"

"Why don't you walk me to the shower instead? I'd love to have a hot shower."

"Not today. Tomorrow maybe."

She raised his bed and then rubbed his skin with a sponge soaked in warm water. She lifted his arm and then held his head up to wipe his neck. Her touch was gentle. After, she dabbed his skin with a soft towel. Then helped him with his supper. Before leaving she gave him two pills again and this time he swallowed them; he did want to sleep and forget.

But even in his slumber, the thought of Silvia did not abandon him. He saw her in her short, blue skirt, arriving at the dance club, dancing tightly with Benito, laughing at his whispered suggestions. Then sitting at her desk, a piece of white paper in front of her and pen in hand, staring into space, incapable of writing a single line to Roberto.

Nurse Foster voice woke him up "Wake up sailor," she said jokingly as she pulled the curtains, "your boat is in port."

Roberto recognized the smell of eggs and coffee. "Good morning" he said, "is it already breakfast time?"

"It sure is. I'm glad to see you slept well last night."

He was glad too; that his nightmarish dreams had only been that, that despite it all, another day had dawned.

After he had his breakfast, nurse Foster left and he spent the day thinking and listening to the radio and waiting for Catherine.

"Hallo Roberto" she sang, entering the room. "Are you ready for your sponge bath?"

She was already near him and felt her gentle touch over his skin. "Please let me have a shower" he said, "you promised."

"Do you feel up to it?"

"I think so. Let me try." He pulled up his pajama pants and swung his legs outwards. He stood up and, outside of a throbbing head ache where the cut was, he felt reasonably well.

"Sit down a moment, I'll undo your bandages and then replace them after your shower."

He sat and she came between his legs and worked on his head bandage first, coming close to his face with her breasts as she unwrapped the rear part. He could feel the warmth of her body, inhale the fragrance of her skin. She seemed to have used an even higher dose of perfume; or was it his imagination? He wished he knew if she was good looking as Luciano said.

"There!" she said letting the last section drop, "don't open your eyes yet, I'll wash them with a solution first."

"Okay" He said, wondering if he'd be able to see her.

She placed her hand under his chin and gently raised his head. She rubbed his eyes and drops of odorless fluid ran down his cheeks and fell on his naked chest. She wiped them with her hand and it felt more like a lingering caress.

"Now you can open them" she finally said.

He blinked a few times, and the image that appeared in the still hazy, dark background, he distinguished a young and pretty face, blond hair, a small impertinent nose and green or blue eyes. As she moved away, he saw a well proportioned figure and movements that had the grace of a model.

There was no doubt, Luciano's comments had been quite appropriate.

Catherine returned with a towel, clasped his arm, took him to the shower and opened the taps.

"I'll leave the towel here" she said placing his hand over the chair. "I'll be back in a few minutes."

When she returned, he had finished and had made his way to the bed. She rubbed his shoulders and chest with the towel and said:

"I'm off now. I'll see you tomorrow."

Roberto would have liked her to stay or return, but a different nurse brought him supper. Roberto was disappointed and all he could do was think of Catherine, envision how he'd like to undress and make love to her.

The next day, Doctor Schmidt came with a different nurse and, after a quick examination, said: "Your eyes irritation is getting a bit better, but it's still too soon to know if the cornea has been damaged. After we unwrap you again, you'll be able to tell us how your vision is."

Shortly afterwards, Catherine came, followed by his friends.

This time with Cicci, who had finished his period of punishment, was with them.

"You lucky dog" he said to Roberto in Italian. Then turning to Luciano and Toto, added, "Have you seen the piece of ass they assigned to him?"

- XXXV -

NO BANDAGES

Finally, Cathy announced that she would undo his bandages, freshen the medication and test his vision.

When she finished, Roberto couldn't stop staring at her. She was really dazzling; a perfect oval face, sumptuous lips, silky blond hair pulled back in a bun, a small band of hair falling on her forehead and definitely green eyes. A tight belt over her white gown revealed a narrow waist and well pronounced hips. He imagined his hands over those hips.

"You like what you see?" she said jokingly.

"Sorry Catherine. I certainly do. I didn't think I was so obvious."

"I don't mind. I too like what I see. How is your vision?"

"Much better."

"Good. After your shower I'll replace the bandage, we need to be cautious for another few days. Now remove your pants."

"Don't worry" she added laughing at his expression, "I've already seen all there is to see." Her voice was matter of fact, sweet and serene.

He turned around and complied. Then she helped him to the shower.

"You can gently shampoo your hair, even around the stitches. And your arm too."

She sounded very close, but although tempting he did not dare turn around. He was afraid that her agreeable manners and his wishful thinking, had given him the wrong idea. Wouldn't it be nice though, he thought.

As he lathered his short hair he felt the bumpy stitches on the side of his head and kept thinking about Catherine, just a couple of feet away from his naked body; was she looking at him? He switched off the tap, turned around and saw her attractive silhouette against the light colored window shades. She was facing him and holding a bath towel.

"Come" she said invitingly, "I'll help you dry yourself."

He started moving towards her when he heard some noises in the corridor, took the towel and pulled back one step.

"I can manage" he said. He moved to the edge of the bed, sat down and dropped the towel over his legs.

"Let me put some ointment on the wounds before I replace the bandages" she calmly said.

"Do you have to cover my eyes again?"

"As I said, only for another few days."

"It's unfair. I can't see you then…"

He wanted to say something more. Her nearness was giving him courage, but the noises in the corridor and even more the possibility of misinterpreting her friendliness made him hesitant. She was so close that he could have pushed his arm forward and put his hand under her skirt, feel the warm, naked flesh of her thighs, above her white stockings, or even higher.

He briefly thought of Silvia, but the urge of the here and now seemed stronger than her distant image. Besides, hadn't she gone dancing?

Cathy did not answer his last comment. She wiped drops of water from his chest. Her hand continued to descend across his stomach. A sudden excitement went through his body and reached his maleness. He took her hand, then he turned it upward and placed a kiss on her palm.

"I'll have to go soon" she said keeping her hand in his, "I have other patients to care for…"

She read his disappointment and added, "Later I'll be back and visit you."

Her voice had acquired a husky tone.

Then, in an unexpected impulsive gesture, she knelt between his knees, pulled his towel aside and uncovered him. "Lie down" she whispered pushing him gently backwards and, as he did, her tongue teased the tip of his erect penis, and then, as he became fully aroused, her soft, moist lips embraced his member. He squeezed his eyes and reached for her head, his fingers entwined in her silken hair.

At supper time, Catherine returned.

"I hope you like baked chicken and baked potatoes" she said in her usual joyful tone, "I brought you a double portion."

"I love it" he said thinking of their earlier intimate act. "When do you get off work tonight?"

She sat on the edge of his bed again and said: "Open your mouth and don't worry. I said I'll be here didn't I? Now eat and after try to sleep awhile, you need rest."

He ate eagerly and sometimes he intercepted her hand, holding it while he finished chewing his food or asking another question:

"Who is singing now?"... "What's the name of this song?"... "Would you help me write down the words of this song? There are some that I don't understand."

"Too many questions" she said with a smile in her voice, "Everything in its own time. Now open your mouth and eat."

When he finished, she unwrapped his bandage and changed the dressing over the wound. He forced his eyes open and gazed at her silently for a long moment. Then exclaimed, "Catherine, you are beautiful."

"Thank you. But now you have to lie down and hold these cups over your eyes, so that they are completely cleansed. Then I'll put some medication and bandage you again. Tomorrow the doctor may be able to tell you how long we must carry on this routine. Now be good and rest, I'll come visit you in a couple of hours."

"I'll be waiting right here," he said jokingly. Given the six hours difference with Italy, Silvia would be sound asleep. Yet, even thinking of her, the distance, place and time, his background, he would have no difficulty making love to another woman. That's the way it is with men, he thought.

At least in Italy.

And, here in America women seem to be the same as men. Don't I know it? He thought of the many stories heard from his friends and his own experience with Manuela in San Antonio, and with Catherine right here. In both cases the females had initiated flirting and behaving in a playfully alluring way. He didn't mind being the beneficiary of that interest but, typically, he wouldn't have been able to accept this promiscuity from any girl he would consider for marriage. 'Yes,' he conceded, 'it is a double standard, but what can I do? In these matters I'm just a product of my society; I didn't make the rules, I just follow them. I'm glad to be a man.'

The radio had begun a program of music from the Big Bands Orchestras: Tommy Dorsey, Artie Shaw, Count Basie. The last piece was from Benny Goodman: "Estrellita!"

His heart pounded in his chest, remembering the last time he had heard it. It was while making love to Silvia. She had come to pick him up upon his return from the tests in Caserta and they had stopped below the banks of the Arno River. He revisited the scene in his memory and fell asleep savoring her kisses.

He woke up awhile later wondering what the time would be and when the radio announced it he realized he had slept about four hours. Had Catherine been back? Had he missed her? She did say that she worked the night shift, but when did she get off work?

The silence of his room was only broken by the odd whine of sirens echoing in the night; police cars rushing to an accident? Firemen hurrying to put out a fire? Toto, Pat and a few others would be asleep at the base by now. Cicci, would be with his woman, probably making love, but where? At a Motel? At her house? And what about Franco? He had been out a lot lately. He had seen him with a pretty young girl. "This is Louise" he had said introducing her. They were getting out of the P.EX. holding a bunch of records.

He held his breath, his door had been carefully opened.

"Catherine, Is that you?" he whispered.

"Yes, it's me, Roberto. It's my rest hour and I thought I'll spend it here with you."

"I was afraid to have missed your visit."

"No, my dear." She was near his bed. "Technically it's already 'tomorrow', so if you wish I can remove your bandage for a while.

"That would be wonderful; I want to see your."

"Can you sit up? I'll help you."

"No problem." He heard something fall to the floor, a sheet or blanket, perhaps.

Then she was beside him, unwrapping his bandage. He imagined her breasts inches from his face as he could feel the warmth of her skin and breathe her alluring fragrance. When the last piece of gauze was pealed, he opened his eyes and in the dim light of the radio dial he saw the sculptural naked body of Catherine, only inches from his face. She had one knee over his bed as though she wanted to climb on top. She pushed him gently down, "Let me do it this way," she said, "I don't want you to exert yourself just yet."

He was immediately aroused and, as she crossed over with the other leg, he caressed her well-modeled breasts. She rubbed herself against his hardness and pressed the length of his penis against her vagina, moaning softly. He raised his head to kiss her turgid nipples. "Bite them," she said, "bite them". He did it, gently at first and then a bit harder as she seemed to enjoy it. After awhile she rose on her knees and then slowly descended over him guiding his manhood totally inside her body.

They came together and she collapsed over his chest, relaxed and hard breathing. He kissed her neck and caressed her shoulder, tenderly, like the quiet state of mind he had suddenly fallen in. "Catherine!" he whispered in her ear, "I don't deserve this much love, but I'm glad you're giving it to me." Then he let a soft giggle, "Perhaps when I'm released, I should consider hurting myself again, to return here."

"Don't be silly," she said, "if you want we can see each other after you're dismissed."

"If I want…?" he said squeezing her to his chest.

She finally rolled to one side, "Now rest for awhile" she said. "Tell the doctor, the bandages fell down. Here leave them beside your pillow, they'll replace them in the morning."

After another week both the wounds and the eyes inflammation were much better and Roberto was released from the hospital. What a relief! The latent fear of having his eyes damaged and his life destroyed had never completely abandoned him. Now he felt as though a huge stone had been removed from his chest.

Roberto was released from the hospital.

He poured over the notes of his friends and in a few days he was able to catch up with the program.

- XXXVI -

THE END OF THE COURSE

A few days later, Roberto returned to the hospital to have his stitches taken out and to get another small bottle of ointment for his eyes. He asked about Cathy.

"She has been urgently transferred to a unit assigned to Korea" her superintendent said.

"Are you Roberto?" she then asked. "She said she will write you."

He was very disappointed. Making love to a woman without worrying of consequences, was a new experience for him. However, he came to the conclusion that, perhaps, due to his imminent return to Italy, it was better that way.

Some of his colleagues were so much involved in love affairs that they left their studies behind. Some had even abandoned the base without authorization and received heavy punishments.

Dreams must end.

On Friday he met Ray who apologized for not coming to the hospital to pay a visit to him. "I was in Washington."

"Don't worry Ray, it's the thought that counts. Besides, you're here now."

Especially now that Catherine had gone, Ray was his best American friend. Roberto wished to maintain the relationship.

"If you feel like, we could spend the weekend together, at my house" said Ray. "We could chat and listen to Italian music."

Roberto accepted the invitation.

Ray came to fetch Roberto as agreed, and told him he lived in a bungalow a half hour drive from the base. "On top of Monte Sano" he said.

"Why do you call it mount?" Roberto asked when they arrived.

"Are you saying it's a bit of an exaggeration?"

"Yes." Roberto answered smiling, "you call something which is barely a hill a mountain; World Series baseball finals, played only by Americans, etcetera, etcetera…"

"Maybe you're right" said Ray while making a detour from the main road to a narrow dirt road winding for about two hundred feet under high plane trees.

"I suppose sometimes we act as though we were the only ones in the world who count" he continued while parking his car near the bungalow. "Having won the war, has inflated our opinion of ourselves."

Roberto did not answer. He was absorbed looking at Ray's pleasing wood dwelling. Ray opened the door into a spacious living room with sofas, some wooden furniture and a piano in a corner. "Take a seat and make yourself at home."

"Talking about the war" Roberto continued, "I cannot certainly deny the Americans showed bravery, and organization. However…"

"Go on" said Ray opening the door of the refrigerator, "I'm getting us a couple of beers."

"In addition to bravery, at times it was Goddess Fortune which won the day: at Midway when the Japanese fleet was discovered by chance; in Normandy where Hitler persisted in not using his panzers 'D' day. Also remember that three quarters of the western world, plus the mighty Russians fought on your side."

Ray listened without interrupting and Roberto concluded softening his tone: "I'm saying this because one day your military may overestimate your strength and drive you to a disastrous war."

"Dear Roberto" said Ray putting his beer down on the table and sighing deeply, "sometimes the things you say are provoking, but also interesting and honest. What else about our character has struck you?"

Roberto took a sip of beer answered and, encouraged by his friend's high- minded attitude, continued: "The other thing that surprised me is that people here talk a great lot about the Great Depression. In Italy, although we suffered like you or more than you, people rarely speak about it. Maybe because we had many and more recent hard times to worry about."

"I'm listening" said Ray kicking off his shoes and stretching his legs. "The rare times our old people talk about that era, it's like hearing them describe an old, healed injury. In this Country, people of all ages talk about it as though it were an open and threatening wound. Never before I heard about harvest destruction, slaughtering and burial of cattle to keep prices high, throwing away milk and other commodities while millions of people starved to death. Maybe" he concluded, "in poor Italy, that period wasn't much different from the previous ones. Perhaps, after the poverty suffered following the Great War and Fascism, even the 'depression' seemed like normal rain after a thunderstorm. People were able and willing to share the little they possessed and had fewer traumatic effects. Who knows…?"

"Very interesting" said Ray getting up and heading toward the record player. "And now that you have so dispassionately reappraised us, what about some Italian opera?"

"It's a good idea. And on this subject it's I who have to be updated. As an Italian I'm a bit ashamed to be less knowledgeable than you on the subject. But before we do, Ray, please let me apologize for being so brutal in my comments. It's the way I am with real friends. And please, do the same with me when we talk about Italy and Italians. Promise me."

The evening proceeded with Roberto avoiding to be critical or dismissive.

Three days before his departure, Ray came to the base to say goodbye Roberto gave him two LP: "*La Cavalleria Rusticana*" and "*Turandot*" by Puccini he had bought at the P. Ex. They were interpreted by tenor Mario del Monaco, soprano Renata Tebaldi and mezzosoprano Giulietta Simionato; directed by Herbert Von Karajan.

Ray was very appreciative.

"As I already told you" he reminded Roberto hugging him, "here in America a young man with your talent and specialisation would make a good living. And, after work you could attend university. Think about it."

He then pulled a sheet of paper out of his pocket and added: "This is my address. Send me yours when you know your final destination. We'll keep in touch."

* * * * *

The courses had come to an end and Toto had scored the higher marks. Roberto had also attained very good results, especially taking into account that he had, of late, studied very little.

Within a few days they would return home. They would be soon assigned to launch bases located in southern Italy. The usual 'well informed' sources talked about the Apulia region and Roberto heard of Gioia del Colle, Acquaviva delle Fonti, Mottola, Laterza, Gravina, Irsina, Spinazzola, Altamura...and other towns he had never known before.

Those airmen who came from the southern part of Italy, were pleased to be stationed near home. The ones from the north, naturally, were not.

"They are small country villages" they commented while consulting a map to spot nearby cities which offered railroad connections to return home when on leave.

Roberto realized that unfortunately wherever he would be stationed in that region, he would be farther away from Tuscany than he had been when he was in Caserta. How many hours would it take for him to go home by train? How far would he be from main centres like Bari or Taranto? Toto was happy because it was his region and he would be near home. The only relief for everybody was that before being assigned to the final base, they would be granted a few days leave to go home.

* * * * *

After about a year, the American adventure was drawing to a close.

It was customary for the departing group to invite to dinner the civilian instructors who ran the last course.

Warrant Officer Napolitano discussed with his colleagues on a suitable place for the event. Roberto suggested a few good restaurants where he had been with Ray, including one that gave them a good discount because there was a piano bar and Ray used to sing "O sole mio" and other classical Neapolitan songs to the delight of the patrons and the owner.

"It would be too expensive" someone argued.

"But we'll share the bill" said Roberto, "it won't break anyone's account."

"We should go to a closer and cheaper place" said Napolitano who, despite his gaffes, was still with them, "something like that Mexican Grill not far from here."

They argued some more and ended up choosing an even worse one.

When they told the instructors, a visible grimace showed on their faces.

"It's goddamned dump" whispered one of them, but they did not oppose the selection.

"I'm afraid we couldn't have chosen a shittier place" Roberto told Toto. We will look like a band of ungrateful misers. They'll think all Italians are like that!"

His resentment for Napolitano, for causing him to crash from the missile, increased exponentially after this disastrous culinary choice.

- XXXVII -

Toto a New York

THE RETURN

They were again in New York.
Everyone took the opportunity to visit the most famous places.
During evening conversations it was evident that, notwithstanding the remarkable American experience, the older airmen were anxious to return home, embrace wife and children and tell friends about their beautiful adventure.

Some of the young ones, once completed their tour of duty, intended to return to the States, marry girls they had met in Texas or Alabama and settle in the USA.

Regardless of age and status, every one had enjoyed America.

Also Roberto was glad to return home, but not as much as he would have previously thought. He was contemplating Ray's invitation and the more numerous opportunities he would have in America.

Had it all been real?

He anticipated with pleasure his reunion with Mauro and Giovanni. His mother however, would not be there to partake of his experiences.

And Silvia? He had not yet decided if or when to see her. Perhaps he would do it, but he wasn't sure.

On his last day he visited the Moma museum, bought several postcards, wrote short notes and mailed them. He did not reveal the exact date of his return; he wanted it to be a surprise.

The return flight was smoother and faster than the previous one, as Alitalia had just introduced the speedier DC-8 powered by four jet engines, making the crossing in about eight hours. There was a happy atmosphere and chatter on the plane, and someone even looking forward to eating a good plate of spaghetti *al dente* and drinking a 'real' cup of espresso coffe.

They landed at Fiumicino airport, outside the Italian capital, and the bags were delivered with the customary Roman delay. Being a special flight, they had to place their luggage on a long table and drag it along while showing the passport to customs officials who carried out random inspections.

"Anything to declare? Any cigarettes?" the officer asked. "No I don't smoke. would you like me to open my knapsack?"

"No. it's not necessary. Next! Said the officer turning away, "Next!" he repeated looking at the airman first class behind Roberto.

"Anything to declare?"

"No. Nothing to declare. Just my record player."

Roberto was about to move away, but a loud noise made him turn around; the airman had dropped a large loudspeaker. It had broken open on impact, spilling dozens of cigarette boxes. The customs officials did not say a word. He opened a drawer, lifted the speaker box over it, shook it and several more packs fell inside.

"In that case" he told the airman while appropriating more packs from the floor, "you might as well run along."

Roberto shook his head. 'Justice Italian style' he thought.

* * * * *

When Roberto arrived in Castelvecchio, the town seemed smaller than when he had left, almost like an old jacket, it had shrunk and no longer fit.

He called on the Gianis and then he met with the people who rented his house and listened to their complaints: humidity stains, walls to be repainted, Persian shutters to be painted, and other deficiencies, were all brought up to lower the rent.

Though aggravated, Roberto accepted their requests anyway. He hated arguing about money.

He went to see his friend Mauro's who told him his parents wanted him to stay with them until the end of his furlough. Roberto spent long hours with his friend, telling him of the things he had appreciated in America, making comparisons between the two cultures and emphasizing the opportunities that someone as young as they were, would have had there.

"No, I'm not enamored with that Country" he said, "but I can't overlook the chances to work and complete my studies at one of the many universities, or have a career in one of the many aeronautical industries."

Mauro understood that for Roberto, it would not be easy to renounce to all that.

* * * * *

Finally, three days after his arrival, Roberto was able to arrange a meeting with Silvia in Santa Chiara.

They met on the elevated street on the south side of the town that ran for several blocks along the right bank of the Arno River. As soon as he saw her, he noticed how more mature she looked from the last time he had seen her.

They embraced formally and then walked along the pebbled paths of the public gardens, up to the bridge.

At the beginning, both seemed self-conscious, like two persons who have just met. Silvia did not seem angry or offended but she talked in a formal, almost detached way. She asked him about his experience in America and listened to him courteously.

Though replying politely, his mind wandered off to other places, to other times. He thought of Silvia happily dancing with others, perhaps even enjoying Benito's company. He felt angry but he tried to appear unemotional.

They were side by side, but it was as though between them there was a vast distance. As though the Roberto and Silvia of time past, who loved, made love, and could not live far from each other, no longer existed.

'How is it possible that my strong feelings have changed this much?' Roberto thought. 'How could what seemed a certainty, an immovable reference point, an incomparable tenderness, become what it is now?'

He felt as though walking a tight rope; everything was possible, even a fatal fall. He didn't want to mortgage his future, lock himself into a situation before reaching the end of his path. And he didn't want to deceive anyone, least of all Silvia.

They sat in one of the wrought iron benches facing the river, it was shaded by a mature oak tree.

They talked a lot, and then, suddenly she asked: "What are you doing tomorrow?"

"Why? We can meet again if you want."

"Of course I do. Come to my place for lunch."

Surprised and slow to react, Roberto stared at Silvia: "To your place?" he repeated, "and what about your parents?"

"I told them about us. I couldn't continue with the silly subterfuge. I'm too old for that. I feel childish every time I ask Mauro if he got any mail for me."

Roberto did not immediately reply. On the one hand he appreciated Silvia's point. Among other things meeting her parents might allow him to to write her at home and meet her more openly. On the other, in the contest of the small town, it would still be interpreted as a firm commitment towards a common future. Was he prepared to do that at this time?

"It was a simple question…" Silvia pressed. "You are not afraid to meet my father, are you?"

"No, I'm not afraid. I just thought it better to wait a while longer."

"Roberto, you know me well. I wouldn't ask you if I thought I could wait. My parents are getting older, they are eager to meet the man I love, hear your ideas about our future. I told them you'll soon leave again and…"

"I understand, but we knew all that from the beginning and you accepted the consequences."

"Yes, but we didn't know about America and your prolonged time away. We thought that after the course you'd be posted in a nearby base, Pisa for instance. Not in a god-forsaken place in the heel of Italy. My parents keep dropping hints about their desire to see grandchildren and they have difficulty understanding why I can't even tell them when I'll be married. The least you can do is meet them and help me make them appreciate the situation…"

It sounded reasonable but Roberto felt trapped. He hadn't imagined his meeting with Silvia would turn out like this. He felt as though he was walking a tight rope. He didn't want to deceive anyone but, was he prepared to mortgage his future? How about his plan to resume his studies? What about America? If Silvia was reluctant to leave her parents, she would become an anchor. On the other hand…

"I understand" he said sharply, "what time should I come?"

The next day, Roberto took the bus to Santa Chiara and got off in Market Square. As he proceeded towards Silvia's house, he was still strongly bothered by her insistence that he meet her parents now.

He walked through the very streets he travelled when going to school and later to the tannery; bittersweet recollections of another life. He smiled remembering that Benito had told him about 'this beautiful girl' who had just enrolled at the school, afterwards revealing he had followed her and discovered where she lived. As he got closer to her home, he tried to imagine the meeting with Silvia's parents. He had seen them once or twice at the school, when they came to meet the teachers, but he had never talked to them. He was a bit apprehensive and wondered about the outcome of their encounter.

He rang the bell and Silvia came to the gate to meet him. She seemed excited.

"Please don't overreact to my father" she whispered as they crossed the small but well kept garden.

"Don't worry, I'll be polite."

Roberto was introduced to Mr. and Mrs. Corradi. After the preliminaries, Silvia's mother seemed to be taken aback by Roberto cold formality and returned to the kitchen. Her father went to sit in a corner armchair and switched the radio on. It was broadcasting the midday news.

"Don't mind me for a few minutes" he said lowering the volume, "it's always the same crap, but I'm addicted to it."

"Don't worry papa" said Silvia, Roberto and I will sit on the sofa and chat."

Roberto looked around. It was a comfortable, tastefully furnished place, with Persian carpets, aniline leather sofas, teak table and chairs plus other expensive looking pieces of furniture.

How long would it take him to provide Silvia with similar surroundings?

Shortly, Mrs. Corradi returned with a large soup-tureen and said to Roberto: "I hope you'll like this, it's a *minestra di verdure* – vegetable soup, all with fresh things from my garden."

"I'm sure I will, madam. Don't worry."

"She is a good cook" her husband pitched in, "and for the main course we have my favorite dish, a juicy steak from a local Chanina cow. Eating meat helps our leather industry" he added with a chuckle.

"I agree with that, Mr. Corradi" said Roberto smiling.

"Don't be so formal, son. Call me Pietro."

"I don't think I can" Roberto replied. "My parents, were they still alive, would strongly disapprove.'

There were few other passing comments but, between eating and listening to the music coming from the radio, there was little opportunity to approach the matter of his intentions with Silvia.

When the espresso coffee wa served, Roberto pondered whether he should approach the topic first or wait for the father to do so.

"The meal was excellent" he told Mrs. Corradi.

Mr. Corradi gulped down his coffee and looking straight at the youth said: "So Roberto, my daughter tells me you've known each other for a while. In fact, since you were going to school together."

"Yes, but we lost contact and then, when we met again, I left for the Air Force. So, in effect, we've seen very little of each other."

"But enough to write and know you have feelings..."

"Yes, of course."

"Well, Roberto, it didn't come as a surprise when Silvia asked permission to receive your mail. Honestly, if I may say so myself, a beautiful girl like this, should have already been married, let alone engaged."

"Papa" Silvia exclaimed, "could you be a bit more subtle?"

"What? You want me to talk about the weather? Am I wrong in wanting to understand what you two are planning? Me and your mother aren't *gonna* live for ever, you know?"

"Don't exaggerate now papa" said Silvia, "You're not that old."

"Old enough to want to see you married.'

"And enjoy our grandchildren" added Mrs. Corradi looking at her daughter with pleading eyes.

Roberto cleared his throat, took a deep breath and said: "I love Silvia and I wouldn't do anything to hurt her. However, my present position doesn't allow me to give you a swift commitment. For one thing, the Air Force would not allow me to get married until the renewal of my term of service. Secondly, even if I did, I would not be in a financial position to do it for another couple of years. My intentions are serious but, as I said, I'm bound by my obligation with the *Aviazione*."

"If that is the problem, why don't you get out of the Army?"

"The Air Force, you mean. And what would I do then?"

"Nowadays there is plenty of work in Santa Chiara, there are over 400 tanneries and..."

"Sir" Roberto interrupted, "I joined the Air Force to escape the tannery. How could I possibly return to it?"

"I didn't mean as a worker. You could do other things or even join me as an agent and sell leather to sofa and shoe manufacturers. There is good money to be made son, let me tell you."

"I thank you for the offer, but I wouldn't be a good salesman. Beside, money is not my primary motivation."

"What is then?"

"A position or career that enables me to grow, to learn more."

"Listen to me, Roberto. Don't delude yourself, comfort helps make life easier" he said looking around the room as though taking an inventory of the expensive furniture, "and money is what gets it."

"Father" Silvia interrupted, "can we stop talking about money? I'm sure Roberto understands its value."

"Listen kid, you are my only daughter and I am bloody well entitled to be concerned about your future."

There were a few more exchanges of this nature, but finally it was evedent tha nothing would be gained by continuing the conversation.

"Sorry" said Roberto abruptly, "but I have to go." Then turning towards Mrs. Corradi, "I thank you for the beautiful meal and hope to see you again at my next furlough."

"And when would that be?" Mr. Corradi asked.

"I'm not sure, but as soon as I know I'll tell Silvia." He got up and stretched his arm towards him. "Goodbye, sir. I appreciate your concern for your daughter. I'll try to give you more concrete answers next time."

"Goodbye, Roberto. Behave yourself and hurry back."

"I'll accompany him to the bus stop" said Silvia.

Out in the street, Silvia took Roberto's arm.

He couldn't escape the warm feeling of her touch and the satisfaction of walking like that as though they were officially engaged. All the same, he was still riled by her insistence that he meet her parents. He knew their encounter would be inconclusive.

He checked his watch, "There is still an hour before next bus for Castelvecchio"

He said, "let's walk a bit."

They strolled towards the Arno River and then sat in one of the wrought iron benches shaded by mature oak trees far from the path. They could talk undisturbed, but their thoughts were muddled by the emotions and the words were slow to come.

"I hope my father didn't upset you" said Silvia after a long silence.

"No. It didn't. But you should have known our meeting was going to be like that."

"But at least now you have met and you can write me at home" said Silvia holding Roberto's hand. "I love you Roberto, and think we made a little progress."

I love you too, Roberto thought, but marriage and children? What about my ambitions? She is still part of the Old World, I've seen the New one, how could I possibly return to this place and live a 'Corradi' life?

They promised each other to write and say how they envisioned their future

He left again.

- XXXVIII -

CASERTA

Warrant officer Busato welcomed Roberto as though he was genuinely happy to see him. Especially when he gave him an envelope with American stamps.

He assigned him to a new dormitory and told him he was the first of the group to arrive. He also told him that he had been promoted to airman first class and he could therefore add another red stripe to the sleeves of his shirt. A small increase in salary would follow.

Once unpacked, Roberto started towards the gym. He was anxious to see the old instructor and tell him about his experience with the Japanese *Kodanska*, or judo experts. He found his as he was starting a course with a new group of enlisted men.

"How nice to see you" said the instructor upon seeing him. Then turning to his class added, "This is my favorite *judoka*. f you are not on duty remove your uniform, take a *judogi* and give me a hand. I would like to show these students a real *randori*."

Roberto went to change and when he returned to the mat, the instructor said: "Please explain to them what's a *randori*."

"It is a training fight" said Roberto, "in which, in order to acquire experience and perfect ones throws, both contenders put up only relative resistance." He knelt over the *totami* mat and knotted his belt loosely, as Onishi had taught him.

"Ready?" asked the instructor pulling on both ends of his black belt. "How about demonstrating that series of non orthodox throws you invented for our exhibition?"

They went to the center of the *tatami* and stopped at a few steps distance from one another. After the required ceremonial bow, Roberto jumped in the air and hit his opponent on his chest with both feet sending him to the floor. The maestro remained there and when Roberto got close enough, he hit him with a scissor movement, one leg behind the knees and the other on the lower part of the chest causing Roberto to fall backwards. They both got up and continued with a series of throws, emphasizing the swiftness of the execution and the safe completion of the fall, to reduce the impact.

After a while, the aggressor became the defender and, during the course of the fight, a variety of holds, throws, falls, immobilization and strangulation moves, were shown.

At the end, with a knee over the *tatami*, they straightened their *judoji*, tightened the now loose belts, got up and, facing each other, bowed again.

Roberto went to the edge of the *tatami* and sat among the new trainees.

"What you just witnessed" said the instructor, "is an advance technique for training and exhibitions. Do not try any of those throws before you have acquired sufficient dexterity in *ukemi* or fall procedure and above all, before understanding the merits of limited resistance during *randori*. First airman Lanzi, explain to them what i mean."

"In addition to what the maestro said, remember that during a *randori*, and sometimes even during a real fight, when your adversary has unbalanced and is about to throw you, opposing resistance can only cause you harm. When it is obvious that you are about to be overpowered and thrown, it's better to think how to limit the damage. This way your adversary will help you to facilitate a clean fall. In case you don't, feeling your resistance, he won't protect you during the fall and you may be harmed beyond his intention. Also" he continued, "don't overestimate your ability. I did during the championship in America, and it cost me the loss of a fight I should have won. Be humble."

"Soon we'll be sent to our new base" he told Cicci when he arrived from home.

"I hope they'll tell us soon which one" Cicci replied.

These bases, part of a defense system the American set up in response to the Russian's advanced status in the missile field. They were strategically placed in England, in Turkey and in southern Italy. The names of the ten towns were known, but they still ignored which one they would be assigned to.

What the boys had seen in the States had only been sections of mock-up of 'real' missile's bases, suitable for training; next they would see the real ones.

However, since they were part of the 'American system', they hoped that, from a logistic and organizational standpoint, they would reflect their high quality.

Roberto knew that, for the next several months, his distance from Silvia, would not allow much progress towards their common future. However, his most immediate step, was to transfer to the new base and then... hope for the better.

- XXXIX -

GIOIA DEL COLLE

Finally, the rest of the airmen returned from America arrived at the school.
Days later, some of them received the transfer order for the new destination. Roberto Lanzi, Vito Falci (Cicci), Pat Maestroni and Luciano Canali, (Long-pole), would soon leave Caserta to report to Gioia del Colle, primary support base of the entire missile system in the south of Italy. Others would follow from other bases or from home if still on furlough.

From Gioia, they would be selected according to their specialties and then allocated to one of the ten launch bases scattered in the Apulian countryside in a seventy five kilometer radius from the main base.

Before entering the train station, Roberto turned around to give a last look at the King Palace.

"I wonder if we will ever come back again" he said. "Now that we are leaving it, never to return, you won't believe it but a feel a bit nostalgic."

"Go screw yourself" said Cicci, "nostalgia my ass! I really hope I'll never come back. Or better, I don't even want to see it in a postcard."

"Same here" confirmed Canali.

When the train arrived, the four friend pushed through the crowd, they took the first free compartment and placed they knapsacks on the spare seats to prevent anybody else from entering. They would cross the entire boot of Italy almost at ankle height, from the Tyrrhenian sea to the Adriatic, up to the deep Apulian region. The train would stop almost in every station and the trip, of less than three hundred kilometers, between mountain passes, tunnels crossed at slow speed and pauses to give precedence to express trains, would last all night.

After eating sandwiches they had purchased at the station and smoking a cigarette, Cicci, Pat and Longpole, tried to carve themselves a comfortable position among the knapsacks to rest a few hours.

Roberto was not sleepy. He got out of the compartment, pulled down the window, and resting his back against the corridor's wall he watched the monotonous passage of barren countryside. He was trying to imagine what Gioa del Colle may look like. He knew it o be only thirty nine kilometers from Bari and forty three from Taranto. Hence, sometimes, he might be able to go to the seaside on Sundays. He also wondered which final base he would be assigned to, which of his friends would be part of the same group and who would be sent somewhere else, perhaps never to be seen again. He thought of America, to the possibilities he would have in that Country, he thought of his old friends in Castelvecchio, and even the old ones at the tannery.

The moon had appeared in the sky.

The uncultivated fields were scattered with stones and weeds. Every now and then, a patch of land would be strewn with olive trees with ancient, twisted trunks and branches that seemed the imploring arms of tormented souls. Then, suddenly out of the countryside, a small cluster of hovels, emerged in the distance, perhaps a shepherd's or a farmer's village.

When the train stopped at a station, one or two people alighted, one or two came aboard.

After a monotonous repetition of shuddering stops, jerky departures and long repetitive swathes of dull scenery, Roberto returned inside the compartment and, ignoring the stale air, he removed his boots, placed his feet over the seat across and soon fell asleep.

They arrived at Gioia del Colle at dawn.

The sun had just risen over the horizon and it already glowed with intensity.

Surprisingly, there was no one waiting for them. They crossed the little square in front of the station and entered the only bar open at that time.

"Excuse me" they said to the barman, "how far is the Air Force base from here?"

"*Abbout fo' kilometer.*"

"*Fo'* fuck sake" exclaimed Cicci parroting the barman, "I place my ass *inhere* and I *don'* move *'til* they come and *fech* me with a coach."

They ordered espresso coffee and after over an hour they began to wonder how, under that ferocious sun and that heavy gear, they would reach the base.

"Do you ever see a military bus in front of the station?" Roberto asked the barman.

"*Somme time.*"

"What should we do?" he asked his friends.

"It sure as hell doesn't resemble the American organization" said Cicci, "who knows if the missiles are carton copies of the real ones."

"Bunch of ass holes" exclaimed Patrizio.

"Let's hope" said Canali shaking his head, "our base is real."

They left the café, placed their knapsacks on the ground and sat in the shaded part of the sidewalk. Cicci pulled the visor of his hat over his eyes and pretended to be asleep. Pat and Long-pole lit a cigarette and Roberto entertained himself doing crosswords puzzles. After about thirty minutes several aviators exited the train station and came across the street.

"Hello guys" said Roberto, "Would you know how to get to the base?"

"Yah. The military bus should come by around nine."

"Another ten minutes" said another fellow looking at his watch, "usually it stops right here."

"Are you guys stationed there?" Pat asked.

"Yes. We're just returning from leave."

"How's life here?" Cicci asked lifting his hat.

"Let's not talk about it" said the first fellow. "The only good thing is that there is complete chaos and you can come and go, even for many days, without being noticed or looked for. To tell you the truth, that's what we did. We are returning from a self-authorized furlough."

"Ah, a real paradise" Roberto exclaimed.

The airman looked at him. He couldn't understand whether Roberto's was sarcasm. He was about to say something else when Cicci said:

"Here is the bus of the Imperial Aviation, gentlemen. All aboard please."

They left the station and the inhabited area and after a few minutes they were travelling over a double lane road, boarded by trees and on one side a tall metal fence stretching for as long as one could see. Beyond it, the slender silhouette of several F- 84 and F- 86 jet fighters. Many hangars were regularly spaced along the runway and many brick structures, that could have been offices or dormitories, were perpendicularly aligned with the street. Few airmen were leisurely walking over the cement paths connecting the buildings and a couple of Jeeps drove in opposite direction.

When they reached the main entrance, they noticed that the gate was guarded by enlisted men, while a sergeant was smoking and reading a daily newspaper inside the guard-house. The bus slowed down and passed the gate, without stopping for identification of the occupants. Now Roberto understood what he was told at the station, no one really seemed to care!

The bus stopped in front of one of the buildings identified as "*Uffici*- Offices" and everyone got out.

"Where are we supposed to report?" Roberto asked one of the fellows encountered at the station.

"Wherever the fuck you want."

"What do you mean? Where do they assign the sleeping quarters?"

"Theoretically upstairs, in the orderly room. Ask for Warrant Officer Ierullo. See if you can find him… and good luck to you."

The four comrades started to climb the stairs exchanging, at every step, comments indicative of their appreciation for the reception.

"And it's only the beginning" said Roberto.

"Fuck" replied Cicci, "I can imagine the rest!"

In the orderly office there was only a sergeant who, confronted by the request, said he didn't know if or when Ierullo would return.

"We have just arrived from Caserta after travelling all night long" said Roberto, "you must at least assign us to a dormitory. We need to wash and rest."

"*And to miself they moost give a premio Nobelle. How can I give you a dormitory if I don't got one?*"

"Where do you suggest we go, then?"

"*You don wanna to know where I tell you to go.*"

Roberto was about to argue, but Long-pole took him by the arm. "Come on, Rob. Let's go see if we can find some of our comrades arrived before us. Maybe they can give us a hand to find a place."

"Gee" Cicci exclaimed, "this is just like America… South America!"

After a couple of hours spent visiting one overcrowded place after the other, it was evident that there was no space available. Roberto, tired of that pilgrimage, threw his knapsack over the sidewalk. He sat on the steps outside an office grumbling, "if they knew this base wasn't yet ready, why on earth didn't they leave us in Caserta?"

"Lanzi" Cicci yelled towards his friend, "that is the fucking one hundred million dollar question. Not even the heavenly *'effin'* father knows that."

They were all sitting down on the steps when a Warrant Officer with black, thin mustaches, a-la-David-Niven walked towards them:

"*If yous guys wanna sleepe tonightte*" he said without preamble, "*you'dde bettar get yourself a cot at the depotte, and arrange yousself in a roomme in the olde base.*"

"Where exactly?"

"*Whereva you wanna. There ain't almost nobody there.*"

Swearing like Turks, the four friends assembled one cot and placed the other three on top, with the canvass still rolled up around the wooden lateral poles. They also loaded all the knapsacks and, each holding one corner of the wooden frame started walking towards the old base. Given the weight and the distance, they stopped several times.

During one of these rests, an officer driving a black Fiat stopped: "What on earth are you doing with those folding beds?" he asked, "it looks as though you carry a dead body."

"We've just arrived from Caserta. We have been told there is no space on this side of the base, to go to the old one and manage whichever way we can…"

The officer shook his head, engaged the gearshift and left followed by a cloud of dust.

The four airmen continued their pilgrimage. They skirted the guardhouse, crossed the main gate without being checked or questioned and crossed the paved motorway. The entrance to the 'old base' was completely unguarded. At the end of a wide space with graveled paths intersected by untidy flowerbeds full of wild weeds, stood a dozen old low-rise constructions in obvious disrepair. Probably, pre-war lodgings for army personnel.

"Holly fuck!" Cicci exclaimed upon entering the first edifice.

It was completely dark and a heavy smell of decay fluttered in the air. They placed the cot on the ground and then, since the light switches did not function, they proceeded gropingly towards the inside.

In one of the first rooms they found two airmen sitting on one cot, that they had moved below a window, so they could see; they were playing rummy.

"Hi guys" said Long-pole recognizing the two. They were Tony and Sandro, wireless operators from his course. "There is four of us, where can we go?"

"Hello, tall one. Welcome to the Ritz Hotel of *'Gioia del cazzo'*. Here beside us there is a half dozen first category rooms, but I don't know if you can afford them. Anyway, choose whichever one you want and drop a few cigarettes for the valuable information."

"Is there any electricity?" Roberto asked.

"No. Neither light, nor hot water or soap."

"So, how do we manage?"

"You are from Tuscany, yes?" Tony asked. "I'm from Napoli and we have an adage that says:

'Face fridde e nun me lave, e si face chiù fridde ancora ietto via pure 'u sapone.'

You probably don't understand our dialect, but it means: 'It's cold and I don't wash, and if gets colder yet, I'll throw away even the soap.

In our case, we don't even have to throw it; we never got it.

Roberto left the room without commenting and a couple of hours later they had organized their new dwelling; Roberto with Cicci and the other two in the one next door. Rummaging around the edifice they had found two chairs and a small table. They planned to hunt for more furniture the following day as now it was supper time.

They crossed the motorway again and entered the new base. They asked which of the numerous mess halls they should attend.

In the U.S.A., mess halls were not categorized according to rank, but here the grouping was great: there was a mess-hall for superior officers, one for lower officers, one for warrant officers, one for specialists airmen, one for enlisted men and perhaps others yet.

It seemed that the quality of the food needed to be earned, like rank and seniority.

Finally, after they identified theirs Mess hall, they met with other comrades and they received information regarding the missing components of their group.

"As anyone heard from or about Toto Marciano?" Roberto asked.

"Yes. I understand he was temporarily sent to the base of Mottola, to substitute a warrant officer who pretend to be sick to avoid that posting."

"Too bad. I hope he'll eventually join us at Acquaviva."

"Who is us?"

"I, you, and all the group who was together in the States" replied Marcolin between energetic nose sniffs, "if you go to the personnel office you can see the list of the ten groups and their final destination to the operative bases."

"Is Acquaviva the closest to Gioia del Colle?" Luciano asked.

"Yes"

"When do they foresee we move to the launch bases?" Roberto asked.

"No one knows that. It will be weeks I think, even months. I heard some of them aren't even ready yet."

"And in the meantime what do we do?"

"As little as possible" replied Franco Vannelli.

After supper they all went to the bar and continued to exchange thoughts and information while smoking and sipping coffee. Roberto decided to return to his room. Someone must have changed a fuse because now, a low wattage bulb was shedding a weak gleam of light over the mold stained walls. Unfortunately, it made the ambiance seem even more depressing.

He went to his room, removed his shoes and trousers. then touched the bed sheets:

"Shit!" they were ice cold and damp. He decided to leave his shirt on. Still too uncomfortable.

He looked around, then he pushed his cot near the electric plug, put a chair under the blankets, picked up the hair-drier from his knapsack, he secured it to the chair's frame, plugged it and turned it on. When the vapor cloud ceased to rise from the sheets, he removed the chair and the drier and went to bed.

He remembered when young, in cold winter nights, it was his *nonna* who made sure his bed would be warm. She used a clay warming-pan with red hot coals thinly covered with ashes, which hung from an elliptic wooden structure and, who knows why, they called it *'prete'* or priest. Thinking about his dear old *nonna*, always brought to him melancholy thoughts.

He couldn't fall asleep and thought that after so many dreams and expectations he couldn't have imagined a more humiliating situation than the present one. Instead of being treated like the chosen, specialized personnel they had become, capable of becoming in short, the pivot of that organization, they were treated like dirt.

How could this be the place he had dreamed about?!

* * * * *

Weeks went by and almost every day new negative experiences were added to the previous ones. Many people thought like Roberto, and several were starting to vent their displeasure and threatened not renew their tour of duty.

"This is a joke" Carlo said, "I'll leave this place as soon as I can."

"Me too" echoed Rebuli, "I can't live in this shit-hole."

'What a pity' Roberto mused, 'to have chosen the best at the academy, sent and trained them in the States in forefront technical subjects, to then treat them like this; if they left, it would be a terrible loss for the Missile's Group, for the Air force.

Still many were not unhappy about the disorganization and the confusion that allowed them to do whatever they wanted. They could leave the premises without authorization, play cards or table soccer all day long, read magazines and lie down for hours on end.

Roberto's bitterness and disappointment were so deep that he often needed to state them aloud.

"You always complain" a wireless technician of his course told him once, "you lack patriotic spirit."

'Patriotism! How many wars and calamities had happened because of that abstraction? Was it not a synonym with nationalism, parochialism, of us against them.' This is what he would have liked to answer, but he knew it would have been useless.

"If my Country treats me like this" he said instead, "I have no reason to find affection in my heart."

He couldn't remember any days in his life when he felt so discouraged and dejected. Not even in his early days at the tannery.

And yet he must endure.

What other alternative did he have?

- XL -

ACQUAVIVA

Finally they were told that they would meet their commander.
Perhaps there was light at the end of the tunnel.

A senior warrant officer gathered the group in a large office with only one desk and two chairs. The boys kept talking, speculating how soon they would go to their final base.

Suddenly the warrant officer ordered "Att...tention!" and their chief officer came through the door; fortyish, medium height, splendid uniform, no hat and hair too long for a military man.

"At... ease" he said after a moment.

"I'm major pilot Fernando Perini. Finally we meet." He glanced at the group, paused and frowned. "I've never seen a worse bunch of soldiers in my life. Your uniforms are not regulation, your boots are not shined, your shirts and belts are of American issue, your hair too long and if you, as they tell me, are really the very best we've got, I don't even want to know what the rest are like."

His face reddened and his voice grew in volume with every phrase. "You look as though you came from a prison camp, and..."

He was about to continue when Roberto stepped forward, "Sir!" he said assertively, "Do I have your permission to speak?"

"Yes, you may. But I don't take exception to your appearance."

"All the same, sir, if my colleagues are too stupid or too afraid to speak, I'm not. You are right, we do look like a band of desperadoes. However, since we have come to this base – which in my opinion is worse than a prison camp – we haven't seen a bar of soap, a tin of shoe-shine, a new shirt or even new shoe laces which, if I am correct, it's all material which we are to receive regularly. Our shirts are from the American P.X. because in this climate ours are unbearable. In order to find a place to sleep we had to steel a cot in the main base and carry it to an abandoned hut across the street. If I want to take a shower I must do it with water that, if it were any colder, it'd be called ice. We have asked many questions, and received no answers. In short sir, we are as disgusted as you are, but we have been unable to do anything about it."

He stopped. He didn't know if had dared too much. He had spoken the truth but, as he found out in Caserta, in the military, truth didn't count for much. What counted was the major's reaction.

"Where are you from?" He asked with an even voice.

"From Tuscany, sir. Near Florence."

"It figures."

He turned towards the warrant officer who seemed to shrink a few inches. "And what would be the bloody reason for this?"

"Commander" he said as his neck retracted between his shoulders like a scared turtle, "We haven't received any supplies."

"Get the phone operator to connect me with the provisioning department of the Air Force in Rome. On the double!"

The major moved towards the desk and the boys looked at each other in anticipation.

When the phone rang, he grabbed it with anger. "Who am I talking to?" he asked aggressively. "O.K. captain, now listen to me. General Graziosi asked me to take this goddamned job because he wants the Acquaviva base functional and in a minus fifteen status in an impossibly short time. I said I would do it and staffed my crews with the best young technicians I could find. These are top notch youth, but they won't be for long if we treat them like shit!"

The boys were looking at each other, wondering who he was talking to, how much of the indignation was just for effect, and whether he was really as concerned as he sounded. After all, Italian high ranking military men, like politicians, were always adept at rhetorical speeches.

"My executive officer is going to give you a list" he said concluding, "and, I either get all I'm asking by next week or you people in Rome can take all the missiles and shove them where the moon *don't* shine."

It sounds good, if a ted bombastic, Roberto thought. But at least he seems to have balls.

Major Perini stepped back to the center of the room. "I mean what I say" he stated, "and you'd better remember that!" He went back to the front of the desk, sat on its edge, "Seat down on the floor, we'll have a chat."

They sat on the floor, and he continued.

"You heard what I said. Because of logistics and other reasons, our base has been chosen to be the crown jewel of the lot. You'll find me amenable in many matters, but not in performance. I promise that, if you execute your duties well, we'll all benefit from it. But if you don't, we'll share the blame and I'll make you sorry you were ever born. Understood?"

"Yes, Sir!" they all replied.

"Fine! Tomorrow I'll go and inspect our logistic base and perhaps even the launching pads. I'll need one of you to come with me. What's your name? He asked Roberto."

"Airman first class Roberto Lanzi, Sir."

"Since you seem to have the sharpest tongue, you'll be my liaison with your comrades. Meet me here tomorrow morning at o-eight-hundred."

"Yes Sir."

"Dismissed!"

* * * * *

Roberto walked to the executive offices at the convened time, and major Perini was ready to go. Outside, he picked up his attaché case from inside his brand new blue Lancia Sport and signaled his young driver, to start the jeep parked in the shade of a large poplar tree.

He was a young Neapolitan draftee, named Esposito. He had typical relaxed manners and wore his cap skewed so much to the right that it seemed ready to fall.

Roberto said hello, jumped in the back seat and watched the major, in front of him, remove his hat and pass his hand over his very long hair; not what one could call a military cut, he thought. He removed his as well and felt the brisk air play with his hair; he hated hats.

They left the main base of Gioa del Colle and took the opposite direction of Bari. They skirted the long air field where dozens of American fighter planes, F86 and F104 Starfighters interceptors, were stationed on the side of runways ready to be deployed. In this co-joined base Italians and Americans worked side by side with very specific tasks. The Italians operated the radars, the repair shops and supplied logistic support. The Americans provided the air cover for the ten missiles bases dispersed in the Apulian countryside in a radius of fifty kilometers. Some of the pilots were Italian as well.

They bypassed the dusty town of Gioia and proceeded through a straight road recently paved, and lined on both sides by low 'dry' walls constructed with the stones removed from the fields. Ancient olive trees and cactus plants with fleshy, thorny leaves and brilliantly colored flowers, was all one could see in the sparsely inhabited countryside.

Forty five minutes later, they reached the outskirts to the town of Acquaviva Delle Fonti where fields were arranged with vineyards. Roberto noticed that in this region, the vines were kept low, perhaps because of the arid soil or the torrid climate. They were not as well aligned as in Tuscany and not as cured and supported by canes as those at the Banchini farm. Here and there, a few kitchen-gardens with tomato plants, egg plants and peppers were fashioned against a fence, together with more cactus plants and fig trees.

At a crossroad the major told the driver, "Go to the logistic base first. You know the way."

The driver slowed down as they entered the town, passing by rows of low tenements and intersecting narrow side streets. They went by a church and a long treed square with a raised platform at the center. The usual equestrian statue of Garibaldi stood at the side, with pigeons resting over his shoulders and feces over his head. A small fountain was on ne side and old women dressed in black fetched pails of water; was that all the '*fonti*'- fountains' there were in Acquaviva? And if so, why the name?

"Here" said the major handing a sheet to Roberto, "make yourself useful."

"Yes…?"

"You've been with your classmates for over two years now. I want to know who you think is the most skilled in each specialty. Beside each name, jot down 1, 2, or 3 in order of capability."

"But" said Roberto surprised, "you have all our records, you know how we scored. Why would you need my opinion?"

Major Perini turned on his seat to stare at Roberto, "Don't play modest with me Lanzi, you know why. As I said, you've been with them for over two years now, you can give me a better insight than a piece of paper. By the way" he then added, "the numbers are for technical know-how. Use letters - a, b, c and d - for character, reliability etcetera, etcetera..."

When Roberto gave the sheet back to the major, he observed it for a few moments than asked "So you think airman first class Marciano is the best crew-chief?"

"Yes sir, I do."

"And you granted Canali and Falci equally in electronics, but gave Canali a higher mark for reliability."

"He is more even headed, sir. Besides, I don't think Vito will remain with us long."

The major did not enquire as to the last statement, but asked instead, "And why you didn't rate your skills?"

"It's not up to me to do it."

"I'm asking you to."

"Sir, I don't want to sound immodest, but if you insist... I can rate up there with the best when I want to. But..."

"But?"

"Screwdrivers and wrenches are not my ultimate ideal. I'm more interested in the organizational aspects of operations. Screwdrivers and wrenches can be handled by many people. I prefer to look at the bigger picture..."

"But you know who can solve the individual problems?"

"Yes sir. I have no problems with that."

"Do your comrades recognize that quality?"

"I suppose."

They were silent for a long time and finally the driver said, "Five more minutes, commander."

It was a short ride along winding dusty country roads and after bouncing over an unguarded railroad crossing they came to a stop. The driver blew his horn and momentarily a draftee came out of the guard house lifted the bar across the entrance and saluted.

The gated compound had half a dozen separate structures of similar style. The one closest to and to the right of the entrance, said the major, was for offices and the ambulatory. The first one to the left housed the kitchen and the mess hall. The other two groupings were, one for the service personnel and the other for warrant officers and technical personnel. The officers, who mostly lived in nearby cities, always went home at night.

"Sir, may I have a look at our quarters?" Roberto asked.

"You certainly may."

"I'll be quick" said Roberto beginning to jog towards the building. He entered and faced a wide corridor with several doors evenly spaced on each side of the wall. He opened the first one and saw a neat room with two beds, a desk between them, two chairs, an armoire and a coat rack. A wide window looked into the spacious courtyard. If these are our rooms, he thought, they'd be quite an improvement. He received an equally good impression from the brand new bathrooms clad in white porcelain tiles and marble basins. Contrary to the 'open concept' of those in Redstone, here the toilets had proper doors.

"How do they look?" the major asked.

"Very good, actually. Everyone will be glad to move here. And how are your offices?"

"Far behind schedule, damn it, and not a stitch of furniture is here yet! But I'll be damned if I'll let that, delay our start. Esposito" he then yelled, "start the car, we are going to the launching area."

The bar lifted again, the sentinel saluted and disappeared in the cloud of dust raised by the speeding jeep.

"How far is it?" Roberto asked.

"About three kilometers" Esposito replied, "but sometimes much farther than that."

Roberto was still thinking at the cryptic answer when they stopped again. Exiting a curve, they found themselves behind a cart pulled by a mule. There was no space to pass as the narrow road was squeezed by thick stone walls.

Through the centuries, to reclaim as much lend as they could for their crops and avoid damaging their tools, the poor farmers removed the large stones from their fields and built walls at the edge of the road.

For the next ten minutes they had to proceed at 'mule-speed'. Then, finding a small opening in the wall, the farmer pulled in and the jeep squeezed through.

They drove on until Esposito stepped again on the brakes and a swear word slipped out of his lips.

The gates of a railroad crossing were obstructing the way.

"What on earth!" Roberto exclaimed, "what are we to do in an emergency?"

"We must wait!" said Esposito.

"How long?"

"If it comes from Acquaviva, six or seven minutes. But if it comes from the other direction… it'd be long enough to take a nap."

Roberto looked at the major, who had kept silent. Obviously he was aware of this situation. He had impulsively opened a pack of cigarettes and had begun to smoke, his glance lost in the distance. Perhaps, like Roberto, he was wondering who had allowed the two bases to be separated by a railroad.

Whoever was responsible, had to be either complete morons, or people who had personally gained from the sale and acquisition of these particular parcels of land. Unsolicited, Roberto's mind went back to the anecdotes told by uncle Renato. The stories of 'pre-staged' war exercises, the one of air squadrons flown in from other bases during Mussolini's parades, to give him the illusion of a much greater strength than the real one. Perhaps even the 'eight million bayonets' the dictator used to boast about were a myth. After all, had anyone ever counted them?

Finally, a slow freight train went by, the bars rose, the jeep started again. Fifteen minutes later the flat, cultivated countryside disappeared, replaced by an undulated, rocky environment with low, thorny bushes and tall dried out grass. Shortly, from the slightly elevated approach, they could distinguish a tall radio-transmission tower shooting out of the center of the base. Then, the mushroom shaped lookout towers in concrete, spaced around the high wire fence of the base, and the white tops of three intercontinental ballistic missiles pointed to the sky. As they entered the base they saw the low bunkers for the personnel, and three sets of support trailers scattered at a distance from the missiles; the launching unit, the liquid oxygen and the liquid propellant unit, the generators. Transfer pipes were running from the tanks to the missiles and disappeared at its bases under its skirted protection. Several trucks, semis, jeeps and small refueling tanks for the generators were stationed in front of the bunker-billets.

"Let's take a ride around the base" said the major.

A paved road ran along the entire inner perimeter, rising, dipping, curving and following the undulation of the terrain like a race track. Three bifurcations provided the access to the missiles and the support equipment.

No house or other inhabited structure was visible in the area surrounding the base..

* * * * *

"Back to Gioia" the major said to the driver after a cursory inspection.

As he climbed into the jeep, Roberto noticed two sites where metal frames were partially erected and a dozen or so draftees were sitting around, as though waiting for manna from the skies.

"What's holding up the erection of those tents?" He asked.

"Good question" said the major, "we're going to need them to storage perishables and other goods. But those guys seems to be conscripted people. We don't deal with them" said the major.

"I had a smoke with them," proffered Esposito, "This group is only weeks away from final discharge. There *ain't* much you can do with them. They'll take punishment, rather than work."

"We shall see" said the major crossly. He pushed down the front passenger seat of the jeep and sat at the back beside Roberto.

"I don't want to twist my neck talking to you." he said as soon as the car started. "So tell me, how are we going to solve that problem? The tents I mean."

Roberto thought for a moment and said, "Obviously threatening them with punishment won't do it. We'll have to think of some other way. If you wish, I'll try."

"What are you thinking about?"

"Better you don't know, sir. Leave it up to me, I'll think of something."

"I can send you back tomorrow with Esposito. We need those tents up to complete the job"

"Very well, sir."

They rode in silence for a while and the major asked "Do you like this area?"

"No, sir. It's foreign to me. The people, their dialect, their way of life, even the countryside... it's too different from where I grew up."

"I know, this is not Tuscany. I spent time in Florence at the War Academy, I liked it, but it has flaws as well you know?"

"I don't doubt," Roberto replied politically, "but that is what I was used to."

"I remember a bunch of stupid girls, at the stadium" the major continued, "yelling and vying for the attention of Jullino. Just a common soccer player..."

The comment didn't seem to be quite what Roberto would have expected from the major. It seemed rather petty, unrelated to the subject and out of character. "On the other hand," said Roberto with a mild tone of resentment, "it seems to me this region has not progressed for centuries; it still smells of feudalism."

"Have you seen Bari?" That is a beautiful city."

"No, sir. I haven't had the opportunity yet. But I intend to visit it, I'm curious to discover the traces of its many conquerors."

"Do you know some of its history?"

Roberto did not answer immediately. They were crossing the town of Acquaviva and as he looked around he saw an old man trying to push a donkey through a door. It looked like a ground floor apartment, how could it be? He'd better save the question for later.

"Yes, sir. I know it was a fishing village as far back as 181 B.C. and was controlled first by the Greeks and then by the Romans. It connected the coast with the Via Traiana. After the fall of the Roman Empire was conquered by Goths, Lombards and Bizantines."

"And who came later?" the major asked.

"The Normans. Probably upon their return from one of the unsuccessful crusades. During the Middle ages the city was ruled by the Hohenstaufen and the Sforza. Many religious edifices, including the cathedral, were built during this period."

"You are an arrogant Florentine, but you do know a lot about my city. Obviously you're quite interested in history."

"Yes, sir, it's one of the many subjects I like. Too many perhaps. Sometimes I wish they were fewer" he said thinking of the single-minded pursuit and technical achievements of his father.

"You can't excel at all of them, you know…"

"Yes, I do. But if that's the price I must pay, so be it, in some subjects I'll have to settle for second."

They were silent for a long while. Despite the difference in rank, Roberto thought, I he might be able to parley my rapport with the major into a mutually beneficial relationship.

He knew however, he had to be careful; on one hand, not to rouse the resentment of the lieutenant and the executive officers, and on the other, to use words and manners which would not foster the idea that he took his goodwill for granted. It was going to be an interesting exercise, but with the cooperation of his comrades, it could be done.

The way he saw it, with the base having special 'designation' from the powers that be, it was up to them to make it work. After all, given to the myopic circumstances created by the high command in Rome, it was the lower ranks who held the cards for the good functioning of the missiles. In fact, in addition to having sent too few of them for training in the States, the officers, rather than from technical background, often came from categories with only general office experience; paper pushers.

The first challenge, Roberto thought, would be in succeeding to convince the reluctant draftees to erect the tents.

* * * * *

- XLI -

THE TENTS

The following day commander Perini told Roberto to return to Acquaviva and look after the erection of the tents.

"I'll take crew-chief Marciano with me" he told the major, "I'll need him to supervise the job."

"Good luck" the major replied, "I'm told we tried everything... At any rate, regardless of the results, send back Esposito no later than mid afternoon, I'd like to visit the base again with my executive officer."

"Yes sir, we'll do."

Roberto and Toto walked towards the Jeep. Esposito saw them coming, put off his cigarette and started the engine.

After a while they started to talk and Roberto hoped Esposito, long time driver of the commander, would be a good source of information.

"Where does the Major live? He asked.

"In a beautiful residential area of Bari."

"Is he married?"

"He is, but he has no kids. He fools around with women though." Esposito added laughing.

"Do you know where he was during the war?" Toto asked.

"I heard he was stationed at an airport in Albania, and the 10th of September '43 – just two days after the Italians signed the armistice with the Allies, he was taken prisoner by the Germans and shipped to Poland. After the war, prior to coming to the 36th *Aerobrigata Interdizione Strategica* he was stationed at Gioa del Colle – not far from home – with a group of Vampire aircrafts. Then to America for missiles' courses, and then here."

Esposito had also heard him bragging about his manly prowess with women, while in the company of three or four junior officers.

"What did he say" Toto insisted.

"That while he was in the States, he had…'more than satisfied' a woman that no one else had been able to satiate."

Apparently the junior officers had smiled and nodded obligingly as though their commandant had shot down a dozen enemy planes.

"You're really well informed," Roberto exclaimed, "don't tell me the major has told you all those things."

"Oh no. He hardly speaks to me. I'm just a lowly driver. But when he is with other officers, especially juniors, he never quits. I make myself invisible and listen."

"You are a smart fellow" said Roberto. "How about that?" he said turning to Toto who was leaning forward from his back seat.

"He sure is" he said.

Esposito's account seemed to validate the sketchy opinion that Roberto had started to form on commander Perini, ever since his first meeting and the loud telephone call to Rome. The bragging about women and his flying ability confirmed a certain trait that would leave him vulnerable to compliments and flattery. Helping him to achieve his goals and look good with his superiors, would be greatly appreciated.

They arrived at the missiles' base. From his high turret, the sentinel recognized the commander's car and told the guard on the ground to open the gate. Inside, nothing had changed and the draftees were leisurely sitting around the grassy area near the tent equipment.

"Slow down," Roberto told the driver, "then drive off the road and park yourself right in the middle of that group." Then he turned to Toto, "I'll try to see who's the band leader, but whatever I do, you stick with the main group."

Esposito turned onto the grass and drove towards the draftees. Two or three of them had to scamper out of the way and yelled words of protest against him.

"*Buongiorno* –good morning" said Roberto with a broad smile, "we're here to complete the work and the sooner we're finished, the sooner you can have a leave and go to town."

"Ehi, guys, you hear that?" said a big fellows lying on the grass, "Yesterday they tried to threaten us with prison, and today they try with gifts."

Everybody laughed.

"And what the fuck you want us to do in that cow town anyway?" said another man, his hat pulled almost over his eyes to shield the sun.

"In a few days we'll be home anyway" said the big fellow, "we *ain't* moving."

He had a northern accent, he was the biggest of them all, and since he had used the plural, it was safe to assume the others would follow his example.

"Listen *polenton*" said Roberto with an even voice, "we don't have time to waste, get your ass off the ground and start working."

Suddenly there was silence and everyone looked at the big fellow to see his reaction.

"If you *wasen't* wearing *them* stripes" he said sitting up "I'd kick your ass, man."

Roberto smiled, removed his sweater, rolled up the sleeves of his shirt and said,

"Toto, save those stripes for me, will you?" He gave him the sweater and then turned to the big fellow.

"Come with me *polenton*. What I have to tell you is confidential." Then to Toto again, "Nobody moves until we return."

Ten minutes later they came back, Roberto with his arm around the shoulder of the big fellow, smiling and talking to him as though they had been long time friends.

"Get off your ass guys" Roberto said, "Rocco and I have come to an amicable arrangement, we'll set up the tents and then we'll go to town."

Esposito noticed that Rocco's back was full of bits of dry grass, his shirt was hanging out of his pants and his left eye was almost completely shut.

"Holly fuck!" he exclaimed.

Roberto looked at him, winked and said, "Go get the commandant; we've got work to do here."

Toto unrolled the prints over a box and started to organize the men. Roberto and Rocco, now in undershirts, were working side by side, lifting the heavier beams and dictating the pace. Toto supervised the work and showed the proper usage of tools, to the least skilled, encouraging and helping everyone. Every now and then he checked the drawings to make sure they were proceeding chronologically.

"Don't bother me with those details," Roberto told him, just make sure we don't go ahead of ourselves and make mistakes. Anticipate the next move so that the process is smooth and well organized." Then he went back to his work.

By lunch time, when the service airmen came with the chow, one tent was up and the wooden platform of the second was half laid.

Roberto and Toto, sat on the grass and ate with the men, who by now had become friendlier and well disposed.

"Hey, Airman first class" said Rocco, "do you people eat this kind of crap too?"

"Since in a few days you'll be a civilian, you can call me Roberto. And regarding the food, yes, I'm afraid ours is not much better than this."

"I bet the mess NCO's play footsy with the suppliers and splits the dough."

"It wouldn't surprise me" said Toto, "but let's finish and go back to work, I want to get to town as well, I need a hair cut, badly."

Around three o'clock Major Perini arrived and found, both the draftees plus Roberto and Toto, conversing amicably on the turf in the shade of the two raised tents.

"Atten-tion!" said Toto as the commander neared.

They all stood up until ordered "At- ease."

"This is some feat!" the major exclaimed, "I was told it'd take two or three days."

"Not with a crew like this, sir" said Roberto, "and by the way, sir, given the speed and the effort, I promised them a night leave; I hope you'll agree."

"They can have their leave" said the commander stopping in front of Rocco and looking up to him and his black eye.

"What happened to you?"

"It was an accident, sir" said Roberto, "he hit his face on a metal roof joist."

"*Yessir*," Rocco confirmed, "That's what happened, a damn roof joist."

"And so it seems" said the Major smiling, "and so it seems. But do yourself a favor, pass by the infirmary and get an ice pack."

He didn't think he was going to get a better explanation from either Rocco or Roberto and when he found himself alone with Toto he asked "How on earth did he do it to a big fellow like that?"

"Lanzi is a black belt, sir. He doesn't like to talk about it, but in the States, as part of the foreign team – which included the Japanese – they won the overall Air Force Tournament. I saw him knock down bigger and tougher guys than that. "

"I'll be darned," the major said, "I would have never thought. But… why the black eye?"

"Probably the big fellow wouldn't give up. I've seen a few people make that mistake, and regret it. Or else" Toto continued, "needing a visible proof for the other guys, he thought it better than a broken arm."

The major smiled slyly and said, "All the same, we'd better stick to the story of the joist."

"Understood, sir!"

* * * * *

- XLII -

THE STING

A few days later major Perrini's group moved to the new facility of Acquaviva.

One morning Roberto and Toto were told to meet the commandant in the recreation room.

They found him sitting at the ping-pong table, several papers scattered over the green surface, a hand at his forehead. Warrant officer Ferrillo and lieutenant Giannini standing at his side.

"WHY can't you get a darn reply from those devils in logistics?" the major was yelling.

"We do have a reply, commandant" the lieutenant replied, "but it is the same as before. They are telling us that the furniture for your office has not yet arrived. Actually, they aren't even sure it has been ordered."

"How on earth they expect me to deliver a functioning missile base, missing even elementary things such as office furniture? Perhaps" he continued in a lower tone, "the donkeys in Rome expect me to do it sitting on one of those stone walls which abound around here."

Roberto cleared his throat and the Major raised his eyes.

"Ah, you are here" he said turning on his chair. "First airman Lanzi and Marciano, we are faced with a small, but annoying problem which, so far, no one has been able to solve." The two airmen nodded silently. "In a few days" the major continued, "technical people and high officers from the capital and from Paris will come for a preliminary inspection to the base and as you see, unless we perform a miracle, I would have to receive them in the recreation room. I am tired of empty promises."

He paused and looking attentively at the two airmen. Then he seemed to have found the right words.

"I called you because, even if you used unorthodox manners, you were able to solve the problem of the tents. Now, I need another… miracle and have the furniture for my office appear within the next forty eight hours."

"But how can we do that? Commander… " Toto started.

Roberto elbowed him and Toto said, "Perhaps First Airman Lanzi has an idea…"

The major shifted his attention to Roberto who did not speak for several moments.

"Perhaps, there is a way" he finally said. Then he screwed his forehead and fixing the Major straight into his eyes, said, "But I doubt it would receive your approval."

"Leave me out of it. The problem is yours to solve."

"We would need a few things from you, commander."

"Name them."

"A written permit to enter the Gioa del Colle base, a blank module of requisition, your driver and a truck."

The commander looked at the warrant officer and the lieutenant.

"Give them all they need."

He then turned to the airmen and said "You'll have it for tomorrow morning, now you can go."

* * * * *

"Where the hell are you thinking to get the goddamned furniture?" Toto asked as soon they had left the recreation room, "in a department store?"

"No, Toto, there we would have to pay for it. I know a place where it is free."

Roberto explained to his friend that, knowing the commander needed to furnish his office, he had already spoken to Cicci and, together, they had devised a plan. They would go to Gioa del Colle where, knowing the confusion and lack of control, they would be able to subtract pieces of furniture from any of the unoccupied offices and, if required, even from others.

Toto looked at him unconvinced and Roberto continued:

"We will wear the work clothes of new recruits and will pretend to be new draftees assigned to jobs like cleaning, moving and other menial jobs. You can wear your normal uniform and will remain with the driver and should any problem arise you'll worn you with a whistle."

"But… are you sure this plan will work?"

"I think so. What I don't know is what we will find and where. Somehow though, I'm confident we'll scrape enough to furnish Perrini's office."

Early the following morning, they drove to Gioia del Colle, reaching the town after forty five minutes, and the base ten minutes later. Beyond the metallic fence, the engines of two F86 jets were purring low as though afraid to disturb the peaceful morning air. A few people walked between the hangars and a couple of jeeps were moving at a slow pace toward the mess-hall.

The day, at Gioia, had just begun. Somnolence and lethargy seemed to affect everyone.

At the gate, Toto who sat near the driver, handed the authorization to the sentinel who then signaled the other to lift the bar.

As soon as they were through, Cicci, who was at the back with Pat and Roberto, knocked at the cabin rear window and said:

"Park right under the office complex and if someone asks what you are doing there, you answer that we moving some offices as per the general's order."

"Only a general?" Toto retorted; he was still unconvinced.

"You can say the Minister of Defense, if that pleases you" Cicci replied, "as long as you don't fuck up."

When the truck stopped the three jumped down, Cicci dug an old wrinkled hat from his rear pocket and shoved it on his head crooked. He was unshaved and he looked exactly like one of those untidy draftees destined for the humblest chores.

"Lanzi" he said to his friend, "do something with yourself. Unbutton, open your shirt, mess up your hair; what the hell, you look as though going on parade, for Christ sake!"

Roberto followed his suggestion, and they all moved to the first floor. The listened quietly from the corridor and as soon as they had located an empty office, they entered and selected cabinets, chairs, desks, and small bookcases. Given the easiness of the first few entries, they started to enjoy the process and became more selective. They went from a silent office to the next, taking the newest pieces of furniture, the best accessories. Crossing a warrant officer or a sergeant in the corridor, Cicci would supply the most absurd explanations in one of the many dialects he could imitate, so bizarre that they would not insist. It was difficult not to burst into laughter. Roberto got the maximum satisfaction removing the welcome mat outside the office of general Graziosi.

"We are almost finished" he told the driver, "start the engine." Then he looked at Patrizio and asked: "Where on earth is Cicci?"

"I don't know. Maybe he is still upstairs."

Roberto ran to the second floor, looked at the end of the corridor and almost had a shock. Cicci was holding the general's door wide open and was gesturing for him to join him. The general was sitting at his desk, holding the telephone against his ear. Roberto couldn't imagine what his friend had in mind, but saw him getting close to the desk, pretend he was dusting the top with a wiper, move some papers, while the general, irritated, was gesturing with his free hand, for him to disappear.

"*Joost uno minut generà*" he heard Cicci mutter, "*I got to finisheh my work.*"

Then he saw him going towards the buffet, behind the desk, lift the garbage can, place a large crystal ashtray and other small accessories inside, lift his hat in salute and make for the door. As he reached it he winked at Roberto and said in perfect Neapolitan dialect, "*Iammocenne, aviè, acchi ammo fernuto* – let's go, airman, here we have finished."

Toto, who had observed from the cabin of the truck all that hustle and bustle and seen the amount of furniture moved, couldn't believe his own eyes. Nor, when he was told, could he believe that Cicci had removed those objects from the general's office, right under his nose.

At the gate, the same airman came close to the truck for control. "Where are you going with all that stuff?" he asked.

"Don't waste our time bud" said Cicci, "I need to go very badly and I just may do it right here."

"For God sake" the guard replied, "get lost, it stinks enough in here without you making it worse."

* * * * *

The following day, as soon as commander Perrini arrived from Bari, was invited to his office.

He stopped a few steps away from the door, looked at the mat with the woven word "Welcome", and began to laugh. Then he entered. The office seemed furnished by a team of expert decorators. In addition to the beautiful high-back office chair, mahogany desk, four visitor chairs, several cabinets and other equipment, it was impossible to miss the beautiful maps on the walls, the framed photos of jet airplanes and missiles, the costly crystal accessories accurately placed over a rectangular black leather mat.

"What on earth!" they heard him mutter under his breath. "It was well worth the wait. I didn't expect all this… efficiency."

Then he turned towards Roberto and trying to wipe out his smile from his lips, said:

"Lanzi, but that mat outside my office isn't identical to that of general Graziosi?"

"Almost identical, commander. The general's is a bit smaller."

- XLIII -

THE FALLEN JET

It was about 1:30 p.m. and the 'Launch Team' was returning to the missile's base for routine exercises. Everyone was complaining about the weather. For several days the sky had assumed a brooding aspect. It was as though someone had pulled a dark canopy over the base. The previous day it had rained constantly and looking at the color in the clouds, it was reasonable to anticipate more rain.

The driver stopped the bus as the two service men pushed the gate open. Then engaged the gear and moved forward, but as he was about to accelerate one of the two *carabinieri* permanently at the gate, jumped in front of the bus, gesturing frantically and forcing him to stop.

The sudden braking jolted everyone forwards.

"What the hell is he doing?" The driver exclaimed. He opened the door and the *carabiniere*, looked at lieutenant Bargi, who sat in the front seat just behind the driver, and said, "There has been an accident. One of our jet planes has fallen in a field nearby. The pilot is wounded."

"Who told you that?"

"That farmer over there, speaking to my colleague."

Everyone looked at the middle-aged man near the gate. He wore ragged working clothes, his face and arms burned by the sun, he held an old bicycle by the handlebar. Every now and then he pulled on his pants which were tied with a cord and talked excitedly to the policeman.

Probably he had been working on his fields.

"We'll look into it."

"You cannot go with the bus" said the *carabiniere*. "The old *contadino* said you'd need a tractor to go there, the path is thick with mud and pot holes."

"We've got what we need," said lieutenant Bargi, "Lanzi, Marciano, get the three quarter ton and let's go. The rest of you can proceed for the launch base. We'll join you later."

The three got off the bus and while the officer spoke to the farmer, Roberto and Toto ran to get the big American made Jeep which, like other vehicles at the base, due to their specialization, only they were qualified and authorized to drive.

"This is going to be fun" said Toto, "Do me a favor, Roberto, You drive."

At the gate, they picked up the officer and the farmer with his bicycle, and following his indications they started on a narrow, muddy path, skirted by thick stone walls, which bordered the property.

"If it was an emergency landing" said the lieutenant "he must have nosed in one of those darn walls."

"Yes" the farmer confirmed "the *ting* that stick on the side came off."

"The wing you mean?"

"Yeah."

"I wonder if it is an American F 84 from the Gioia air field," said Toto.

"Oh yeah" replied the old farmer, "It's *Americano*, it *gots* a big white star."

They continued to speculate about the accident and after about three kilometers they arrived near the site. Turning around a cluster of high bushes they saw the small fighter plane. The left wing was completely detached and lay in the middle of the field, the smashed nose rested against a stone wall about 4 feet high and 2 feet thick. Behind it, a short, straight channel had been carved by its belly on the mucky grounds.

"Not a bad crash landing," said Toto "considering the short space."

"Yes" said the lieutenant, "lucky the pilot didn't try to use the landing gear. The plane would have catapulted."

They parked a few meters away and got off the vehicle. The right wing was touching the ground and the air intake was full of leaves, dead birds and other debris.

"I wonder if it lost altitude, sucked in that stuff and stalled the engine" said Roberto.

"Possibly" said the lieutenant, "He couldn't have chosen this place for a landing strip. Maybe he ran out of fuel and couldn't reach Gioa's airfield."

"Perhaps…" said Toto as though following a different thought.

The shape of the air intake and the back slanted wings confirmed it as an F 84-F, he thought. Moreover, these fighters are used by several NATO countries, including Italy. But… the red, green and white identity cockade, running across a five-point star, did not bring to mind any specific Country.

He walked farther toward the rear of the plane, looked up at the tail and suddenly stopped. He threw his arms in the air; incredible as it seemed, he was now sure of what it was.

Ever since he was a young boy, Toto always had a passion for airplanes. During the war, the Germans had established a temporary field near his grandfather's farmland and he spent hours, lying on the grass, watching *Stukas* and *Caproni Campinis* take off and land, dreaming to be one of those pilots. With his first money, he bought subscriptions to the aviation magazine "ALI" and kept up with the newer types of airplanes. Finally, in the States, while his companions were girl-hunting and Roberto was practicing Judo, he picked up collecting kits of small but veritable replicas of fighter airplanes. He spent hours assembling them and becoming familiar with the smallest detail.

As soon as he looked up at the tail of the fallen jet, he noticed that the horizontal tail section was fixed and the traditional rudder was hinged to its rear edge. He remembered that in the F 84-F, it was all one piece – mobile and responsive to the cloche – to control the climb as well as the roll and pitch of the airplane.

"Fuck!" he exclaimed, "F-84 my ass, this is a MIG 17."

"What on earth are you saying?" said lieutenant Baggi, "are you out of your mind?"

Instead of answering, Toto, jumped on the wing followed by Roberto and, upon reaching the cockpit, they immediately noticed all instruments identified with tags in Cyrillic lettering.

"Toto is right" Roberto shouted, "It's a damn Mig!"

The lieutenant seemed still unconvinced. So, Toto leaned inside the cabin and yanked out the metal safety lid of a switch with the unfamiliar symbols. "Look at that" he said tossing it to the lieutenant, "see if I'm dreaming."

"I'll be…" they heard him murmur.

"And look here!" The boys exclaimed in unison as they descended from the wing. There were meters and meters of film on the ground. The Plexiglas cover was shuttered and it had fallen out of the photographic receptacle near the air intake.

"I bet he was taking pictures of our missiles," Roberto said.

"Then… then" the lieutenant mumbled beginning to grasp the gravity of the situation, "then it's from the Iron Curtain!"

"No kidding!" Toto exclaimed.

"We'd better alert Air Command. Let's go boys, let's dash to the base and phone Gioia Del Colle. Maybe they'll send out some interceptors…"

"To do what?" said Robert laughing "to dive bomb the fallen plane?"

He got a nasty side look from the lieutenant, who then turned towards Toto and asked "How did you know it was a Mig 17?"

"It didn't have an 'Elevon.'"

"And what the hell is that?" the lieutenant asked. Both Toto and Roberto gave a strange look at the lieutenant; 'what are we to do with you?' it seemed to say.

"It's a contraction of the words 'elevator' and 'aileron'" Toto answered.

"Because it has that dual function" Roberto explained.

The puzzled expression of the lieutenant, seemed to indicate that the explanation had served little purpose.

At the base they found the jeep of the *carabinieri* with two additional farmers who said they had taken the pilot to the local hospital of Acquaviva and deposited the undeployed pilot's parachute and his Makarov pistol at the local police station.

* * * * *

- XLIV -

THE CRASH SITE

Roberto, Toto and Cicci took another ride to the crash site with a colonel on board. On their way, in order to avoid a deep hole, Roberto drove with two wheels over the shoulder and the vehicle was so inclined that the colonels yelled:

"Are you Russian too? Are you trying to kill us?"

"Not with me on board, sir" Cicci replied.

At the site of the crash the three airmen jumped down from the jeep close to the plane, walked over the muddy terrain and climbed the wing leaving heavy tracks over its surface. The colonels tried to imitate them but, weight, age and gravity worked against his attempts. He remained suspended from the wing, vainly groping at its round cutting edge, his short legs pedaling in mid air. He was about to fall when the *carabiniere* guading the plane, grabbed his legs and tried to push him upward. He continued to slide backward when Cicci took hold of his arms, pulled him over and dragged him over the muddy part of the wing. Toto and Roberto turned around to hide their laughing. When the colonel finally got on his feet, his blue uniform had turned brown. He carefully walked towards Toto and Roberto and Cicci said: "Guys, make room for the commander."

Red in the face from effort and indignation, the colonel, whose 'general services' badge clearly indicated he had never been near a plane, bent over the cockpit and looked inside.

"Is that Russian?" he asked indicating the labels beside the flight instruments. Then, noticing that some instruments were missing, said: " Look how those poor bastards are supposed to fly. No wonder he fell from the sky."

Roberto looked at Toto who, unseen, had already taken his souvenirs.

"Sssshhh! Listen" said Cicci to his friends. "Tic-tac, tic-tac, tic-tac. It's a self destructing mechanism. Let's run."

"No. It's just a wa…" Toto couldn't finish the phrase as Roberto gave him a kick

"Let's run, let's run" he repeated.

They jumped down and ran towards the jeep, followed by the colonel yelling, "Wait for me, wait for me."

* * * * *

Two days later every one was still talking about the event. The local paper reported it and made the most absurd assertions. One stated that the Acquaviva base had shot it down with one of their 'intercontinental ballistic missile'. The other, not as implausible, was that the Bulgarian pilot, who had refused to talk to the military, at the hospital, in order to escape the 'care' of the terrible local doctor, had begun to speak fluently in several languages.

That afternoon Vito received a phone call from a friend who worked at the radar station. "Ehi, Cicci," he said in jest, "stop throwing atom bombs at enemy planes, will you? You're ruining my entertainment."

"What do you mean?"

"Now I have to go blind watching blank screens."

"I still don't get what the hell you're talking about…"

"You think we didn't know about that Russian Mig?"

"It's not Russian its Bulgarian" said Cicci, "but…" he continued, "if you knew why the hell didn't you call the interceptors?"

"It's a long story."

"Well, my term of service doesn't expire for another three years, so, I have the time. Besides, you didn't just call me to say I spoiled your fun. So, if you want to oblige me… I'm all ears."

"It's been coming over for a while" said the radar man lowering his voice. It's always the same routine; it enters Greek air space from the north, when the Athens-Rome Alitalia Comet jet takes off. It uses it as a shield over the Ionian Sea at an angle that makes it difficult for us to detect. Despite that, we often spot him, and then lose again near the Italian coast, when he dives below radar screen."

"So, why don't you call the interceptors?"

"We did a few times, but the *sonofabitch* always comes around lunch time and when we alert our pilots, they tell us to go to hell, or other dark places, and to call them after lunch if he is still around."

"So why don't you alert the Americans at Gioia del Colle?"

"Are you shitting me? They'd be likely to start another war. Besides, we once did and they didn't find anything. They asked us lot of questions and made us feel as though we didn't know our job. So screw them, let the poor Russian take a look at those white birds. What the hell, everyone knows they are there! By the way Cicci, I know you didn't shoot that plane with your missiles, but… what happened?"

"My friend Roberto mistook it for a pheasant and shot it down with a sling shot."

"Fuck you pal, you can tell me."

"Seriously, you know what happened?" said Cicci chuckling, "the poor bastard was flying so low that his engine sucked in a bunch of birds, it lost power, stalled and had to crash land."

"Seriously?"

"I swear it. We found the turbine full of sparrows and tree leaves. The pilot was lucky to be alive. Fortunately he didn't deploy the undercarriage, he landed on the belly, skimmed over a stone walls and smashed its nose on the next. That was it."

"I read in the local papers that he now is beginning to talk to our police."

"I bet" said Cicci. "If he fell in the hands of the same doctor that butchered me, he would speak even Chinese!" He explained that a few months earlier he had dislocated his shoulder falling during a soccer game at the base. After the 'treatment' at the hospital he had a completely broken collar bone and required a surgical operation and a silver pin on his shoulder.

When he stopped laughing, the radar man thanked Vito for the information. "Thanks pal," he said, "I'll let you know if we see another bird."

The following day Toto, Roberto, and Cicci talked of the incident at their breakfast table. A captain – one of the many officers who had come from Rome to nose around about the Mig – came near them and asked: "Who can drive me to the site?"

"What site?" Toto asked while the others continued to eat.

The incident had been another chance for the lower rank to deride and despise the so-called 'high' officials from the capital. In fact, it soon became evident that, instead of being technical people, they were well-connected paper pusher who, hearing of the accident, seized the opportunity to take a few days off from their musty offices and visit the countryside. After a short visit at the crash site, and perhaps a supper with the base commander, they disappeared to Naples or the nearby island of Capri.

"So" insisted the captain, "let me rephrase my question for you dummies. Who the hell is allowed to drive the semi?"

"We are" Roberto and Toto answered in unison. "But" Roberto continued, "we are no dummies, sir."

"O.K. so finish in a hurry and drive me there I have to take some photos."

Roberto saw Toto's expression and kicked him under the table.

"Let's take a joy ride" he said, winking to Cicci. "Do you want to drive?" he then asked Toto.

"No," said Toto, I'll seat at the back with Cicci and enjoy the view."

"Take the right," said Cicci pinching Roberto's arm and said, "the left lane is blocked by a huge farm cart, I saw it yesterday."

Roberto understood and took the country road which he knew full of rocks, deep crevices and huge puddles because of the rain. It was exactly the ride this ass-hole deserved. The captain who was bumping his head on the ceiling of the cabin, removed his hat and placed it on his knees. After a couple of kilometers the road became even muddier and the big puddles concealed the depth of the holes. Suddenly, Roberto pressed the brakes, and almost sent the captain through the windshield.

"What the hell are you doing?" he snapped.

"There is a big hole just ahead. I'm trying to remember exactly where."

"The hole is in your head" said the captain unceremoniously, "go ahead I say."

Roberto raised his eyebrows, turned around and saw Toto's and Cicci's smile, press their feet down and clutch their seats. He engaged the gear and launched ahead. After a few meters, the front wheel fell suddenly into a deep crevice hidden by the muddy water and the captain, unprepared, hit the cabin ceiling violently.

"What the fuck!" he exclaimed.

"That's the hole I was trying to tell you about... sir."

They all got off the vehicle and saw the front wheel sunk in the hole up to the axel.

"And now what?" said the captain.

"Now we're fucked, sir" Cicci replied. "The best thing if you are in a hurry, sir, would be to walk back to the base. We must stay with the vehicle, we are responsible for it."

"*Goddamned it!*"

"You can be there in about twenty minutes" said Roberto who had a hard time remaining serious.

"And you'd better hurry" added Toto, "because it could start raining again very soon."

"That's all I need! Look at my poor shoes." Then he stared at the boys and asked, "You don't think if we push we'd get out of the hole?"

"I doubt it, but we can give it a try."

Roberto climbed into the cabin, starter the motor and yelled, "Now!" He floored the gas pedal and made the wheels spin, plashing everybody."

"Stop it! Stop it for *godsake*, you're covering us with mud." Roberto switched off the engine again.

"Fuck the Mig" said the captain, "I'll go back to the base, you're on your own."

The boys made a jest of resignation.

"So be it, Sir" said Cicci making an ostentatious military salute. The captain brought his hand to his visor, turned around and left.

The three climbed back in the cabin, their belly hurting from laughter and waited until the captain had disappeared behind the olive grove. Then, Roberto engaged the four-wheel drive and the half ton moved smoothly.

Mimicking a famous phrase from a Bond movie, Roberto turned to his friends and said:

"Where to James?"

Back at the base they continues to talk about the accident.

"I'd like to know who sends these morons" said Cicci. "Some of them have a hard time telling the nose of the plane from the tail."

"I'm sure the Air Force has capable people too" snapped an airman whose father worked at the Ministry.

"Why don't they send those guys then?" Cicci retorted. "The ones we've seen so far were pathetic."

"Not the kind of people I'd follow in war" added Roberto.

"But there is no war" countered the same airman.

"But… as it happened in the past, we 'unintentionally' can find ourselves in one. In those circumstances, obeying those kind of people would be a problem for me."

"Then, what the hell are you doing in the Forces?"

"That's exactly what I'm beginning to ask myself."

"You are naïve."

"Don't I know it!"

In one way, the fall of the Bulgarian jet had been a welcome distraction from the dull daily routine. On the other, it had once again emphasized the lack of coordination of the Italian Command, the deep deficiencies of the high ranks. For someone like Roberto, the amusement of the moment did not compensate for the serious consequences such an environment might have in his future.

* * * * *

- XLV -

THE FRANKFURT ZEITUNG

A week after the crash of the Bulgarian jet, upon their return to the logistic base, Toto and Roberto where summoned to the *carabinieri* office.

They were told that three 'foreigners' had been discovered just outside the wire fence of the base, hiding behind the bushes, taking pictures of the missiles.

"We think they are Germans, but we're not sure" said one of the *carabinieri*, "can you help us out and translate?"

Roberto and Toto looked at each other, they only knew a few words in German, but decided to meet the foreign trio anyway.

"*Gude Nacht!*"

"*Gude Nacht, sprehen sie Deusch?*"

"*Ein bishken…*" The limit of their German repertoire was approaching and Roberto asked: "Do you speak English?"

"Oh yes, but the *carabinieri* don't."

"But we do, so there is no problem."

They all laughed and continued the conversation in English while the *carabinieri* stood silently aside.

"They are journalist-reporters of the Frankfurt Zeitung" Roberto explained.

" And what are they doing here?"

"They heard of the Bulgarian airplane and are collecting information to write a story about our base."

"How did they get here?"

"They flew to Bari and, borrowed two cars plus some bulky photographic equipment from their Italian affiliate and came to our site with their paraphernalia."

Had Roberto used the word 'gear' or 'stuff' instead of paraphernalia, perhaps the *carabinieri* would have looked less suspiciously at all those black pieces of equipment spread on the floor. The other problem was that, at this late hour, there was no officer to be found and the *carabinieri,* not wanting to be blamed for possible mistakes, decided to go to the nearest command post. Bari, and unload the responsibility on someone else.

Held again as interpreters, Roberto and Toto gladly embarked in what was becoming an exciting diversion from the dull routine.

Toto, jumped in the Fiat 1300 with one policeman and one German, Roberto followed in the other Fiat with another policeman and two Germans. The last *carabiniere* followed with the small Italian-made-jeep or *'Campagnola'* loaded with all the photographic gear.

Night had fallen and, while driving fast, the mature trees lining both sides of the *Via provinciale* to Bari, seemed to dart by at a frantic speed. Intersecting with another car coming from the opposite direction, the German driver of the leading car, fidgeted with the control buttons and tried to lower his high beams. Not being familiar with the car, instead of lowering the lights, he switched off altogether.

Blinded by the lights of the oncoming car, he panicked and stepped on the brakes violently. The car skidded sideway and stopped, only inches from a large tree trunk.

"*Inshuldig*" said the driver visibly shaken.

"You see?" the *carabiniere* barked from behind, "they *are* spies, he was trying to kill us."

Roberto laughed and waived to the others indicating they were O.K.

They resumed the drive and after another forty five minutes they reached Bari where they took the road which followed the coastline. The *carabiniere* told them to stop in front of a high rise with a large brass sign: Z.A.T.

"*Vhat doez it mean?*" the German asked.

"*Zona Aerea Territoriale*" Roberto translated, "it's the Air Command for this particular zone."

"*I szee.*"

After several debates with the officer in service, they were taken to a large room, told to make themselves comfortable and wait. Finally a gentleman in civilian clothes came and listened a few times to the story. He seemed satisfied and about to release the journalists when one of the *carabinieri* mentioned the MIG 17. He hadn't even read or heard about it and that new prompted a series of phone calls from another room. He too, was trying to unload this hot potato on someone else's plate.

Following further consultation, they were told that after compiling a few documents the Germans would be released. Since they were to move to another room, they thanked and said goodbye to Toto, Roberto and the carabilieri.

The five Italians jumped onto the *Campagnola* and were ready to return home.

It was about eleven o'clock at night and suddenly Roberto realized they had missed supper. Now that the excitement had passed, he realize that he was starving.

"Hey, guys" he said spotting a restaurant sign, "why don't we stop for pizza?"

- XLVI -

THE LAST DROP

Major Perrini had just left. The launching test of the Acquaviva Base had been passed at full marks and he was going for a few days to the NATO headquarter in Paris to receive high commendations as the commander of the best missile base of the southern system.

He would spend two weeks of well deserved rest with his wife on the Italian Riviera. In his absence, captain Quadra would assume command of the base.

No one was happy of that temporary replacement. Least of all Roberto, mindful of Quadra's arrogant approach with Manuela in Lackland, and of his inserting incompetents like W/O Napolitano in the launch test in Redstone.

However, since the team had splendidly overcome all tests, they expected a period of calm.

Before commander Perrini's departure, Roberto, Toto and Long-pole had requested a brief furlough which was promptly granted. Roberto would use the time to go home and seek a long-term agreement with the people renting his house who were withholding payment because of some minor discrepancies. He also had to pay the inheritance taxes, which were almost due.

Toto would go to his town to spend some time with the family and to view the small piece of land his father had bought with the money sent from the United States.

Long-pole, would spend his furlough in Rome with his mother and father.

They anticipated days of calm at the base, perhaps even weeks.

The day after commander Perrini's departure the entire group was convened in the large meeting room. Since captain Quadra was not familiar with all of them, they thought he would want to officially introduce himself to the group and congratulate them for a successful launch. After all, as even the American technicians had confirmed, the base had achieved results which were even better than expected.

The airmen entered the room confident there would be nothing to worry about.

However, the unhappy face of first lieutenant Bargi and lieutenant Giannini, who kept his eyes down as though to avoid the scrutinizing looks of the men, did not seem to match their expectations.

When the captain entered they were called to attention. He silently scrutinized the entire group for several moments, then they were ordered at rest.

"As you already know" he coldly started, "I will be the base commander for the next several weeks. I would hate to think that the results of your last test have gone to your head." He paused, and in the silence that followed one could almost hear the thoughts of the airmen-specialists, not used to be addressed in that tone.

"To start with" he continued, "I have requested General Graziosi to come and witness a second simulated test, which I have scheduled for the day after tomorrow."

At those words, a high buzz rose from the files of the airmen.

"Silence!" the captain yelled, "the general will see that even under my command this base will still perform brilliantly. And now go back to work and prepare for the test."

"Captain, sir" Roberto called.

"You can address me as commander, since that is what I am. What do you want?"

"I only wanted to mention that two of my colleagues and I are about to go away for a few days and we will not be available for the test. Perhaps, it would be better to postpone it a week or two."

"Have you gone mad? How do you dare suggest such a thing? Postpone my ass! I promised the general that the test will be done no saints or devils on earth will prevent me from doing it. From this moment all permits are revoked. We shall see if I am a lesser man than your Major Perrini."

Roberto noted that at those words, lieutenant Giannini raised his eyebrows and first lieutenant Baggi bit his lips.

"Pardon me again, *commander*."

"You again? What on earth do you want?"

"I must go home to take care of urgent matters. I have no family left and no one can do them for me."

"I make no exceptions. First we do the test and then I might take under consideration your requests, but have no illusions, I'm not major Perrini, I won't be fooled or swayed by your tactics".

When he left the room and they saw him disappear behind the door of the commander's office, the buzz changed in open dissention.

"Who the hell does he think he is?" said Toto.

"Now I'm screwed" said Roberto, "but if that turd thinks we are going to help him to look good with the general, he'd better rethink his approach."

Despite having placed his hand in front of his mouth, lieutenant Giannini was heard whispering to Baggi, "I smell a rat. I think captain Quadra is using a pretest and Major Perrini's absence to get this post., Beside the prestige, he'd be much closer to his home."

The comments continued for awhile and then, true to their duty, the two officers requested the men to calm down and begin a list of the necessary things for the count-down.

That evening at supper, the bad humor of the specialists, had reached alarming proportions. No one said anything specific, but even without words it was quite obvious that their support for the success of the launch would be, at best, minimal.

The next morning, the team of specialists went to the operative launching base early. When captain Quadra arrived, all support equipment had been checked and the electronic panels trouble-checked to be sure there were no malfunctions or anomalies.

The day of the test they announced that general Graziosi would arrive at the base of *Acquaviva delle Fonti* around eleven o'clock.

Every one was already at his post and captain Quadra sat in the launch trailer in front of the electronic control panel, already tasting his success. To be sure, he ordered a pre-test and requested to initiate several preliminary sequences.

"Captain, sir" Roberto communicated from his post, "it's not advisable to do what you requested."

"What the hell are you saying? Shut up and proceed as ordered."

Roberto shook his head, swore under his breath, and at the appropriate moment he put in action the pump for the liquid nitrogen."

When the general arrived, he went directly to the launch control trailer and sat besides captain Quadra. The simulated launch started and the fuel transfer was completed in due time. The captain followed the next sequence and the liquid nitrogen began to transform into gas to cool the gyroscopes. Roberto switched again the pump on and seconds later the gyroscopes began to overheat and the process was interrupted for safety reasons.

Captain Quadra swore into the headset.

"Crew chief" he yelled, "go see what the problem is."

There was no need to go, both Roberto and Toto knew exactly what had happened. Regardless, they took the cherry-picker, drove it under the missile, extended the four stabilizing trunnions, jumped inside the cabin and rose to the panel situated on the nose cone where the gyroscopes were lodged. They opened it and Toto checked with his tester, the electric terminals of the pump for the liquid nitrogen.

"Affirmative" he said into the microphone, "the pump's motor is burned like we knew it would."

The captain swore again. "Change it immediately and resume the sequence."

"We need to request it from the NATO depot in Paris" Roberto replied, "it will take at least a week." He than passed the tools to Toto who proceeded to dismantle the pump.

"Take it" he said smiling, and handling it to Roberto, "give him his fucking trophy."

When they got down from the cherry-picker, the general, apparently disappointed in the captain, had already left in a bad mood without even responding to Quadra's salute.

Captain Quadra was enraged.

"You made me look like an ass hole" he shouted, "but you will pay for it. Crew chief Marciano, why did you say 'as we knew it would?'"

"Because" Roberto replied, "we have had the same problem any time we operated that pump in sequence. The pipes leading to it have a negative inclination and if made to function frequently, the gas condenses blocking the valves causing the motor to burn."

"Bunch of beasts, why didn't you tell me then?"

"Actually I tried to tell you and you answered 'what the hell are you saying?' In addition," Roberto continued in a cold tone, "I have also written a very detail technical explanation on this. Commander Perrini has taken it to Paris. I presumed that, even as a 'temporary' commander, you would be aware of it."

"Lieutenant Baggi" captain Quadra yelled, "see that the entire team is consigned to quarters. As far as you two " he said pointing at Toto and Roberto, "I'll let you know tomorrow what to expect."

- XLVII -

CAPT. QUADRA

The day after, the two crew-chief Roberto Lanzi and Salvatore Marciano, were told to report to the office of Captain Quadra.
They were held to attention for about ten minutes while the captain was distractedly shuffling papers over his desk.

The two looked at first lieutenant Baggi who stood in a corner of the room staring at the wall in front of him. In the loaded silence of the room, minutes seemed to pass as slowly as eternity.

Finally, the captain raised his eyes. He stared coldly at the two propulsion specialists, lifted a sheet of paper from his desk and his sharp voice cut through the air.

"This is the transfer order for the two of you. From this moment you will not be part of my team, but you will be transferred to Irsina. That's where all unwanted leftover ends up, and that's where you belong."

"Captain, sir" Roberto said, "I don't believe we deserve this treatment. If you take a look at our records you would see we were chosen for this base because of our capabilities."

"I'm not interested in your records. I know what I see. Perhaps you were in the grace of your commander, but for me you are leftovers."

"Why? It was your blind insistence that caused the failure of the pump, sir."

"Crew chief Lanzi" the captain yelled, "if you don't shut that venomous mouth of yours, instead of Irsina I send you to the prison island of Gaeta. There they would teach you how to have respect for a superior. Lieutenant" he then yelled towards Baggi, "take them away from here before I really get mad."

Roberto took a step forward towards the captain's desk, but Toto held his arm.

"Let's go" he whispered, "this meeting has ended, but tomorrow is another day."

During the trip on the jeep to Irsina, Roberto and Toto did not talk much. They were mad, deluded, sad. Roberto stared at the fields parched by the strong southern sun, the olive trees twisted and contorted as though because of an internal pain, those sparse hovels scattered in the desolate Apulian plain. Every now and then he saw a distant human figure slowly moving among those humble habitats, women dressed in black, with head scarves pulled forward to shade their eyes from the fiery rays of the sun, a lethargic dog, walking through the yard, in search of a bone or a bit of shade, chickens rasping through the gravel. The usual wall made out of stones were lined at the edge of the properties, interrupted every now and then, just enough to allow the passage of the work animals and the farming equipment.

Roberto thought that if Acquaviva had appeared to him as a backward and under-developed town, this place could be classified as a chunk of Dantesque inferno. Yet… at that very moment, he was even envious of those poor people, of those families that in the evening would have met around the supper table, that would have shared a warm meal prepared by a grandmother, that afterwards would go to and sleep in tranquility, without the worry that a captain Quadra would unjustly scold them and send them away.

What have I done? Roberto wondered. And if Toto had not held me back? If I had really fetched captain Quadra by his throat, would I be now directed to the military prison of Gaeta?

He felt a shiver go through his body.

People always talked about the prison-island as of a hellish place, a place of no-return. And then bye-bye Silvia, bye-bye career, bye-bye Tuscany!

He exhaled a long sigh and then he thought about the hardest moments of his past life; his father's departure for the African front, the abandonment of his house because of bombardments, the death of his dear grandmother, his departure for Caserta, the death of his mother. All crises he had overcome and, in time, they had grown bearable in his heart and mind.

Even this sad moment will eventually pass.

"Ehi Toto" he said clearing his voice and forcing himself out of his sullen mood,

"Who do we know in Irsina other than Cicci?"

- XLVIII -

IRSINA BASE

"Look what the cat dragged in" said Cicci with a smirk as soon as he saw his old buddies. "Don't tell me that even you have fallen from the graces of commander. Perrini. Minimum you must have set the base on fire."

"Hello to you too, Cicci *bello*" Toto replied. "No, we didn't set the base in fire, we just caused captain Quadra to look like the ignorant ass hole that he is in front of general Graziosi."

They recounted the story in details, each dressing it with adjectives that would have given a red face to the devil.

"And how does one fare in here?" Roberto asked.

"As well as in hell" Cicci rhymed. "The captain is an idiot, discipline doesn't exist, the base is in disarray, the food stinks, and our bedrooms are like ovens during the day and like fridges at night; it couldn't be better…"

Roberto's mouth twisted as though he had bitten a lemon. "And the town?" he asked.

"The town is at the Avant-guard" Cicci replied sarcastically. "There is no one, but two taverns. Well, actually one and a half, since the other half crumbled down after the last rain. Most of the time they don't have even bread.

Sometimes, on Saturday, the local priests allows the projection of a movie pre-screened by the Holy Sees and if an actor says a s much as… 'Holy Heavens' it gets censured. But what really makes it a world venue, is its advanced and unusual air conditioning system."

"And what the hell is that?" Toto asked.

"When it's hot they open the windows and when it's cold they bring in three or four donkeys who breathe hot air into the place."

"Get lost."

"It's true, and it kind of works, though as you enter you don't know if it is breath or farts."

Roberto and Toto didn't quite know if to laugh at Cicci's stories or to cry for the misery awaiting them.

"In other words" Cicci concluded, "this is such a good place that I have already requested to be released ahead of time."

"And do you think they'll let you go?"

"Of course not, but I have ways..."

After only a few days it was evident that discipline was completely gone from the base and the state of readiness of the missiles was just as bad as the conditions described by Cicci.

Instead of the required fifteen minutes, they would need days or weeks to put a single missile in a 'launch' condition. But the base commander was not worried. He knew that no inspection team would venture to that damned place and when Central Command asked the reason for such inefficiency, he replied with his standard phrase:

"Scarcity of replacement pieces and qualitative deficiency of personnel."

Often, at the base there were accidents that normally would have aroused suspicion at Headquarters. The last few weeks alone, had seen an airman drive so fast within the base that he caused his jeep and the cistern in tow to tumble over and crash against a trailer; a tent where cleaning fluids and other flammable materials were kept, catch fire; three airmen reported strange wounds and had to be sent to hospital and then home to recoup; a crew chief, who had been denied transfer from Irsina, had used the cherry-picker forgetting to extend the trunnions, tipped the vehicle wounding his head and damaging a missile.

But the event that shook the entire organization and echoed in Rome as well as at the NATO headquarters in Paris and Washington, was when, during a launch-test, a nuclear nose-cone fell down to the ground like a ripe pear from a tree.

Fortunately, the safety features worked and the damage was limited to many pairs of soiled underwear, days of investigations, enough written reports to destroy a forest, and a new nose cone with nuclear device; or perhaps, without!

The usual 'high officers' from Rome came to investigate the occurrence, but limited their questions to fellow officers who didn't even come close to understand how a thing like that could possibly happen.

A week after this occurrence, major Perrini and general Graziosi arrived at the Irsina base. After stopping for a half an hour with the local base commander, major Perrini summoned First Airmen Vito Falci- 'Cicci', Salvatore Marciano and Roberto Lanzi.

"Firstly" he said after having answered their salute, "I wish to tell you that you will immediately return to Acquaviva. I don't want to criticize captain Quadra for his… excessive disciplinary action in sending you here. But…from what I heard from lieutenants Baggi and Giannini, it could have been avoided."

The major stopped. Then resorting to the ploy he often used to observe the effect of his words, he pulled out a pack of Marlboros and slowly pulled out a cigarette. Then, perhaps unable to detect any reaction, he continued. "However, I would like very much to know how the nose cone incident came about."

"We can't state anything with certainty" said Cicci repressing a smile, "but during the simulated launch, when we got to the second stage separation, the by-pass malfunctioned and the bolts exploded as during a real launch, causing the cone to fall."

"I am as aware as you are of what happened, but… why? Damn it!"

"The mystery of electronics" replied Roberto, "who knows, perhaps a short circuit caused by humidity, or by who knows what…"

"What, or whom?"

"Commander" Cicci replied, "as every one knows only the American experts have access to the final phases of launch, the blue-prints inherent to that sequence, the target objectives…"

"Boys" the commander said with a deep sigh, "take your personal effects. You'll come back with me with the jeep. The general is going back to Gioia del Colle with the helicopter. But promise me one thing" he said staring each one in the eyes, "I don't want to hear anymore about the 'mystery of electronics' or any other mystery."

Finally, he lighted his cigarette and blew away a long puff of smoke.

- XLIX -

BACK TO ACQUAVIVA

With the return to Acquaviva, the boys should have felt vindicated. Unfortunately, the treatment received from captain Quadra, the state of anarchy seen at Irsina, the uncertainty of when they would receive their next promotion and the negative reports they got from their comrades from other bases, were beginning to take their toll.

Moreover, Roberto was not soothed by the preferential treatment he received thanks to his relationship with commander Perrini.

He had formed a dislike for the organization that he had initially idealized and that now showed an inefficiency, a mediocrity and an apathy that he could not stomach.

That very evening, gathered again with their old friends, they discovered that the three weeks under Quadra's command had been a disaster. There had been cases of insubordination, menaces and punishment. Consequently, none of the three missiles was operative or in a minus fifteen launch condition.

Carlo said he would spend his next furlough trying to find a job up north. Cicci would try to get released ahead of time and return to the USA, others would send job applications to FIAT, Alitalia, Piaggio, Olivetti and wherever else they thought their technical skills could be used.

Rebuli and Livio, revealed they had already contacted a textile industry up north which was computerizing their manufacturing and had received a good initial response. Understanding that many of their comrades, were planning the leave the Air Force, Roberto and Toto began to think in those terms.

A few days later the sergeant on day duties called Roberto and gave him a letter addressed to: Lanzi & Marciano. It had been readdressed at Gioia del Colle, but the sender's address was from a town up north. His name did not immediately ring a bell.

Roberto looked for Toto to open it and read it together. When he found him, Toto smacked his forehead and exclaimed: "Damn it, I think I know who it is. He is the guy that…"

"Calm down a moment" said Roberto, "we'll find out reading the letter."

Dearest comrades:

I don't know if you remember me; my name is Aldo Schiavon and I frequented the course of propulsion system in Caserta prior to yours.

A few days before final exams I fell sick and I was sent home to convalesce. Upon my return I repeated the course and I was given the opportunity to give the exams with your group.

Believe it or not, the matter that most bothered me was the fact that I was awarded the prize for best performance and the gold wrist watch that came with it.

It should have been given to one of you two.

However, perhaps I did you a favor, because it came at a big cost. But let's proceed in order: as the first classified, I had the right to nominate the three airports of my choice. I did and waited for the almost certain confirmation of the one closest to my town. A few days before the end of my furlough (which was part of my prize), a carabiniere of the local detachment brought me a sealed envelope with the travel order.

I was excited and I opened the envelope.

When my eyes fell upon the name of my destination I almost fainted: I was to report to Alghero, in Sardenia.

"Alghero", I repeated as though in a trance, "that's where they send people as punishment."

During my train trip from Olbia to Sassari, thinking of my future, my eyes filled with tears. I hadn't cried since early childhood, but I had to do it to rid of the accumulated anger, the disillusion, the injustice for the nasty treatment received. I asked myself to whom they would give the post I had requested, and wondered who hated me so much to ship me to Alghero, who might be the damn soul who had signed my sentence.

It was useless of course. If you wear a uniform you must obey; there are no ifs or buts.

Now, as soon as I'll reach the end of my engagement period, I'll ask for my final
Release.

Yes, I'll return home, my back pack full of memories and resentment.

Dear Roberto and Toto, I know though mutual friends that, despite your American adventure, you were not spared some negative experiences.

However, I just wanted you to know that damned gold watch, was nothing but a bad omen.

I conclude my rambling soliloquy by wishing you the best and hoping you'll enjoy a safe and long life.

Aldo Schiavon

Roberto folded the letter and handed it to Toto.

"Here" he said," and to think that we wanted to have that prize. Poor Aldo, he has suffered a worse fate than ours."

"For sure" said Toto, "it wasn't his fault. But now, reading his letter I want to leave the Air Force even more."

A few days later, as they spent their time off walking the street of Acquaviva, Toto said:

"How about spending our next furlough in Rome? I could di the round of all Airline offices and you…"

"And I" Roberto interrupted, "I'll go and knock at all embassies. The idea of spending my life inspecting or fixing airplanes doesn't do a damned thing for me."

For days, he thought about his conversation with Ray and the possibility of returning to America as an immigrant. One thing was for sure, he would never return to live and work in his town.

* * * * *

A few weeks elapsed.

The base of Acquaviva became again the best in the system.

However, discomfort and discontent were spreading like a hidden cancer. By now, Roberto thought, even eliminating the most dangerous metastasis, it would be very difficult to save the patient.

After the American experience, they felt as though they had been dropped 'from the stars to the stables.'

What should I do? Roberto wondered.

He decided to write to Silvia; afterword he would also tell his friends Mauro and Giovanni. He immediately wrote a letter and posted it before he would have had the time to change his mind.

He had tossed the dice. Now he could only wait until they stopped rolling and show the results.

He had crossed the Rubicon.

After almost two weeks, Roberto received Silvia's reply. He quickly put it in his pocket nonchalantly and, his heart racing, he walked to his room. He placed the letter over his table and sat, staring at it, trying to think of the words he would have liked to find.

Finally, he opened it.

My dear Roberto

When Mauro gave me your letter I could hardly believe it.
I am sorry to hear that the situation is such as to make you think of leaving the Air Force. I don't know whether to be happy or not, since you did not mention where you would go, what you will do and, most of all, if I am part of your future plans.

Yes I know, you gave me some hints, but too much time has passed for me to feel confident of their interpretation and to reply to you unequivocally.

Among other things, you also mentioned 'America'. Mauro predicted that one day, and despite your initial impression, you would try to return there. I must admit that he knows you better than I do, and if this is what you want to do I wish you success.

But, if you are asking me (in your subtle way) whether I would leave my family and follow you, I can only reply that I do not exclude it. I am sure that if we still love each other, we can overcome any obstacle.

However... yes my dear there is an 'however'... I would like to see you, look into your eyes and hear from your mouth all the answers that I refrain from asking now.

Let me know when you will take your next furlough.

Waiting for you, I remain,
Your Silvia.
P.S. I still love you

Roberto read it a couple of times and then he lay on his bed with his eyes shut.

He didn't know if Silvia's letter had helped him or not. And felt almost as when he was about to leave the tannery. He remembered the enthusiasm, the hopes, the dreams. Now though, he could not anticipate the future and he experienced moments of optimism and confidence, followed by moments of anxiety, worry, even fear. He knew he would leave a sure position with perhaps slow but certain advancement for something that was yet uncertain and unknown.

On the one hand, he was confident that the newly acquired technical skills, the English language – that was becoming the technical lingo of the world – would have opened some doors. On the other, not able to focus on something specific, he felt lost in a thick fog. He had to wait that it would lift or dissolve, or move into a clearing to look at the possibilities in a clear and concrete scenario?

He decided to act.

The day after both he and Toto requested a few day off and, as previously considered, they were going to start their job investigation from Rome.

They acquired a map of the city, they spent hours marking with a pen the location of Airlines offices, Embassies, Consulates. They calculated routes and distances, deciding which were close enough to each other to be approached on foot.

Changed into civilian clothes and armed with hope, determination and copies of all certificates acquired while in the Air Force, they started the long pilgrimage along the roads of the capital.

At the beginning, their tentative way and inexperience, did not allow them to go past the doorman. After a while though, having refined the method and addressing receptionists and clerks in English, they were able to gather more information and in some cases fill up job application forms.

At the end of the first day, they had supper in a small restaurant near Termini train station. Its name was "Da Nazzareno", they had discovered it when in Rome for the English test, and returning to it every time they passed through the city.

Tired and weary by the heat, it was pleasant to rest and have a good meal in that place. The head waiter, that after the first time had always recognized them, made them feel at home and at the end of the meal served them a slice of *'Fedora'* chocolate cake double the normal portion and a digestive liqueur 'on the house'. The boys reciprocated by leaving a generous tip.

"So what do you say?" Roberto asked as they were sipping coffee, "did we made any progress today?"

"Yes, but not as much as I hoped. I thought that young as we are and with our qualifications we would have had a better reception."

"Perhaps there are more people than we imagined looking for a job. The clerks of those companies must be bombarded by requests."

"Tomorrow" said Toto blowing a sigh, "my first stop will be at Trans World Airlines, then Alitalia and Pan American. Since the technical offices of these companies are at Fiumicino airport, I'll take a bus from Termini Station." Then he looked up and said, "And you? What's your program?"

"To start the American Embassy, then the Australian and the Canadian. After we shall see. It's better to go separately, we'll cover more ground."

"Okay, we'll meet here at eight."

The following evening, sitting at their usual table, the two boys were tallying up the result of the day:

"At Alitalia they didn't even look at me," said Toto between sips of red wine. "To get in that company, one may need the recommendation of a fucking cardinal or some other turd already in the inside. My best chance was at Trans World. They made me fill the application and then the manager of maintenance gave me a short interview. Too soon to say, but he gave me the impression that he was satisfied with my credentials. Especially when he saw that I was trained in the United States. However, he seemed a bit hesitant when I told him that I was still in the Air Force. At the end, he shook my hand and said he'll let me know shortly. What about you?"

"At the American and Australian Embassy, they made me feel – forgive my example – as though I was a poor, uneducated *terrone* from the south begging for a piece of stale bread. I almost told them to go fuck themselves. The immigration request for those countries must be so high that they could close their doors for a few years."

"And the Canadian one?"

"They were much better. But there is a problem…"

Toto put his glass down and looked at Roberto.

"In every place they explicitly asked if I had completed the military service? Without the release" Roberto concluded, "I'm afraid, we're screwed."

"Yes, but do you think it's essential even for an application?"

"I'm afraid so."

"So, what can we do?"

"We ask to be released as soon as possible. What else can we do?"

"Without having first been given a job offer?"

"If that is the only way to get it…"

They returned to the base with some hope, but without anything concrete. They now knew for certain that they would receive no job offer without having first been released from the military. It felt like jumping from a trapeze without any safety net underneath.

They continued with their duties, but with less enthusiasm than before. Those tall white missiles, aimed at who knows which soviet city, in a play between opposing political powers called 'cold war', seemed every day more absurd. One read there were thousands on both sides, all armed with atomic bombs, hydrogen bombs, ready and capable to destroy a good chunk of the human race. And if at the red button there were some idiots like they had witnessed themselves? Officers so convinced of righteousness of their own cause that would press the red button at the smallest provocation? When Roberto thought in those terms, he could no longer justify even the reason to wear a uniform.

Their work was reduced to a mere maintenance routine for the equipment and the status quo of the missiles. Roberto and Toto waited for some kind of response from the companies and organization they had contacted, while sending others by mail to new prospective ones. Together with Carlo and Patrizio, they had started to frequent the evening classes in Bari. Toto as a radio technician, Carlo and Roberto for a science degree and Patrizio for accountancy. This way, they would use their free time to study and be better prepared for future eventualities.

By now, the increased request for discharge, had become so serious that it jeopardized the operational status of the bases.

Due to the insufficient amount of men Rome's planners had sent to the courses in the USA, they had now to concoct some remedial action. Unable to resolve the initial mistake, they issued a decree that annulled all future requests of discharge. This included even those who had already finished their thirty six-months of duty as established in the enlisted papers.

Initially, a few early requests had passed unobserved, later though they were all denied on the ground of 'National Emergency'. Some airmen specialists, countered with feign sickness, family emergencies and other excuses concocted to make themselves 'unable' to attend their duties. The rest of the personnel were obligated to work long hours and sometimes to even contribute to the work in other bases near Acquaviva in order to keep the missiles operative.

All crew chief, including Roberto and Toto, were told to double their efforts and consequently they had to drop some of their courses.

"Enough is enough" said Roberto. "Now I will go and give my resignation to commander Perrini."

"What good is it? we already know that we will be held by Ministerial decree?"

"Toto" said Roberto in a gelid tone, "if they will deny our release, I will cease to cooperate and I will convince others to follow my example. I think the commander knows I would do it. Administrative difficulties or not, I think he'll conclude that he'd be better off letting me go!"

- L -

LIUTENANT GIANNINI

That morning lieutenant Giannini looked at Roberto resignation letter. Then looked at him, read it again and held it in his hands, perplexed and unsure of what to do.
"So, you have really decided to leave us?" he said with a forced smile.
"I have decided to leave the Air Force" Roberto clarified.
"But you know, people like you could have a good career."
"Yes, I know, but it is too late for me. It's my fault , I joined the Force with too high expectations, it was inevitable that I'd be deluded."
"But… what more did you expect? You received excelled training, you have been in America, you are part of the most efficient base of the system, part of a chosen unit. What on earth do you want?"
"I already told you, lieutenant, I believe I am too naïve, I had deluded myself to find, under the uniform, the discipline I missed as a civilian."
"Meaning…?"
"More discipline, more efficiency, more sense of justice and above all, superiors that I could admire."
"And you didn't find all that in here? Speak freely, forget my rank."
"No sir. I have been disappointed too many times. You have seen yourself the spectacle of those… officers from Rome who came to investigate the fall of Mig 17. Buffoons in uniform, with scarce or nil technical knowledge, with little if any interest in the implication of the plane crash and no respect for the lower ranks. And the present situation with many inoperative bases because some pen-pusher in Rome could not even project the correct amount of personnel needed. And let's not even talk about sadistic imbeciles like captain Quadra!"

"Lanzi" the lieutenant interrupted, "your intelligence is sometimes dimmed by your arrogance and immoderate sense of righteousness. I am an arrogant bastard myself. In fact, I am the last in a long line of wealthy bastards, small nobility they call it, that have somehow survived the misadventures of our poor Country. But you must consider that we must live with today's realities, alliances and misalliances, on the premise of a grandiose yesterday that no longer exists. You must remember that we have limited resources and we must try to promote a relative influence on… stifling bureaucratic practices that would discourage a saint."

And when the limited means are made even smaller by incompetence and corruption° said Roberto, °even our modest objectives end up in the trash."

"Those are pretty heavy accusations, Roberto. I would avoid mentioning some of those things to major Perrini when he'll call you…"

"I will do my best, lieutenant. I have a certain respect for our commandant, but I cannot forget all the rest."

Lieutenant Giannini blew a sigh, gave the letter back to Roberto.

"Honestly, If I were you I would change some of the wording. It isn't necessary to express your thoughts so bitterly."

"Thanks for your suggestion lieutenant. I'll read it over and see what I can do. May I go now?"

"Yes, you can go, Roberto. Good luck to you."

* * * * *

- LI -

FAREWELL COMMANDER

Towards evening Roberto was told to immediately go to major Perrini's office.

He had been expecting the call, but the immediacy of the encounter forced him to reexamine his decision. He imagined the commander would try to make him change his mind, like he knew he had successfully done with others. It was his duty. He wondered what kind of arguments he would use with him.

The commander responded to Roberto's salute and asked him to sit across from him.

They talked awhile about banal things, the weather, the improved food at the base, the general mood of the squadron. Then, major Perrini picked up Roberto's resignation letter and began to read it aloud. At the end he put it down, smoothed it with the palm of his hand, placed his elbows over the desk and joined both hands under his chin. He remained in this position for a long while, thoughtfully staring at Roberto. He then took a pack of Marlboro out of his pocket, pulled out a cigarette and began to play and tap the filter end over the desk. He put it over the ashtray without lighting it up.

"Do you have anything to add to this?"

"No, sir."

As lieutenant Giannini suggested, Roberto had softened a bit the tenor for his letter requesting the release from the Force. However, it was clear that the commander was perturbed by its decisive tone. He folded it again and sighed.

"I know all that happened during my absence and as you know I've tried to put things right. Both you and your friend are again under my direct command and you will remain there as long as I stay in charge which, as far as I know, it will be for quite some time."

Though acknowledging captain Quadra's misjudgment, the commander was careful not to openly concur with Roberto's opinions.

"I am grateful to you, sir, but I cannot entrust my future to the grace of your presence. I don't like to be part of an ineffective organization with officers who only think of their career, to their own advantages, and who consider the rest of us as mere garbage."

"You know it's not that way with me. Also you seem to forget that, despite the behavior of certain officers and, in your words, an ineffective organization, we are the heirs of a glorious past."

"Excuse me commander but… which past are you referring to? I hope not the usual ancient Rome or the Renaissance. To much time has passed since then and, at least on the battlefield, thanks to the quality of our leaders, we haven't done that well in the last two thousand years."

"Despite that, dear Roberto, we have had many heroic acts, many examples to emulate, and …"

Roberto seemed to have fallen in a dialectic trap, but he was determined to pursue his path.

"What have the few personal acts of heroism" he answered emphatically, "to do with the image left by a nation guided by a bunch of incompetents? With that of an army lead by incapable generals?"

"Let's not denigrate our past. Let us instead respect those who, on whichever front, with deficient armament and inferior equipment has been an exemplary models. Those who gave their life for duty."

"My father was among those who gave their life for a misplaced sense of duty" Roberto replied. "For what? For whom? Do you think I can feel honored by that? Do you think my mother can thank him for giving up his life for a fanatical imbecile who thought bayonets were enough to win a war?"

"Now we don't have people like that. We don't have bayonets, we have missiles."

"Yea" Roberto replied, "missiles located in a place only accessible by country roads that run across railways with access denied by remote control barriers. The Russians couldn't have made things worse for us had they set up our base."

"Roberto" said major Perrini in a harsher tone, "be realistic, we are in Italy not in America. We must do with what we have; we must build our highways on top of those built by ancient Romans, our high-rises over Roman and Etruscan ruins, our airports over swamps only suitable for mosquito. So, what the hell is the difference if our damned missiles' bases are built between railroad tracks at the end of inaccessible country roads? Who cares if a dishonest politician purchases inappropriate land for our bases? Do you think it was different under the king?

Or under Mussolini? Or that the system would change if the communists took over the government? Let me tell you my boy, it has always been and it will always be this way. We have been blessed and damned by the same stroke, we are and always will be Italians!"

There was a pause. Then major Perini lowered his voice and said: "And one last thing, Roberto, don't deceive yourself; other nations are not better than ours. Only smarter, they don't wash their dirty laundry in public."

During the next moment of silence, Roberto thought of the many people, including Silvia's father, who had told him he was naïve.

"But let's not waste any more time in useless skirmishes" the major continued. "I am sure you understand me as I understand you. I cannot say that you are completely wrong, nor can I state that you are right. My duty is to do whatever I can to improve on the little we have."

He lifted his cigarette from the ashtray and finally lighted it.

"We have just exited a disastrous war" he continued while blowing smoke towards the ceiling, "Lost, but in some ways we have redeemed some of that honor that you so earnestly mention. Our soldiers have fought the best they could, our Country is slowly progressing. Perhaps you don't realize it now, but in our modest way, we are participating in an important phase of contemporary history. One day people will realize that our efforts and sacrifices have born fruit. It is an experience you will remember as a significant factor for the rest of your life.

We need young, promising men like you" he continued with renewed emphasis, "in front of you there is a bright future and, if you pursue it, it will be useful to you to the Air Force, to the country. Don't throw away these years. I know you are studying to get your diploma. As soon as you get it, I have already decided to recommend you for an officer course at the *Scuola di Guerra Aerea* of Florence."

The major put the cigarette on his lips and took another drag. Perhaps, to better observe the impact the mentioning of his native city would make upon Roberto.

"After, you would return to my squadron" he added calmly, "I speak to you as though you were my own son… that son that God never gave me."

Roberto felt moved by that appeal which seemed sincere. He made an effort to conceal his feelings, he cleared his voice, but remained silent. Despite the attraction of a career for which, at the time of his enlistment would have given ten years of his life, now, after all he had seen, his moral code would impose a refusal.

It seemed impossible even to him!

He remembered the distant day when, going through the center of Santa Chiara, he had noticed the advertisement for enrolment in the Air Force; his chance to leave the tannery, his chance for a better life.

That evening, he immediately sent his request to the Ministry. And that night, before falling to sleep, he day-dreamed to be wearing that beautiful blue uniform and have a successful career. He also remembered the movie with Rock Hudson he had seen in Caserta, and later when, after passing his exams at full marks, a colonel had congratulated him and his friends.

"Of all the military categories" he said, "the Air Force is by far the better. It offers the best opportunities to a young promising youth like you. The Air Force is a young Corps, not encumbered by centuries of old traditions. Since pilots are kept flying by specialists like you will be, the best will always be rewarded. Given the high responsibilities, the remuneration is higher than in the other services."

It had sounded very promising.

Unfortunately, there had been too many disappointments; the humiliating experience in Caserta, the frustration of the English exam in Rome, the return from America to the unfinished bases in Italy, and after additional setbacks, the final awareness that his ideals could not be reached in the military, and perhaps, not even in his Country.

How could he possibly be part of a system which was more interested to maintain a status quo and the privileges so dear to the upper echelons? How could he, under those conditions, obey and expect to be obeyed by subordinates who were treated unfairly?

"Commander" he finally said in a hoarse voice, "I am truly grateful to you, both for the offer of the Academy in Florence and even more for considering me like a son. I feel honored and I must say that for me as well, you have been more than just a superior. But it is too late now. I do realize that, whatever I chose, I'll have to begin anew, follow my destiny in fields other than this, perhaps even far from my own Country. I am sorry…"

"Then you will not stay?"

In the few seconds that followed, Roberto perceived this to be his last chance to achieve what he had dreamed upon joining the Air Force. He saw the sleeves of his jacket adorned with the officer's golden bars, the prestige and the economic status that went with it.

It was but a moment, for swiftly came his reply:

"No sir, I will not."

Someone knocked at the door.

"Yes?"

Esposito peeked from the door, "Commander" he said removing his hat, "if you wish to be in Bari by seven, we should leave now."

Major Perrini let out a sigh and began to get up. Roberto jumped to his feet, stood at attention and smartly saluted.

The major straightened up and answered the salute.

The two men remained like this, one in front of the other for a long instant, looking into each other's eyes, right hand tensed at the side of the forehead. Then, the commander lowered his arm and extended his hand to Roberto, who shook it and held it a moment. He then turned on his heels, opened the office door and let his superior by.

He thought his eyes were moist.

He remained on the threshold of the door and followed him with his eyes until he disappeared inside the *Giulietta* Sprint, he heard the door close shut and saw the car take off in a cloud of dust.

Then, he again put his hand to his forehead, and held it there, in a military salute, until the car disappeared as though swallowed by the night.

THE END

EPILOGUE

(The end of the Italian missiles bases)

In 1958, Fidel Castro interrupted the dictatorship of Fulgenzio Batista in Cuba and the United States of America cut their economic assistance to the new regime. Then Castro formed an alliance with the Soviet Union who was inclined to buy Cuban sugar and supply economic and military assistance.

Many Cubans who opposed Castro found refuge in Florida and, on April 17, 1961, 1500 of them, trained in the U.S.A. and helped by the CIA, attempted to land in Cuba near the Bahia de cochinos-Bay of pigs. The venture failed miserably.

By then the spies operating in Cuba were fewer and unreliable, consequently, the Americans resorted to high altitude photographic reconnaissance of the island by means of their U-2 Airplanes. Soon they discovered that, contrary to their assurance to the Americans, the Russians were installing a network of SAM (ground-air defensive missiles) to protect what looked like medium-range ballistic missiles. The latter was a serious threat as they would have easily reached most areas of North America.

J.F. Kennedy, then president of the United States, gathered his cabinet to discuss several alternatives that were soon reduced to two:

1- aerial attack of the Cuban bases
2- total blockade of the island.

The president favored the second because he was told that even a very heavy aerial bombardment would have not destroyed 100% of the bases. Also, it would have undoubtedly caused casualties among Cuban civilians and Russian soldiers with a consequent military retaliation by the latter.

With the still high tension regarding the city of Berlin, the American president did not want to add another crucial situation versus the Soviets.

As the embargo was put into place, Krushchev, the president of the Soviet Union, accused Kennedy of risking another world war, while insisting that no Russian missiles were in Cuba. The arm-wrestling between the two presidents lasted a couple of weeks and finally the Russians, after requesting that the Americans would not invade Cuba, decide to withdraw the ships sailing towards the island. On October 27, 1962, the Americans officially ended the blockade and avoided a possible nuclear conflict.

Unknown to most, Kennedy had also secretly agreed to remove the Jupiter missiles from Turkey and Italy, since by then they were considered obsolete and also easily subject to sabotage.

Consequently, the 10 operational bases part of the 36^ Brigade, in which Roberto Lanzi had served, were finally dismantled. Following the dissolution of the base and the dismantling of the launch sites, some of the aviators-specialists were sent to new destinations in Italy. Others, disillusioned, left the Air Force and a few found employment with Alitalia, Fiat Avio, Selenia or emigrated to the United States and Canada. A homogeneous group, under a technical-operative profile, was disintegrated and scattered all over the world.

Therefore, with the 'dispersed' materials and well-trained personnel, Italy lost a patrimony which, if suitably used, could have contributed to the development of the national industry in the field of space research.

www.ingramcontent.com/pod-product-compliance
Lightning Source LLC
LaVergne TN
LVHW091535060526
838200LV00036B/613